"How did he die, John?" Yolanda asked. I'd almost forgotten she was there, which was surprising given her propensity to dominate any conversation within a city block. I looked closer at her. She was a bit pale.

JT noticed, too. "You ladies should go in the house. I promise we won't dig up anything without asking you first, Molly."

I watched the ambulance carrying Sam away. "You're sure?"

JT nodded. "Go inside. I'll check with you before we start digging."

Mark put a hand under Yolanda's arm. They started toward the side steps that led into the kitchen. I followed, then paused to glance back at JT. "How did he die? You didn't say."

JT was watching the ambulance trundle down my lane. Then he swung his gaze to me, his expression unreadable. "Looks like somebody stabbed him with a pitchfork. Did one go missing, Molly?"

I gulped and took a step back, almost landing on my ass as I hit an icy patch. I'd been missing my favorite pitchfork since the day Sam disappeared. I considered lying, then knew I had no choice. I nodded dumbly, feeling as though I was choking.

JT turned to stare at the gaping hole where Sam had lain. "Looks like we found it."

Reviews for *Your Saving Grace*

"The story is well-paced with excellent dialogue, intriguing suspense, and an exciting ending. Of special interest are the protagonists who are a little older than in your usual romantic suspense, but sexy and still in their prime. YOUR SAVING GRACE is a tale to enjoy and savor. This reviewer will be looking for more books by this talented author."

Romance Reviews Today ~Marilyn Heyman

"The world that YOUR SAVING GRACE envelops you in will leave you curious and astounded as the case of Hannah's attacker unwinds. Hannah is as tenderhearted as she is bullheaded, while Jude learns to love for the first time by her example. J. L. Wilson did an excellent job keeping me guessing until the very end of the 'who done it' story. Comprised of great writing and a wonderful story, YOUR SAVING GRACE isn't to be missed. Thumbs up for J L Wilson for writing a shocking end!"

Romance Junkies ~Lacey

Review for *Brownies, Bodies, and Breaking the Code*

"The tension builds to a suspenseful finale, and the reader is made to really care about Jessie and Gus. The supporting cast is also intriguing, and it is difficult for Jessie (and the reader) to discern the truth early on. These are mature characters. Gus is a silver-haired professorial type and Jessie is 51 years old. I love it that she is a topnotch computer gal, up on modern technology. She can also be a bit flaky, and I like that, too. Gus is secretive, but tender, and attractive in a somewhat nerdy fashion. J L Wilson has created an original story, peopled by a highly original cast."

The Romance Studio ~Lynn Bushey

Candy, Corpses, And Classified Ads

by

J L Wilson

Candy, Corpses, And Classified Ads

COPYRIGHT © 2007 by J L Wilson

Contact Information: info@thewildrosepress.com

Cover Art by *Kim Mendoza*

The Wild Rose Press
PO Box 708
Adams Basin, NY 14410-0706
Visit us at www.thewildrosepress.com

Publishing History
First Crimson Rose Edition, 2008
Print ISBN 1-60154-201-1

Published in the United States of America

Dedication

To Maggie: thanks for the idea!
And to the rest of the STBP gang,
who helped me whip this pig into shape.

Chapter 1

"Oh my God. The Death card." Amelia Gray looked at the Tarot spread she'd dealt, then at me with a stricken expression on her plain, Cover-Girl-powdered face.

"Of course there's a death card," I said. "I'm going to kill that damn pig."

"Now, now," Ike Bernstein, my boss, chided. "Melvin is someone's pet."

"He's also tearing up my azaleas, digging out my garlic and decimating my chives. Not that chives are a problem, they grow like weeds, but—"

"This is serious, Molly," Amelia insisted, tapping the Sleeping Beauty portrayed on the card. Amelia used the Whimsical Tarot, which had fairy tales for its theme. "Very serious."

I waved it away, pausing to take two blue M&Ms from the tray on my nearby desk. "I'm not worried. There is death in my future. Porcine death."

I joined Ike at his desk where he was busy laying out tomorrow's newspaper. "Aren't you done yet? I want to see the Tuesday Teasers." The Teasers were the *Tangle Butte Daily Tribune*'s ("daily" meaning Monday through Friday) version of personal ads. Since the TBTrib served a population of about ten thousand, including the outlying counties, the Teasers were often meager. Until lately, that is.

"Looking to see what your boyfriend says this week?"

1

Ike's pale blue eyes glinted with mischief. Age hadn't diminished Ike's sense of humor. It had only honed it to a cutting edge. After thirty years of ownership, he still managed the TBTrib, wrote many of the features and edited the articles Amelia, Danny, and I contributed.

"He's not my boyfriend." I tried to peer over Ike's bony shoulder. "I don't know any man who's that romantic."

"He must know you." Amelia swept up her Tarot cards from the old oak counter separating the TBTrib 'staff' from the 'public.' She came through the drop gate to stand at Ike's other side. "So many of the clues are tailored to you, Molly."

I remembered the first personal ad, which had come to the TBTrib two months previously. *You once loved me as much as you love M&Ms. Can you love me again?* It was signed, Your Lost Love. This had been followed by others, like, *Our love was made to last, please forgive me. Your Lost Love* and *Please tend my heart the way you tend your roses, if you did, I'd bloom for you. Your Lost Love.* The ads had been paid for in cash, three months in advance, and were sent to Ike personally via anonymous email.

I stretched for my desk and my M&M stash. "A lot of people like M&Ms." I popped a green one in my mouth, then nudged Ike. "Come on, show me."

He tilted the computer monitor so I could see the highlighted box on the mockup of the Tuesday Teaser page.

DWM, 49+ years old, seeking 45-year-old WWF. Must love cats, gardening, M&Ms, and books. Please be willing to take a chance on a guy who used to be a jerk. Your Lost Love.

This required several yellow M&Ms. I was forty-five, widowed, white, female. I loved cats, gardening, M&Ms, and books. "Well, it can't be anybody I know." I turned back to my desk and the feature story awaiting my deathless prose. "No man I know likes cats. I don't know a man who even tolerates cats, much less likes them."

"But maybe JT has had a change of heart and—"

I shot Amelia a glare. We'd had this discussion before. "When JT and I broke up twenty years ago, words

2

were said that can't be unsaid. It isn't him. And even if it was, there's no turning back the clock. Now let me finish this." I sat down and stared at the chunky computer monitor festooned with yellow sticky notes. The story hadn't written itself in the time it took for Amelia to do my Tarot reading for the day. I stared gloomily at the headline. *New Police Chief No Stranger to Tangle Butte.* With a weary sigh, I carefully aligned my fingers on my keyboard. I'd long since worn away the letters, and when my hands strayed, I wrote gobbledygook.

"The new Chief of Police, J.T. McCord, has come home to Tangle Butte after leaving eighteen years ago to pursue a career in law enforcement." Leaving after he jilted me, left me in the lurch, then married and was divorced by that bimbo with all the money, Shirley Corcoran, who to this day still lorded it over me that she snatched JT away from me. Every time I met Shirley in the Shop 'n' Save Food Boutique, she gave me a smirky smile and flashed the mega-carat diamond on her left hand, a gift from Mark, her third husband.

I considered my CD player, wondering if a bit of old metal music might kick my brain into gear. Then I shook my head and pounded the keys, gamely determined to finish the Assignment From Hell. "Chief McCord has spent the intervening years in Kansas City, where he served on the police force and worked for the county prosecutor's office as an investigator."

That sounded lukewarm, even to me. I didn't have much to go on. The Tangle Butte City Council had hired JT, but wouldn't release his credentials, citing employment confidentiality. Clyde Burdett, the City Manager, had smugly told me, "We were lucky to get somebody like JT, who was willing to come back here and work for the little pay we could give him."

Of course, I couldn't quote that in the TBTrib. I glared at my screen.

"It would go a lot easier if you'd just interview him," Ike commented. His desk was a few feet from mine. His sharp eyes zeroed in on the pitifully few words on my screen.

Amelia, shuffling her Tarot cards at her own desk, piped up. "It's a legitimate reason to see him. You shouldn't be shy."

Both Ike and I snorted at the same moment. Shyness was a trait with which I was unfamiliar. "It's hard to write a story about somebody you don't respect," I muttered, propping my head in my hands and leaning my elbows on my desk. "The police can't even keep a stupid pot-bellied pig from trespassing." What I wasn't saying was that JT had been in his new job for three days and I'd so far avoided him. It was inevitable that I'd run into him, of course, but I was trying to postpone the awful moment as long as possible.

"I doubt Melvin is high on the priority list for the Tangle Butte PD." Ike stared at his own computer monitor. "JT looks like his daddy."

Curiosity warred with dignity. Curiosity won. I scooted over to Ike's desk, propelling my wheeled chair with a few well-placed pushes of my stockinged feet on the worn oak floor. Munching some green M&Ms, I peered at his computer screen.

Oh, Lord. There he was, JT McCord, looking all brisk and businesslike in a dark gray suit with official police insignia on it. He had short-cut white hair now, but his daddy had been white-haired when he was in his forties, too. JT would never be called handsome, but he had an interesting, angular face with unreadable dark eyes and a harsh-looking mouth. His face was long and narrow, darkly tanned, with the high cheekbones, dark eyes, and the flat nose of his Ojibwa mother. I remembered how his eyes would flash with laughter and how devastating his rare smiles could be.

I pushed away from Ike's desk a bit too briskly and went colliding into the counter. Amelia finished shuffling her cards and went to Ike's desk. "Time for your reading."

He shot me a long-suffering look, but obediently cut the deck and appeared interested as Amelia set out the cards in a pattern of her own invention. Amelia had been trying various fortune-telling techniques since I'd known her, which was now pushing eight years. Tarot cards had stuck around the longest. It seemed like the Death card came up in just about every reading she did for me, so much so that I insisted on checking the deck to make sure it wasn't stacked. It wasn't. I just kept getting dealt

Death.

I tuned out her murmured conversation with Ike and focused on the feature story that wasn't. I didn't want to write about JT but I had to. He was, after all, News and I was the News Editor (and the business reporter, news reporter, photographer, and archivist). I wished I could foist him on Amelia, but she was Community, Entertainment, and Home. Dan Bailey, a high school senior, was Sports, Automotive, and Outdoor Living. No, JT was my cross to bear.

I positioned my hands on the keyboard, prepared to take the plunge again when the front door opened. My desk was at the back of the room so I spied him before he saw me. Snow glistened on his topcoat as he paused in the doorway. Then he closed the glass-fronted door and stepped up to the counter. I tried to slide inconspicuously under my desk, but my keyboard tray prevented my descent.

Ike bounded to his feet. "JT, how are you?"

JT McCord shook snow off his dark blue topcoat, then tugged off his navy gloves. "Ike, it's good to see you. It's been a long time." He leaned over the counter and stuck out his hand.

I attempted to ooze out of sight but although I am a small person, I wasn't small enough. My sorted M&Ms rattled alarmingly in their watercolor artist's tray, balanced in the lazy Susan on top of the books on my desk. I gave up on anonymity in favor of maintaining chocolate harmony.

"I've come to see Margaret if she's—" JT's dark eyes scanned our cramped quarters. Five desks were jammed into the main office and the oak counter took up its own share of space. The November sun didn't have enough strength to light the far corner where I was slouched in my chair. But trust JT to home in on me. I swear it felt like two searchlights were beaming out, trying to snag me.

"Hey, JT." My hands were trembling and my stomach was doing flip-flops. I wasn't sure if it was fear, excitement or anger that made me go on the offensive. "I hope you've come here about Melvin."

He leaned on the counter on the public side. Ike

leaned on the staff side. They looked like two mismatched peas in a pod—JT, tall and lean, still young-looking despite his cropped white hair, and Ike, short and hunched with his thick, curly white hair. "Melvin?" JT asked, smiling politely at Amelia, who'd leapt to her feet and was brandishing her Tarot cards as though ready to do a reading for the New Guy In Town.

"I've sworn out complaints about him." I slouched in my chair and tried to counter the intensity of JT's stare. I knew I couldn't do it, though. My green eyes were no match for his obsidian ones. "He's destroying property."

"Mrs. Dalworthy's pot-bellied pig," Ike said in a low voice. "He gets out on a tear now and again."

"Now and again?" I fumbled for an M&M, coming up with a brown one. I frowned and put it back. Brown was not what I needed now. I needed red or yellow, something with punch. JT watched me with that unnerving stare, seemingly relaxed as he leaned on the counter. But I knew better. I knew that casual pose hid the body of a—

Okay, let's not go there. I had once been intimately acquainted with JT McCord's body. "How about every week?" I demanded, anxious to divert my brain from a trip down Erotica Lane. "That pig has come into my yard just about every day this week. He's dug up my chives, he's tried to root up my azaleas, he's—"

"You live in Yolanda's house, is that right, Margaret?"

Hardly anybody called me Margaret any more, not even Yolanda, my mother. Everybody used my nickname, which was essentially an acronym. "That's right, John." I emphasized his first name. Two could play this name game. "When Mom moved into a senior townhouse, I moved into the old house."

"That's the house at the end of 4th Street?"

He knew damn well where my family lived. He'd come to pick me up on dates at that house many times in the past.

Ike beat me to the punch. "You know where Molly lives, JT," he said in a mild, reproving voice. "What's this about?"

"It's that pig, isn't it?" I kicked away from my desk and stood, taking several pink M&Ms to bolster my courage. "What has he done now? Did he dig up my roses? I was going to enter those roses next year in the flower show. I just tipped 'em a few weeks ago. If he dug them—"

"Tipped?" JT asked.

I popped the M&Ms as I advanced on the counter. "You know, half-burying them in the ground so they'll survive the winter. I had to dig a trench and—" I had a horrifying thought. "That pig didn't dig around my new plumbing, did he? Son of a bitch, I'll shoot him. I just had that septic system put in a few years ago, when Sam—" I ground to a halt when JT's alert black eyes focused on me.

"Sam? Your husband?"

Did I detect a note of jealousy in that low, calm voice? Nah. I must have imagined it. "My ex-husband," I said with what I hoped was a certain amount of dignity. "The one who ran off with a hairdresser." Unspoken but mentally shouted was *Like you.* "I divorced him in absentia. I was having the new septic system put in when that asshole ran away, leaving me holding the bill for the entire thing." I stood next to Ike and glared over the counter at JT. "Anyway, Sam's got nothing to do with this. Did that stupid pig do something to my plumbing?"

JT looked down at me. His face was as hard as I remembered it, all lines and planes and strength. "I'm afraid your husband does have something to do with this. The pig dug him up."

"Huh?" I looked at Ike, who was taller than me, even though he'd shrunk with age. He and I both turned our gazes on JT. "Melvin dug up who?"

"Your husband."

It took a minute for the words to sink in. Then Amelia said in a faint voice, "I knew that Death card was serious, Molly. You shouldn't laugh at Death."

JT's gaze fastened on her. I breathed a sigh of relief at some other poor unsuspecting schmuck coming under his scrutiny. "What do you mean?" he asked.

Poor Amelia looked like she'd faint, but, then, she always looked poorly. She was nearly seventy and everything about her was pale, from her pale brown hair to her pale skin to her pale green sweater and matching slacks. I intervened before she dropped.

"Amelia Gray, this is JT McCord. He's a cop, so you

shouldn't incriminate yourself any further. What do you mean, Melvin dug up Sam?"

"When was the last time you saw Sam Ferris?"

Ike shifted beside me. "Maybe I should call Mark Devlin. He's your lawyer, right? He handled your divorce. I think you should have a lawyer present."

"Oh, for heaven's sake." I longed for a red M&M but they were too far away to snatch easily. "Everybody knows the last time I saw Sam. We were at the Flower Show, five years ago in September. I was judging the dahlias. I caught him and Bobbi Jo doing the deed in the potting shed and I read him the riot act. When I got home I found he'd cleaned out some of his clothes and was gone—with, I might add, Bobbi Jo Rinderhoff, that slut from the Clip Joint Beauty Salon." I leveled a malevolent glare at JT, but it bounced right off.

He stared down at me. "I suppose there were witnesses," he said in that calm, low voice I remembered so well.

"I suppose there were," I spat back. I gave up on being inconspicuous and lunged for my M&Ms, grabbing two red and one yellow, a powerful combination. "Like most of Ottertail County and a few hundred folks from Blue Earth County as well." I popped the M&Ms and resumed glaring at him.

"Probably some folks from Iowa, too," Amelia ventured. "That garden club from Winnebago County came up." She trembled when JT turned his dark eyes on her.

Ike asked, "What's this about? You say Sam's body has turned up? How can that be?"

"We got a call down at the station about two hours ago. The pig's owner thought she heard him—Melvin—in distress. She went looking for him."

"And—?" I prompted when JT appeared stalled.

"Apparently Melvin was rooting around near your house. If I remember correctly, he was right outside the living room. He must have dug into a small chamber and fell in. When we went to get him out, we found your husband." He paused. "And the septic tank."

"How do you know it's Sam?" I demanded. "I mean, maybe it's—" JT was shaking his head. "What?"

"One of the deputies identified him. Bucky Thornton."

"Well, shit." I threw caution to the wind and grabbed four red M&Ms. If ever a woman needed strength, I did. "What did he—how—what—"

It was starting to sink in.

Sam was dead.

I'd always assumed he was off screwing Bobbi Jo Rinderhoff somewhere, laughing all the way to the bank with the money he'd stolen from me. Instead, he'd been right outside my living room window, composting next to the septic tank and the lilac bushes. I sat down. Luckily there was a chair to catch me.

Ike hurried to my side. "You're looking white, Molly." He gestured to Amelia. "Get her some water."

Sam was dead. Handsome, blond, laughing Sam was dead. I may have regretted marrying him, but the first few months were fun, with non-stop sex in just about every spot in town.

That started to pale, however, when I spotted him and Bobbi Jo in my arbor, Bobbi Jo with her skirt hitched up as she gyrated on Sam's naked lap. Sam and I argued and he swore it would never happen again. But then I found them at the Flower Show and told him to pack up and get out ...

... only to reappear now, five years later, landing in JT McCord's In Box. "Was it an accident?" I asked. "Did he fall in the sewer hole? That was a big hole. How did he die?"

JT watched as Amelia pressed a glass of water into my hand. "We're working on that. I'll need you to come with me."

I nodded. "Of course. Let me get my notepad and—" He gave me an odd look. "Well, it's news, isn't it? I'm a reporter, aren't I?"

"It's your ex-husband."

"And the keyword is 'ex'," I snapped. "I haven't seen or heard from Sam for five years. Time wounds all heels."

JT looked like he was trying not to smile. His mouth twitched and there was a suspicious twinkle in his dark eyes. "My car is just outside. You can ride with me."

"I don't think so." I took three yellow M&Ms as a

fortifier. "I'll drive myself."

"And I'll have Mark meet you." Ike went to his phone. JT sighed dramatically. "She's not under arrest."

"No, she isn't." I stuffed my notepad into my bag and my feet into my L.L. Bean mukluks as I grabbed my TBHS Boys Football letter jacket. "She's doing her civic duty and upholding the First Amendment." I reached for the drop-gate, but JT beat me to it. He lifted it in such a way I had to walk under his arm. I glared at his armpit for good measure, then swept ahead of him, out the door.

We emerged onto the sidewalk. A chill wind was hustling down the street, coming off the Tangle River with typical Minnesota fury. We'd already had six inches of snow and it was three days before Thanksgiving. It was going to be a long winter. I avoided the squad car parked in front of the building and headed toward my five-year-old flame-red Audi station wagon, parked just down the street.

"You're looking good, Molly," JT said.

I paused to shoot him a suspicious look. "What's that mean?"

He held up a hand. "Just what I said. I like your cut—that style suits you. And I'd forgotten just how black your hair was."

I automatically ran a hand through my thick, blunt-cut hair, making it spike up the way I liked. "It's easy to take care of."

"I see you're still wearing that letter jacket, too."

Oh, shit. I'd completely forgotten the jacket's history. This was his letter jacket, given to me one night in the back seat of a Chevy convertible. "It keeps me warm."

"They made those things to last," he commented. "I see you still like M&Ms."

I attempted a nonchalant shrug, but that little niggling doubt about *Your Lost Love* made me wonder. "What's not to like? It's a food group."

He smiled. It was as devastating as I remembered. Dimples flashed and his hard, inflexible mouth softened. My insides quivered at the sight. "Indeed it is. I'll see you at the house."

I paused with my hand on Augie the Audi's door. "House?"

"Your place, not mine." He winked. "Not yet at least." He slid into the squad car and was gone before I could close my gaping mouth.

Chapter 2

Surely my ears were deceiving me. Was JT McCord ... flirting with me? My heart was hammering so hard I felt like the shocks had gone out on the car. I positively twitched when I remembered the sight of JT McCord's depthless dark eyes.

I turned up the volume on the "Greatest Hits of the 80s" compilation in my CD player, hoping to jumpstart my mind. Discombobulated thoughts zinged around my cranium as I lurched out of my parking space, following JT's car to my house on the edge of town.

JT was not a flirty man. He didn't have a romantic bone in his body (a body I remembered very well). JT's idea of showing me a good time had been to let me play Backseat Cowgirl in his Chevy. His idea of romance was burgers and beer, then slap-and-tickle at the Route 8 Drive-In.

I drove like a zombie on autopilot through the four blocks of Main Street, took the left at 4th Street and headed over the bridge to the old farmhouse I called home. Of course, I reasoned, that was twenty years ago. Maybe he'd changed. Maybe he was lusting after my forty-five-year-old, five-foot-one, one-hundred-thirty-something-pound body. Maybe he was writing sappy, romantic personal ads in an attempt to woo me back into his saddle.

And maybe I was losing my mind. No way, Jose. JT

had dumped me for tall, slinky, blonde Shirley. He wouldn't be interested in short, black-haired, unslinky me. I was no match for Shirley's slender curves, killer fashion sense, or good taste. My idea of haute cuisine was the Wendy's drive-through and haute couture was L.L. Bean. Look at the overcoat JT was wearing, for cryin' out loud—it looked tailored. The only people who even wore suits in Tangle Butte, Minnesota, were lawyers and real estate salesmen. JT had always cared about junk like what was hip and what was stylish. He'd always angled for one step up, one more rung on the social ladder.

Which sort of begged the question: why did he come back to Tangle Butte, Minnesota, population 4,145? Why didn't he stay in Kansas City and work his way up that social ladder? I fumbled for my notepad and jotted a quick note, which I impaled on the nail I'd Super-Glued to Augie's dash. I needed to call some friends in Kansas City.

I slid into the entrance to my lane and fishtailed down the quarter-mile drive to the farmhouse, braking just in time as JT came to a stop near the garage, which was about twenty yards west of the house. Nearer the house, some men were standing by an ambulance, doors open. There was also a black station wagon, two squad cars, and a van all huddled in front of my garage. Then I saw the small backhoe and I got really pissed off.

"What do you think you're doing?" I demanded, flinging myself out of Augie and striding up to JT. "You can't just go around digging up my yard. You can't—"

He handed me something. I fumbled it open, my mittens making the job tricky. It was a search warrant. "You son of a bitch, how dare you lure me out here and—"

"Lure? I lured you?"

I was prepared to give him a seething retort when the backhoe started moving. "Stop!" I screamed. "You'll dig up Cassie!" I ran across the frozen gravel, slipping and sliding. JT made a grab for me, but he wasn't fast enough. I darted by the four men standing around the area I'd laboriously dug out days before and flung myself in front of the bucket of the backhoe as it prepared to strike.

"Jesus, Molly, get out of there!" JT shouted.

I couldn't answer, all my breath knocked out as he came down on top of me, covering me as the big bucket wavered overhead. I smelled wool coat, aftershave and JT's warm, minty, breath, tickling my ear.

"What the hell are you doing, Molly?"

I shivered and twisted. Our faces were inches apart. "I buried her two days ago, JT," I said and to my mortification I started to cry. "It took me almost two days to dig that grave. Now you're going to dig it up. My poor cat is—"

JT propped up on his elbows and stared down at me. I realized we were in the classic man-on-top lovers' pose. "Your cat?"

His eyes were searching my face, his mouth just a breath away from mine. I wondered if he wanted to kiss me as bad as I wanted to kiss him. I sniffled. "Cassiopeia, my cat. She died on Saturday morning. I had to dig her grave by hand. It took me most of Saturday and Sunday. The coffin I made isn't strong. If you put that backhoe bucket down there, it'll—"

"Okay, okay." He rolled off me, jumped to his feet, then reached down to haul me up by my lapels. "Your cat is buried there?"

I swiped at my nose, knowing how I must look. I have very pale skin to start with, and the combination of the cold and crying had probably left me with raccoon eyes and a Shriner-red clown nose. Then I shoved my beauty concerns aside as I confronted JT. I knew with fatalistic certainty that it didn't matter what I looked like.

"Yes," I said, looking down at the disturbed earth. "I buried all my pets here. There's Herbert the gerbil, Anthony and Cleo, my three parakeets, Simba, Ginny Hound, my—"

"Ginny?" JT looked briefly pained. "I remember that basset hound."

One of the men standing around the hole said, "That's a lotta animals."

"I've lived here off and on for forty-five years." I found a damp tissue in my pocket and dabbed at my nose. "This place has a lot of memories."

"We saw the fresh hole and figured—"

I glared at the speaker. "What, you figured I'd tucked away another husband? In case you've forgotten, Bucky Thornton, Delbert died of natural causes and is buried at the Tangle Butte Restful Hill Memorial Cemetery. And Sam—" I looked up at the house.

"Sorry, Molly," he said, looking a bit ashamed. "Guess we got carried away."

"I'll say you did." I slapped the paper clutched in my hand against my thigh, then I remembered the contents. "This doesn't give you the right to tear up my pet cemetery or my garden," I said, waving the search warrant in JT's face. "This doesn't give you—"

"Actually, it does," he said mildly.

We both looked around as a Cadillac SUV pulled into the driveway, parking behind JT's squad car. Mark Devlin, one of TB's four practicing attorneys, got out. "We'll see about that," I said, so mad I could barely talk. "We'll see what my attorney says." I stomped over to Mark, who always looked like he'd stepped out of the pages of GQ. He had George Clooney eyes, Robert Redford hair, and a libido that wouldn't quit. I knew, because I'd been on the receiving end of his propositions a few times.

"Mark, they've got this thing and—" I thrust the search warrant at him.

"Are you okay?" he asked, taking it, then sweeping me with a look.

I followed his glance. Two buttons on my flannel shirt had come undone at the top, which explained why my boobs were so cold all of a sudden. I tugged my jacket tighter around me. "I'm fine. I had to throw myself in front of that machine because they were getting ready to—"

He put an arm around me and gave me a little shake. It was almost condescending, but I didn't care by that point. I just wanted somebody to stop this madness. "Let me handle it." He released me and went to JT, holding out his hand.

The Meeting of the Male Models, I thought sourly, as I watched the two men talk. They'd been classmates in school, graduating from opposite ends of the social spectrum. Both were well-dressed, tall, broad-shouldered and long-legged. Mark was the golden-haired lawyer's boy who'd gone away to school, come back and went into legal practice with his daddy. JT was from the wrong side of the tracks, half-Indian, and a troublemaker in school who went away and now had come back to lead our bumbling law enforcement team. Presumably, he and Mark would be working together—or be at odds with each other—in the future. That would be interesting, since Mark had married JT's ex-wife. After the lovely Shirley divorced JT, she married Calvin Pritchard, who died and left her a fortune. She then moved on, marrying Mark Devlin. From what I'd heard, it was a troubled marriage.

Yes, indeedy. It should be interesting. I sidled closer, aching to pull out my reporter's notebook, but knowing I didn't dare.

Bucky smiled apologetically at me. "Sorry, Molly. I thought JT had served the warrant."

Ah ha. They screwed up. I hoped Mark would pick up on that. I decided to act forgiving, hoping to lull Bucky into even more stupidity. "I'm glad I got here in time. Honestly, Bucky, you know Delbert's not buried here."

"It wasn't Delbert we were looking for." He scuffed at the ground with his Timberlines, dislodging a frozen clod of dirt. Bucky was short and plump, his plain face red and blotchy from the cold.

"Not Delbert?" I asked. "Then who?"

"Well, Bobbi Jo left town with Sam, so—"

"Deputy." JT looked over at us, his hard face looking even harder in the meager light of late November. "Why don't you help Dr. Norcross?"

"Doc Norcross?" I looked beyond the idling backhoe, noticing for the first time the bright yellow tape fluttering in the wind near the shrubs by my living room window. "You mean Sam's still out here?" I started across the frozen driveway to the house, but JT put up an arm, blocking me from moving.

"Molly, they have a warrant to search the house and the grounds," Mark said as I glared at JT. "If you'll tell us where—"

We all turned to look as a yellow VW Bug came shooting down the driveway to skid to a stop by Mark's Cadillac. To his credit, Mark didn't look worried at the thought of an impending crash. Of course, he could afford three Caddies—one for him, one for Shirley the Queen Bitch, and one for his daughter Belinda, the Bitch Princess.

"Oh, Lord," I muttered as Yolanda sprang out of the Bug and started scurrying toward us, dressed, as always, in her faux leopard coat and pillbox hat. She seemed to remember she was supposed to be infirm and paused, tottering. I went to her side.

"Margaret Olivia Lawson, what is going on?" she demanded, grabbing for my arm to negotiate a tricky spot of ice.

Yolanda is eighty years old, looks sixty and acts forty. I often accuse her of trying to be my younger sister. We look remarkably alike, except Yolanda's hair is permed and thick while mine is straight and thick. We both have oval faces with high cheekbones and what my father used to laughingly call 'a generous mouth.' My older brother Don, who lives in Texas, claims Yolanda has a portrait aging for her in the attic. There are times when I agree.

Yolanda danced a bit as snow edged into her black ballerina pumps. Trust my mother to come to a crime scene dressed to kill, no pun intended. "I have no idea what's going on," I said as we approached JT and Mark. "All I know is the cops came to my house and want to dig up my garden, my yard, my pet cemetery, my—"

"Hello, John, how are you?" Yolanda said, in such a sweet voice I almost retched. "It's so nice to see you after all these years. Where are you staying? I hope you can come over for dinner sometime. We need to get caught up. What's it been, eighteen years? Twenty?"

"This is not a social call." I resisted the urge to strangle her with her faux pearls.

"I'm renting the Watson place," JT said, giving Yolanda a hug that almost lifted the old woman off her feet. "It's good to see you, Landie."

"Hell of a welcome to town," she said, peering past him to the yellow crime scene tape fluttering in the breeze. "You've been Chief for what—three days? And look what we have." Her bright green eyes looked expectantly at JT.

"Yeah, what do we have?" I asked, trying to edge past him.

JT and Mark exchanged a look, then JT shrugged. "Found Sam in a hole next to the house. Is that where the new septic was put in, Molly?"

I started walking toward the hole. "Just about. It was a bit closer to the house." I paused a few yards away. I could see Doc Norcross leaning over, blocking my view of the site.

"It looks like somebody dug a small grave near the septic," Mark said behind me. "The body wasn't buried as deep as the septic, so what with frost heave and all ..."

I nodded. Frost heave was a common occurrence in Minnesota, where temperatures could fluctuate from eighty below zero to eighty above, sometimes all within a week. If you didn't bury things—flower bulbs, pipes, building footings, and, I realized, bodies—deep enough, they'd eventually work their way to the surface. We'd had brutally hot summers for the last four years and last winter was cold, even by Minnesota standards.

"So that means Melvin was able to get to him." I looked around. "Where is that pig? Isn't he a witness or something?"

Once again, I was surprised to see something like humor in JT's normally humorless eyes. "He was released into the custody of his owner."

I watched as Doc Norcross said something to the other men standing around, then a dark, long object was lifted up out of the hole. "Is that—?" I couldn't talk.

JT moved in front of me, blocking the view. "Yeah. We had some trouble getting him out. The ground's pretty frozen."

"Tell me about it," I said, tugging off one mitten to show him my blisters. "I had to keep lighting my barbecue grill over Cassie's grave just to get the ground warm enough to dig."

"Should have rented a post-hole digger," Mark commented, his dark blue eyes watching the morbid scene.

I snorted. "I can't handle a post-hole digger, Mark."

He seemed surprised, then grinned in an 'aw shucks' way. "Sorry, Molly. I keep forgetting you aren't normal-sized. You act big."

I decided that was a compliment. "So what do we do now?" I asked, trying to peek around JT's blue topcoat.

"Now we go in the house," Yolanda said, putting an arm around me.

"No way. They can't be digging up—"

"Okay," JT said with theatrical patience. "We won't dig up the pet cemetery and we won't dig up the roses. Anything else?"

"I'm president of the Garden Club. Everything is sacred in my garden. You can't just dig, willy-nilly, anyplace you want to. You might—"

"Are you president of the Literary Society, too?" he asked.

"Shirley made sure I wasn't accepted into the Literary Society." I gave up trying to peer around him. "Why would I be president of the Literary Society?"

"Well, you being a published author and all."

I looked up at him. "How did you know about that?" I had a modest celebrity status in town, but JT had only been here a few days. How did he know I'd sold some books?

"I've read all your books. They're good, Molly. You sure know how to write a good murder." He turned to look at the crime scene. I followed his gaze and saw a long black bag being hoisted out of a small hole. I could see now that the hole wasn't that deep, certainly not as deep as the septic hole had been, five years earlier.

Then JT's words penetrated. "What? A good murder?"

He nodded. "Yeah, I've read all three of your books. You sure know how to murder somebody. You got it all down right, including the police procedures and—"

"Now just a minute," I sputtered. "I did a lot of research. I talked to homicide detectives in Des Moines when I lived there, and in Minneapolis after I moved back here."

"Oh, I'm sure. You said the last time you saw Sam was at the Flower Show, five years ago?"

"Am I supposed to answer that?" I asked Mark, who was staring in fascination at the gurney being manhandled into the waiting ambulance.

"You've got nothing to hide," Mark said, jerking his attention back to us.

Thank God my attorney was back on track. I felt so protected.

Not.

"I saw Sam at the Ottertail County Flower Show five

years ago. He and Bobbi Jo were in the potting shed, having sex. I read him the riot act in front of God and everybody, then I went back to judge the dahlias." I recognized the unbelieving look in JT's eyes. "It wasn't the first time I'd caught him and Bobbi Jo doing the tango. I told him if I ever caught him again, he was out. I caught him. He was out."

"And you're a woman of your word, aren't you, Molly?" JT said softly.

My face got hot with embarrassment. I'd said almost exactly the same thing to him twenty years ago when I'd seen him and Shirley coming out of the Tangle Butte Palace Theater, their arms around each other. My stomach clenched at the memory of pain and humiliation. "Yes, I am." I met his eyes. I was surprised to see no hint of anger, just an expression of perplexed sadness that suddenly made me melancholy.

The look vanished and the hard cop was back. "What did you see when you returned to the house from the show?"

"Shit, JT, it was five years ago." I tugged off my other mitten and fumbled in my pocket for my emergency stash of M&Ms. These were all my brown rejects, which didn't provide me with any psychic boost, but the chocolate would help.

"Well, did you see a body?" he prodded, watching me extract four candies from the round zipped pocket dispenser I'd gotten at M&M World in Las Vegas.

"Of course I didn't see a body. The hole was filled in when I got home. I remember, because the crew told me they'd fill it in while I was gone and I was surprised to find they'd really done it when I got back." I glanced at Mark. "It was Jimmy Hunt's crew."

He nodded. "They're not the sharpest tacks in the box."

"You don't have to be sharp to dig a septic hole." I tucked my stash away, then tugged my mitten back on. I jumped when the door slammed on the ambulance. "Where are they taking him? Am I supposed to identify him or something?"

JT put a hand on my arm and pulled me aside as the ambulance began a stately crawl down my drive. "That won't be necessary."

"How did he die, John?" Yolanda asked. I'd almost forgotten she was there, which was surprising given her propensity to dominate any conversation within a city block. I looked closer at her. She was a bit pale.

JT noticed, too. "You ladies should go in the house. I promise we won't dig up anything without asking you first, Molly."

I watched the ambulance carrying Sam away. "You're sure?"

JT nodded. "Go inside. I'll check with you before we start digging."

Mark put a hand under Yolanda's arm. They started toward the side steps that led into the kitchen. I followed, then paused to glance back at JT. "How did he die? You didn't say."

JT was watching the ambulance trundle down my lane. Then he swung his gaze to me, his expression unreadable. "Looks like somebody stabbed him with a pitchfork. Did one go missing, Molly?"

I gulped and took a step back, almost landing on my ass as I hit an icy patch. I'd been missing my favorite pitchfork since the day Sam disappeared. I considered lying, then knew I had no choice. I nodded dumbly, feeling as though I was choking.

JT turned to stare at the gaping hole where Sam had lain. "Looks like we found it."

Chapter 3

"They think I killed him."

"Don't jump to conclusions, Molly," Mark said.

We were sitting in the living room drinking coffee laced with Maker's Mark bourbon and, in my case, an M&M chaser. There is nothing like bourbon and chocolate. Well, maybe bourbon, chocolates, and sex could beat it, but other than that ...

I went to the window for the tenth time and peeked out. It was starting to get the dusky gray feeling of nightfall. The backhoe was gone and Bucky was walking around my yard holding some kind of contraption that was shaped like a divining rod. "What are they doing?"

"Searching for more bodies," Yolanda said. She was on her second 'coffee.' I suspected I'd have overnight company if she didn't cut back on the booze.

"Why would I kill Sam?" I asked the world at large. "I just wanted a divorce. And would somebody tell me why JT is investigating this? He's a boss, for cryin' out loud. Don't they have deputies to do this kind of stuff?"

"I don't think any of our deputies have ever investigated a murder," Mark said. "Not to mention the fact two of them are part-time. From what I hear, JT has had plenty of experience with this kind of thing. Besides, he's new here. He wants to make an impression."

"He's doing that," I muttered.

"At least you have nothing to worry about," Yolanda

said. "When you left the Flower Show, Amelia and I were with you, Reverend Potter came over, Ike called—"

I turned and stared at her in amazement. She was right. I'd forgotten that I'd had company that day—a little entourage had followed me home, probably worried that I'd do Sam bodily harm. I sagged into the chintz armchair nearest the window, almost squishing Mr. T, my tuxedo cat, who grumbled and made room for me.

I popped two M&Ms and followed them with a strong sip of coffee. The back door slammed. We heard footsteps in the kitchen, then JT paused in the doorway to the living room.

"I have an alibi," I blurted.

He raised his eyebrows in surprise. "Is there any coffee left?"

I waved a hand toward the kitchen. "You know where it is." He turned to go back the way he'd come. "I have an alibi," I called out happily. "After the Flower Show."

"I know." I heard him opening cupboards. "Bucky Thornton and Doc both said that Reverend Potter came over here. They remembered him telling how Sam had cleaned you out. Once again, you were the talk of the town for a week or two."

I decided to ignore that little 'once again'—for now, at least. "Yeah, he left me a note and took my checkbook, savings book, my credit cards, my—" I stopped. "Maybe this explains why those credit cards were never used. I called to cancel them right away."

"What was in the note?" JT asked, coming back into the room. He'd shed his blue overcoat somewhere. Mark assessed JT's gray tweed suit coat, dark gray shirt and striped tie, black slacks, and shiny black boots. From the glance Mark gave him, I assumed it was an expensive outfit. I had to admit, it looked good on JT.

"It was printed on the computer—just something like *Molly, this isn't working, it's best that I leave. Sam.* Something like that." I shrugged. "He didn't even sign it. I didn't even keep it."

"What about the bank account?"

"What about it?" I felt liquid with happiness and bourbon. I had an alibi.

JT sipped his coffee, watching me over the rim of his

Tangle Butte Festive Fling 50th Anniversary mug. "Did he take money out of your bank account?"

I sat up straighter. "Yes, out of my savings account. Where's the money?"

"How much?"

"Almost ten thousand," I said. "Damn, where's my money? I always assumed he and Bobbi Jo used it to travel to some beach somewhere. Sam always hated the winters here. I just assumed he'd gone to the Keys or someplace warm." I considered making a play for the M&Ms in the candy dish on the coffee table, but inertia and fourteen pounds of black-and-white cat kept me pinned to the chair.

"Bobbi Jo was a pretty girl," Yolanda said. When I shot her a dagger-filled glance, she added, "In a cheap, floozy sort of way."

"Maybe Bobbi Jo killed him," I said. "Maybe she killed him, took the money, and ran away with some other man. She was such a slut. She probably had two or three men on the side. Kind of like—"

"Get me more coffee, dear," Yolanda demanded, brandishing her mug. I almost snapped at her, then I noticed the expression on her face.

Oops. I'd almost opened my mouth and inserted my foot. I'd almost said 'Shirley' and the two men who were still alive to attest to Shirley's sluttishness were right here in my living room. "I can't." I rubbed my cat, who vibrated on my knees. "Mr. T commands that I stay."

"Mr. T?" JT asked, bending over to pet my tuxedo monster.

I waved my hand. "It stands for Mr. Toasty, Mr. Tentative, Mr. Terrified, Mr. Terrific—depends on his mood and mine." I watched JT's hand stroke Mr. T., who responded with claws in my knee. JT's hands were big, with knobby knuckles and heavy veins on the back. They appeared clumsy, but I knew they weren't. I had vivid memories of what those hands could do.

I looked up. He was staring at me. My face got hot as I wondered if he could see the memories in my eyes. I struggled for a change of thought. "What did you mean, 'once again I had the town talking'?"

JT straightened up. "Well, you sort of set tongues

wagging when you married Delbert."

"What the hell do you know about it?" I demanded. My mother gave me a warning glance but I was too pissed off to heed her. "You dumped me like a hot potato, married Shirley and were off on your honeymoon to Acapulco."

His eyes got hard. "And a day later you married Delbert and two weeks later he was dead." He took a sip of coffee. "To be expected, I guess, when a seventy-five-year-old man marries a twenty-five-year-old woman."

My ears were burning with temper and embarrassment. Everybody assumed I'd killed Delbert with sex, and I never bothered to correct those assumptions. The truth was Delbert and I had cuddled, him trying to comfort my broken heart and me trying to comfort him as he faced the death he knew was coming from terminal cancer.

"I suppose Sam wanted to get his hands on Delbert's money," JT commented.

This was an assumption I could easily correct. "I didn't get a dime from Delbert." It was the literal truth. "His kids made sure of that."

Mark cleared this throat. I'd forgotten he and Yolanda were in the room. "That's the truth, JT. My father handled the pre-nuptial agreement. Janet, Sharon, and Claudia Langford made sure that none of Delbert's cash went to Molly." His eyes met mine and I almost laughed at the conspiratorial mischief there. Again, it was the literal truth.

JT pulled back. I realized he'd probably figured me for a gold-digger all those years ago. I waved a hand in what I hoped was airy dismissal. "Anyway, that's old history. After Delbert died, I went to Des Moines and made a reasonably good life for myself. I came back to town eight years ago when Yolanda had surgery. Ike offered me a job and before I knew it, I was a resident of Tangle Butte again. Then I met Sam and ..."

I let my voice trail off, trying to sound wistful and sad. It must have worked. JT looked like he was doing a slow burn. "Sam knew how to treat a girl to a good time. He was fun. I was sorry when he screwed around." I shot JT a haughty glance. "However, screwing around seems to be a habit with some men."

Both he and Mark shifted uncomfortably. My mother, bless her heart, decided it was time to intervene. "Don't you have Mr. Sex tonight, dear?"

Damn. She was right. It was Monday. The Monday Readers Social EXchange was a book group I'd formed when Shirley blackballed me from the TB Literary Society. "I forgot all about it. You're right. We're here tonight." I glanced at my Timex. "In an hour."

Mark stood up. I suppose it embarrassed him that I'd been forced to start a rival book club when his wife had banished me from the oldest book club in town. I nudged Mr. T off my lap. "Mark, thanks for coming out, I appreciate it." I struggled out of my comfortable chair, turned—and saw the expression on JT's face.

Like those credit card commercials say—priceless. I considered correcting his misconceptions about who Mr. Sex was, but I discarded the idea. Let him blow a gasket. See if I cared. "Is there anything else you need, Chief McCord?" I asked as Mark and I ambled toward the kitchen and the outside door.

JT shook himself loose from his trance and followed us, taking his topcoat from the dining room chair where he'd left it. "This isn't over, Molly." He set his coffee mug in the kitchen sink.

"It's over for tonight, though, isn't it?"

If looks could kill, I'd have been foaming at the mouth while I twitched on the kitchen floor. "Don't disturb the scene," he snapped. "We'll be out first thing in the morning, when it's light, to keep processing the evidence."

"Not much evidence after five years, is there?"

He shot me a venomous glance and went out the door. Mark watched, then turned to me with a little laugh. "You've got his Jockeys in a jam."

"I doubt it. Seriously, Mark. Thanks for coming out. Bill me, okay?"

"I will." He winked at me. "I know you can afford it. See you later."

I closed the door on him, peeking out the curtains as he paused on the top step and said something to JT, who'd just started across the drive. Oh, I wished I were a mouse hiding under the stoop so I could hear that conversation.

"Technically it's true," Yolanda said behind me.

I jumped, almost peeing my pants. She was sneaky for an old woman. "What is?"

"Delbert didn't leave you any cash."

I went to the fridge. I'd shopped the day before so I was well prepared for Mr. Sex's Ladies, as we called ourselves. "No, he didn't. The Three Witches of Langford made sure of that." I brought out the vegetable platter, containers of dip, plastic-wrapped cold meat platter, and tray of condiments. "All he left me was three hundred shares of original Microsoft stock, some Xerox stock and Shell Oil stock." I staggered to the kitchen table and set down my load. Then I caught a glimpse of Yolanda's expression and we both burst out laughing.

"I need to move my car so the boys can get out." She gave me a brisk hug. "If you need anything, you let me know."

"Are you okay to drive?" I asked, visions dancing in my head of a yellow VW Bug wavering into the ditch.

"I'm fine. I'll call you when I get home. Have fun tonight, dear." She paused with her hand on the doorknob. "Don't let your past feelings for JT get in the way."

She was gone before I could question her about that cryptic comment. As soon as she left, I called Ike, giving him an eyewitness account to the biggest news to hit Tangle Butte since Marlene Burke absconded with five hundred dollars from the Lutheran Church's Poor Fund and went to Reno to gamble. I promised Ike I'd get pictures of the crime scene in the morning.

"Guess this means I can't do the interview with the Chief," I said.

Ike sighed. "Conflict of interest. You're right. I'll handle it. See you tomorrow."

I laid out my buffet on the dining room table, then went upstairs to wash my face and change my shirt. I glanced out the bedroom window and saw the yellow tape in the light from the living room. That's when it hit me like a ton of bricks.

Sam hadn't left with Bobbi Jo, like I'd thought. Somebody had actually killed him and left him lying out by my window. I sat on the bed, overwhelmed by memory. He and I had made love on this bed, in that shower, on the back porch—the house was permeated with memories, all of a sudden. When I thought he was a whoring bastard, I had banished those memories, but they came rushing back now.

Poor Sam. Why had someone killed him and dumped him in that hole? All in all, he was inoffensive, just another real estate salesman who charmed the ladies. I think I'd known from the start it wouldn't work. Sam tried to be monogamous, but he just wasn't the kind of man to settle down with one woman. I had ignored my doubts, though. I'd been lonely, approaching forty and getting scared I'd never have love again in my life. Sex with Sam was fun, and marrying him had solved a lot of problems for me.

What about Bobbi Jo? No one had really mentioned her. We'd all assumed she left town with Sam five years ago. Was she dead, too? Or did she kill Sam and flee? But why would she kill him? What was her motive? The writer in me—the one who'd penned three murder mysteries and was struggling with her fourth—was intrigued. Bobbi Jo's sister was still in town. I wondered if Sue Anne had ever heard from Bobbi Jo. I scribbled a note to myself on the pad by the bed to call Sue Anne in the morning.

The glare of headlights illuminated the room. Shaking loose from my memories, I went downstairs to greet Mr. Sex's Ladies. My literary group was not as economically advantaged as Shirley's group. Instead of doctor wives, lawyer wives, and business execs, we had waitresses, checkout clerks, cleaning ladies, and stay-at-home moms. Of course, we didn't read literary masterpieces and I'd banned Oprah's Book Club selections because they were all too 'uplifting.' No, Mr. Sex's Ladies read romance novels, murder mysteries and sci-fi. The only rules were that the book had to be readable in a month, have no dismemberments and no gratuitous sex. Other than that, anything went, and frequently did.

We met on the first Monday of the month at the Brew 'n' Chew Café in town, and the third Monday of the month at a member's house. We had strict rules of behavior, rigorously enforced by Paula Belkin, our seventy-five-year-old secretary. The first hour was for food and gossip. The next hour was for Book Talk. Anything after that was a free-for-all. I knew that we'd have no trouble filling the Gossip Hour tonight.

The Ladies arrived promptly at six-thirty. Coats were shed, plates were filled, then we gathered in the living room, younger members on the floor using the coffee table, others using trays or balancing plates on their laps.

"Tell all," Darlene Abernathy commanded. She was a clerk at the Git 'n' Go convenience store/gas station on the outskirts of town. The Git gas station and the Brew café were the hubs of our gossip universe. This was flattery, for her to ask me for an update.

I reveled in my brief moment of fame, telling them about the Pig, the Body, the Cops and the Alibi. Women crowded my window, angling for a view of the Pit, which had been covered by a large tarp and what I thought was an inordinate amount of yellow Crime Scene tape. I finished my summary as we started on coffee and the cake provided by Mavis Fairchild, clerk at the Ace Hardware store in town.

"Somebody killed him?" Carla Baxter asked, shoveling down Chocolate Dream Swirl Delight. "Who would do that? Why?"

I shrugged. "Wasn't me. I've got an alibi."

"Couldn't be a jealous husband, Bobbi Jo wasn't married," Barb Thayer said. "Besides, everybody knows Sam messed around. It was never serious."

Charlene Anderson coughed and waved a hand dramatically. "Swallowed wrong," she gasped. This necessitated thumps on her back. Charlene was a young stay-at-home mom, pretty in a tired, worn-out way. She had joined the club a year or two earlier, but missed almost as many meetings as she attended due to 'Bobby's cold' or 'Nancy's croup.' I didn't envy Charlene her stay-at-home-mom life.

Ruth Michaels, Mr. Sex president and manager of the Yard and Feed Home Improvement store, called the ladies to order at seven-thirty and we began our discussion of the latest James Patterson book. We trounced it thoroughly for an hour, then voted on December's book, deciding on the latest Martha Grimes offering. The talk turned once again to the resident Mystery.

"I'm surprised you didn't smell him," Peggy Calder said. She was a major spoke on the Gossip Universe Wheel because she waitressed at the Brew 'n' Chew. "He wasn't buried that deep. You'd think he'd bloat up or something."

"Bucky said it was three feet down. Apparently, there was some kind of plywood top or something. Melvin broke through that. Otherwise they wouldn't have found him."

"How did he die?" Charlene asked. Her voice was so low I barely heard her. She seemed as white as a ghost. I wondered if she was breeding again, poor girl. She'd been deathly ill with both of her pregnancies.

"They'll do an autopsy," Mavis said before I could answer. "They always do one when there's suspicious death."

I remembered JT's comment about the pitchfork. I didn't think he'd want me to share that information. "JT didn't say anything about an autopsy. I suppose you're right."

"So JT is investigating this?" Kathy Fahr asked with a laugh in her voice. Kathy had taught English for almost thirty years. She'd watched me moon over JT McCord all through high school and beyond.

"Yeah, I guess so," I said.

"How about that?" Barb said. "JT investigating who killed Molly's husband. It's almost poetic justice, isn't it?"

We all paused to consider that. "It's poetic something," I agreed.

A cell phone rang somewhere. "Oh, I'm sorry," Charlene mumbled, pawing through a big blue cloth bag. "It must be Chuck."

Chuck Anderson, Charlene's husband, had started as a teller at the bank and was now in some sort of middle management position. I'd chatted with him occasionally and he'd helped me try to trace the money when Sam decamped with my cash. Chuck was nice, but I thought he was a little too protective of Charlene. But then her brothers, the Hunt construction boys, had been overly protective, too. And let's face it, what did I know about protective men? Delbert was the only man who'd tried to protect me, but his daughters had overridden him.

"I heard—" Peggy paused dramatically, "—that Shirley has her eye on JT McCord again."

"Not," someone said in disbelief. "She divorced him so fast his head spun."

Peggy shook her head. "Ellen Dawkins is a hairdresser over at the Clip Joint. She said Shirley was in there, talking about JT. Said it sounded to her like Shirley was setting her sights on JT again." Peggy shrugged. "He's a fine hunk of man."

All eyes turned to me. I tried to appear innocent. "I'm more concerned with the hunk of man they found outside my house."

People chuckled. Charlene closed her phone, looking a bit ill. I regretted my flip words. I hadn't really loved Sam, but I'd liked him. He didn't deserve to end up like this. I soon forgot it, though, as people got up and stretched, taking used dishes out to the kitchen. I got the coats I'd stored in the downstairs den, grabbing my zip-up sweatshirt jacket on the way.

Peggy watched me take my foot-long flashlight from the hook near the kitchen door as I walked out to the cars with them. "Where are you going?"

"There's a cat hanging around." I gestured toward the tool shed across the drive, twenty yards away. "Cassie adopted the poor critter. What with all the uproar today, I thought I'd check on it. I think the cat gave birth a while ago and I'm not sure where she's hiding the kittens."

Peggy gave me a brief hug. "Sorry about Cassie, but at least she's not in pain anymore."

I nodded, which was all I could do. I still got choked up at the thought of my poor calico cat, who had died in my arms just days before. She wasn't the first pet who'd died that way and wouldn't be the last, but it was always hard.

I watched as people piled into the cars they'd brought, waving them good-bye with my flashlight. Then I went down the frozen drive, picking my way carefully until the motion lights over first the garage, then the shed, came on to illuminate my way. I'd lived here most of my life and knew the place well, but in the fitful moonlight it was hard to see the path.

I went into the old wooden shed, flipping on the overhead light that swung on a chain above. It was a fifteen-by-fifteen space, somewhat tidy, with my riding mower taking up most of the room. I moved inside slowly, not anxious to startle the starved cat I'd seen lurking around for the past month. I'd set out food and water and bedding in various spots, but the coons might have gotten those offerings or her babies, if indeed she'd had them.

A noise behind me made me jump. A short piece of two-by-four clattered against my garden tool rack, rattling the hoe against my spading fork. I shone my flashlight into the corner, expecting to see the cat.

Nothing was there. The hairs on my arms tingled and my mouth was suddenly dry. I decided to put out some more food and water, then continue the search in the morning. I pushed against the door—

— and it didn't budge.

That was weird. This door didn't have a lock. It had an outside padlock, but I never used it. The padlock just dangled on the hasp. I pushed harder on the door but it wouldn't move.

That's when I smelled the smoke.

Chapter 4

I pushed on the door. It held fast. My father built this shed long before I was born. It was weatherworn but sturdy, with a few gaps in the floorboards and the walls. I searched for something to use as a battering ram. The mower? No, I'd drained it of oil and gas, in preparation for winter. Hoe, hammer, rake, shovel—all solid, but not battering-ram-solid. Wheelbarrow? Nope, mine was the fold-up kind, the only type I could manage because I was so short.

Was it the barbeque grill? I'd removed its legs and set it on the ground, keeping a fire going so I could warm up the dirt to dig Cassie's grave. I'd started on Saturday, digging off and on, moving the grill as the ground thawed. I finished in the bitter cold of Sunday morning. I'd set the grill to one side to burn itself out. It was now Monday night.

Had it smoldered all this time? Where had I left it? Once I got the grave dug, I'd forgotten about it. Surely I didn't set it near the shed, did I? I wasn't having Senior Moments already, was I? Hell, I was only forty-five—I was too young to be so absent-minded, wasn't I?

Smoke started to edge under the door and my feet. I stepped back, coughing. I wasn't panicked—yet. I swung the flashlight around, highlighting those dark corners. I had an axe somewhere. Where was it?

The smoke was thicker and dense, the way a grill is

when it's starting to die and grease is sputtering in it. Plumes of gray now rose in the flashlight beam. I ran against the door and bounced off, landing with a bruising thump on the ground when I slipped. I jumped up, anxious to get away from the boiling smoke.

I heard something. I pressed against the wall of the shed. A car? Was someone pulling into the driveway? I pounded on the wall. "I'm in here!" I shouted as loud as I could, but my voice cracked as I choked on the smoke. "Hey!"

What was that sound? Was it voices? I grabbed the hoe and started pounding on the side of the building, near where I thought the voices were coming from.

"Look, what's that?" The voice was faint but audible.

I almost fainted with relief. Finally—there were footsteps outside, then someone pounded on the shed.

"I'm in here," I called out, dropping the hoe. The smoke was so thick I could barely breathe. "The door's stuck."

"It's locked."

It was Paula, our elderly secretary. Geez, she wouldn't be able to help me. Then I heard Charlene's voice. They must have ridden together to our meeting. "I'm in here," I called out. "I don't know how the door closed."

"What's the combination?"

Combination—to what? Then I remembered—the padlock. "I'm not sure. Check on the back, maybe I wrote it down on a piece of tape." I started coughing again, the smoke thick and swirling around me.

"There's nothing here." Charlene sounded scared. Someone rattled the door.

"There's smoke coming in," I called out. "I thought it was coming from the door."

"No, there's nothing here. I can see the smoke but—wait."

The smoke was everywhere now. I'd thought at first that it was coming in under the door but now I realized it was coming from near the door, probably under the ancient floorboards.

"I called the fire department." It was Paula's voice, brisk and professional. "You try to get away from the door, Molly. Get away from the smoke. We'll see if we can't find the fire and knock it out with something. Come on, Charlene. Let's get some snow."

Thank you, God, for Paula's calm, straightforward thinking. I was a mile outside of town. It would take time for the trucks to reach me. How long could a person last with smoke inhalation? I tried not to think about it. I tugged my sweatshirt around my face, trying to block out the smoke as I huddled in a corner, my back to the worst of the smell. For a few minutes, I felt relief, then the smoke started to edge up under my jacket. I pulled it tighter, then peeked out, wondering if I should find the axe and try to hack my way out.

The thick, choking smoke drove me back to the confines of my sweatshirt. I leaned against the wall, pressing to a small crack, trying to get fresh air. My eyes were running as I gasped. My ears were roaring. Were there flames? I felt warmer. Was it just the sweatshirt, wrapped so tightly around me I couldn't breathe? What was—

The screeching wail of sirens shattered my thoughts, jerking me upright. I made a mistake and raised my head, gagging as fumes enclosed me. I staggered nearer the door, stumbling over garden tools, my Wellington boots, and some boxes. Shouting voices were outside but I didn't try to understand what they were saying. I wanted to vomit. Bile rose in my throat and I bent over, retching, my eyes streaming. I covered my face with my hands, careening as I tried to get away from the pain in my throat, face, and eyes.

Strong hands grabbed me. I was jerked out of the vaporous cloud, picked up and carried. I heaved, sucking in deep lungs full of clear, cold Minnesota farm air. Then I choked, crying as I buried my face in someone's shoulder, trying to get the pain out of my eyes as I kicked feebly.

"I've got you, Molly," JT said, his face pressed against mine. "It's okay, I've got you."

I rubbed harder, feeling his soft shirt against my face. "It hurts, JT. My eyes."

"It's okay, it's just the smoke. It'll go away."

I nuzzled into his shoulder, drinking in warm smells of man, sweat, aftershave. *Anything but that damn smoke,*

I thought, as I scrubbed my face against his collarbone. I peered out, my face pressed under his chin. I moved my head and he moved his at the same moment. We stared into each other's eyes from inches away.

"Are you all right?" JT shifted slightly.

That's when I realized he was carrying me. I kicked some more. "Put me down."

His arms loosened and I thought he'd drop me. I grabbed his neck, holding on for dear life. He smiled, his dark eyes glinting in the headlights of a truck parked a few feet away. "Gotcha." He let one arm sag slowly.

I was solidly against him, staring up into his face with my arms around his neck. A long, hard, warm male pressed against my body. He put both hands on my waist, digging in gently and caressing me. Then I released my hold and slid the rest of the way to stand, wobbling, on the ground.

"What happened? How'd you get here?" I grabbed some snow, rubbing it on my streaming eyes. He was dressed in denims and a long-sleeved dark blue shirt, but he wasn't wearing a coat. He must have run out of the house like a bat out of hell.

JT's gaze swung to the shed then down the farm lane, where a fire truck was cautiously picking its way along the ruts. "I heard it on the scanner," he said as he walked back to the shed.

"JT, where's your coat?" I called after him.

He looked down at his shirt, then veered to the dark pickup truck with its door ajar, parked near Augie. He grabbed a coat from the truck before going to the shed where smoke billowed.

Charlene and Paula slid their way to me and we had a group hug. "Thank you so much," I babbled. "How did you know?"

Charlene gave a shaky laugh. "I left my purse and we had to come back. Oh, I'm so glad I did, I'm so glad you're okay." She grabbed me and hugged me again. Charlene wasn't a big person, but she wore one of those Michelin Tire-Woman coats so she nearly suffocated me. I pushed her away, pulling them both to one side as the small fire truck edged into my turnaround.

I swiped at my face. "Where's that smoke coming

from?" I shivered, tugging my sweatshirt around me.

"Come on, let's move." Paula put an arm around my shoulders and steered me toward the garage where we could watch.

The volunteer fire fighters approached the building cautiously. I'd lost sight of JT, who vanished into the shadows at the back of the shed, which butted up against the windbreak of spruce trees on the north side of my property. The men surrounded the building. JT soon emerged, pointing toward the windbreak. I started to follow the firemen, but Paula tugged me back. "Let them do their job, Molly. We'd just be in the way."

I knew she was right but I wanted to know if I'd done something so stupid as leave that grill where it could smolder. Soon JT and John Hite, the fire chief, walked out of the darkness to join us.

"Why don't you go on inside?" JT said.

I recognized a command when I heard it. "What was it?" I demanded.

John answered. "It might be that grill but I don't know how it—" He stopped talking when JT shot him a glance.

"What?"

JT put a hand on my arm and started toward the house. "We'll need to examine it closer, tomorrow, when it's light outside. It's okay now."

"Damn it, JT, talk to me." I wiggled but couldn't escape.

"Go inside, have some tea, and I'll be there in a minute."

"Tea, hell, I'm having some bourbon." I gave up fighting him, jerking my arm out of his grasp. I gestured to Paula and Charlene. "Come on, girls. Charlene, where did you leave your purse?" We went inside, Charlene moving ahead of me to the living room where she grabbed the lumpy blue bag half-hidden by the afghan draped on the couch arm.

"You're sure you're okay?" Paula asked.

I nodded, pulling my Maker's Mark out of the Booze Stash in the pantry. The bottle had gotten a workout today. "I'll be fine. I don't know how that door got locked. The padlock must have slipped." I paused as I poured a healthy tot into a glass. "Wait a minute. How did you get the door open?"

"JT kicked it open," Paula said.

"He what?"

"He kicked it open." Paula pulled on her mittens. "Fear gives a man strength."

I sipped the bourbon. "Fear?"

Paula smiled at me. "I've never seen a man look so panicked since I had my last child and my husband was with me in the delivery room. I swear he thought I was going to die." Paula patted my hand. "It's tough on men when someone they love is in danger."

"Love?"

"Oh, yes." Paula turned as JT came through the back door. "JT, it's a good thing you're keeping an eye on Molly. I don't know what we would have done."

"It's just second nature for me to monitor the scanner," he said, moving past Charlene to stand near me.

"Uh-huh," Paula said. "We'll leave you now, dear. If you need anything, you just call."

Charlene was rooted to the spot, clutching her lumpy bag to her puffy coat. "I'm so sorry, Molly," she whispered. "We tried to get you out."

I waved it away. "Not your fault that you couldn't open the door. Don't worry. Go on home now." I turned to JT. "Are the fire guys still there?" I heard voices as Charlene opened the door from the mudroom and went outside.

"They'll be here for a bit. Don't go out there tonight, okay? I want to examine it tomorrow. That reminds me, what were you doing out there?"

I bristled at his snappish tone. "It's my house, I can go where I want."

He checked his watch. "It's past ten at night."

"Okay, okay. There's a cat I'm keeping an eye on." I saw his exasperated expression. "She's sort of moved in and I think she had kittens. She's probably run away after all the fuss today with that stupid backhoe. Did you see her this afternoon?"

JT leaned against the counter, his hands dug deep into his leather jacket pockets. I suspected he wanted to strangle me and this was his way of stopping himself.

"No, we didn't."

I sipped deeply at my bourbon. "Well, if you do, don't scare her away, okay?"

He closed his eyes briefly. I was surprised by how tired he appeared. There were lines around his eyes and mouth. Of course, he was frowning like crazy, so that may have had something to do with it.

"Promise me you won't leave the house again tonight?"

He made it sound like I was planning to sneak away to go gambling or drinking. I opened my mouth to give him a scathing reply.

"Please."

I shut my mouth again. He sounded sincere. "Oh, okay." I sipped my bourbon. "What was it, JT? What happened out there?"

He pushed away from the counter, his shoulders hunched. "I'm not sure, Molly."

I looked up at him. "Was it an accident?"

He shook his head. "We'll talk tomorrow. Lock your door tonight."

I followed him to the door. "Am I in danger?"

He hesitated. "I doubt it." Then he suddenly smiled, his dark eyes dancing with laughter. "If I say you're in danger, can I stay?"

"Sure," I said with a grand gesture toward the living room. "You'll fit on my couch."

"That's not the spot I had in mind." Before I could move, he bent over and nuzzled my face, his whiskered cheeks rasping me. "See you tomorrow, Molly." He kissed me quickly on the lips, then was gone.

I leaned against the door, surprise making me weak. What was that about? Honestly, JT McCord coming on to me was the last thing I'd expected. I had hardened my heart to the idea that he'd come back into my life at any time, much less now when I was facing middle age and enjoying a comfortable spinsterhood.

I downed the rest of my drink. It was probably just nostalgia, an old friend thing. I decided to do a Scarlett and think about it tomorrow. Mr. T ambled out to the kitchen to join me and we locked up, turned out the lights and went upstairs.

My bedroom was at the front of the house, connected to a spare bedroom via a bathroom that both rooms shared. What a day it had been. It started with that pig rooting around in my shrubs and ended with JT McCord kissing me. In between there was a dead body and—

What happened in the shed? I crossed the hall and went into my den, which faced the north side of my property and the shed. The fire truck was leaving, the big spotlights on top bouncing as the truck inched down my snow-packed drive. I peered out but saw no obvious sign of damage. I suppose the shed would be all smoky for a while, but it didn't really matter. I sniffed my shirt and grimaced. I definitely smelled smoky.

I had a quick shower, then applied my nightly Oil of Olay, my brain churning. I always left that padlock hanging on the hasp. I couldn't remember the last time the shed had been locked. In fact, I was surprised the padlock still worked. I considered running out there to check on it, then decided it could wait until morning. I dragged on my "Poison World Tour" T-shirt, now worn and ancient, then pushed Mr. T over and climbed into bed.

Despite my best intentions, JT popped immediately into my mind. What business did he have coming back into my life like this? I had successfully put him behind me, relegating him to that little corner of my life labeled *fantastic sex, probably because of youth and too many hormones.'* I was settling into pre-menopause without a glimmer of concern and had learned to satisfy myself with BOB, my battery-operated-boyfriend or the Shower Massage. The last eight years in Tangle Butte had been okay, despite Sam's infidelities.

In fact, the last five years without Sam had been very nice. I liked living in the small town and even my run-ins with Shirley and the In Crowd added a bit of spice to an otherwise ordinary life.

I yawned and snuggled deeper into my pillows. T-cat rumbled happily next to me, his tuna breath barely noticeable. JT would probably find Tangle Butte boring and dull after Kansas City or wherever he'd lived. And let's face it, there was a dearth of available female companionship in a small town, especially when he was in such a visible position as Police Chief. It wasn't an elected office, like Sheriff, but he still had to maintain some sort of community standards or something.

Mr. T growled. I was just close enough to sleep to realize he was growling, but too far gone to care. I roused myself, poking my head out of the covers. A clanging noise outside rang out loudly in the night.

T sat up, his black ears like little radar dishes. He growled again. I sat up, too. A distinctive yowl-noise filled the air. "Damn raccoons." I flopped back in my bed, glad to know what had alerted the T-man. I nestled deep in my soft pillow as my eyes closed. A last thought flitted through my head. *I gotta check the garbage cans in the morning. It wouldn't do to have trash all over the crime scenes.*

Chapter 5

As soon as I woke, I called in my news story to Ike. At this rate, I'd lead the headlines for a week. "Are you coming in today?" he asked.

I glanced at the clock. It was eight in the morning. I wasn't sure if I was supposed to wait for JT or not. He said he'd see me, but he didn't say if he'd stop by. "Yeah, I will." JT could always catch up to me in town if needed.

I went outside and checked the shed, seeing no obvious signs of damage. A big tarp covered something behind the shed, festooned with more yellow Crime Scene tape. I resisted the impulse to pull it aside. With my luck, JT would find out I'd done it and read me the riot act. I peeked into the garage where Augie was sitting, but didn't spot the cat or her kittens. She might have taken shelter in the barn where I'd put out some blankets. If she were there, she'd be comfortable for the day. I set out food and water in the dishes near the garage, then went to town.

It was probably my imagination, but it felt like people stared at me as I drove down Main Street. I parked in my usual spot and hurried into the TBTrib office. Amelia was lying in wait for me. "You poor thing," she exclaimed as I shed my letter jacket and kicked off my boots. "I can't believe what you've gone through in the last day."

Ike glanced up from his computer monitor. "You're on

42

Social today. We had to switch. Amelia's doing editing, you're on Social, and I'm doing News. All the big news items have you in them, so you can't write them."

"I could give you the first-hand account of ..." My voice trailed off as he shook his head. I hated the Social beat, but he was in a bind and I knew it. I shrugged. "Whatever. What do you need me to do?" I dropped into my chair as I grabbed three red M&Ms. It was a red kind of day.

"There's the Festive Fling committee meeting at the Country Club, engagements and weddings to proofread, and the Community News column to update. But first we have to do your cards," Amelia said, shoving papers aside on my desk so she could set down her well-thumbed Tarot deck next to my keyboard.

I obediently cut the cards. "What's in Community News this week?"

"All the folks visiting from out of town for Thanksgiving," Ike said from his desk. "It's a big one this week."

I accessed my account on the computer and found the News folder icon. I'd just opened the Notes file when Amelia said, "Oh, The Lovers. What a good card in that position."

I glanced down. Amelia had laid out her usual five cards. The one with Beauty and the Beast was at the end of the small row. "There's the Death card again." I shook my head. "What's that mean, I'm going to die of love or something?"

"No, no, that means your true love will enter your life and change everything." Amelia was excited. I could tell by the way she tapped the desk with one pale pink fingernail. She always tapped when excited or nervous.

"Oh boy," I muttered, peering at my computer screen. "I can't wait for that. What does this mean?" I pointed to the screen. "JoeH xSIL Susie w/fam?"

Amelia peered around my shoulder. "Oh. Joe Hunt's ex-sister-in-law is coming to town and wants to stay with the family. But Joe wasn't sure if he wanted her there."

The rest of the Notes file had similar cryptic notations. I gave up. "Amelia, you're going to have to write this, I can't decipher your shorthand. I'll edit 'em when you're done."

She nodded, still tapping her Tarot cards. "I can do that. Look, Molly. You've got the Emperor, the King of Swords, the Queen of Cups, the Lovers, and Death." She beamed at me. "This is a great spread. Really great."

"Lots of royalty." I checked the rest of the Notes file. It was all in Amelia's bizarre shorthand. There was no way I could put together a readable column from this.

"JT is obviously the King of Swords and you're the Queen of Cups," she declared. "And the Emperor signifies sound advice based on past experience. Probably from an older man." She glanced at Ike, who stoically ignored her.

I peered down at the cards. The Lovers were Beauty and the Beast. The Queen was some woman staring out at the ocean. The Emperor was maybe Santa Claus. I wondered if that meant I'd have a good Christmas this year. "I'm a queen? You never told me I was a queen before."

"In this spread you are. This is so auspicious, so auspicious. It means—"

"It would appear the King is coming to see his Queen," Ike commented.

JT walked in the front door. "Did you know you're the King of Swords?" I asked, grabbing a green M&M.

"Really?" He lifted one eyebrow. "Says who?"

"Says my fortune-teller." I nodded toward Amelia, who was gathering her cards and heading for the edge of Ike's desk for her next foray into the future.

"I've told you, Molly. I interpret the signs. I don't tell fortunes." Amelia sounded peeved, or at least as peeved as someone as timid as her could be.

"Sorry. Why don't you interpret JT's signs?" I eyed him as he leaned on the counter that protected us working peons from the public. He'd apparently left his topcoat at home. He wore the gray tweedy sports coat again, but this time with a white shirt and black and white striped tie. I had to admit, he looked good.

"I'm sure Chief McCord is here on business," Amelia said.

"He's here to talk to me," Ike said, pushing away from his desk. "Come on, JT. Let's go back to the office."

"I thought you were here to report to me about my

almost-fire," I said, swiveling my chair to watch them go into one of the three private offices in the back.

"In a few minutes," JT said over his shoulder. "I promised Ike this interview."

"Interview?" I popped two blue M&Ms, seeking a bit of calm. "You're glory hunting while the perpetrator or perpetrators unknown are—" The door slammed.

"Ike has been wanting to get that article in the paper," Amelia said in a placating voice.

"Yeah, yeah." The article I'd been avoiding. Oh well. I continued skimming the Community News, then shook my head. "I can't do this, Amelia. You'll have to do at least a draft. Sorry. It's just too—"

The door opened again. Belinda Devlin, Mark's daughter by his first wife, paused dramatically on the threshold, the November light behind her like a spotlight on a diva. She held the pose long enough for us to accord her suitable admiration, then she came in and closed the door behind her.

Amelia sidled up to the counter, smiling. "Can I help you?"

Belinda's gaze nailed me. She was a tall girl, about twenty-six years old with thick brown-blonde hair that hung in coifed waves to her shoulders. Her makeup was flawless and her brown ski jacket, brown stretch pants and stylish boots exactly matched the brown of her eyes. She was a DKNY ad come to life. She had divorced well, marrying a doctor in Minneapolis, then getting a huge settlement when they split up a couple of years later. "I came to see Molly."

I pushed away from my desk, taking a brown M&M to stay with her color scheme. "What's up, Belinda? News to report?" I leaned on the counter. I couldn't pull it off as well as she did since she was six inches taller than me and wearing heels while I was in my stocking feet.

"In a way." She glanced at Amelia, who watched us with alert curiosity. Amelia got the hint and wandered to the other end of the counter, politely far away but well within earshot. "I just came to tell you—I've got my eye on JT McCord. I don't believe in beating around the bush when it comes to things like love."

It took me a long minute to figure out what she was

saying. When I finally did, I started to grin. "So you've set your cap for JT, hmm?" I glanced behind me at the closed door of the office, where the object of our conversation sat. "Isn't there a bit of an age difference?"

She gave a cocky toss of her head, her tawny hair bouncing on her shoulders. "Everybody knows older men are better." Then she shot me a bitter little smile. "You should know that, Molly. After all, Delbert was older than you, and so was Sam, wasn't he? Everybody said you married them for their money, but I wonder about that."

Ooh. That was a hole in one. Belinda scored big points with that one. "Yep, you're right. They were older." I shrugged. "No need to tell me your plans, Belinda. JT isn't my property."

"Everybody knows he's writing those personal ads to you." She tugged off her gloves, the leather so supple it appeared alive.

"Seems like everybody knows a lot," Amelia muttered, her voice just barely loud enough to be heard.

I was surprised. It wasn't like Amelia to be so brave. Belinda shot Amelia a murderous glance and I hastened to intervene. "Doesn't matter who's writing personal ads to who," I said. "JT and I aren't seeing each other, nor do we have anything going except a professional relationship."

Belinda peered down her nose at me. "Really?"

"Read about it in the newspaper," Amelia said, the shuffling of her Tarot cards sounding as loud as gunshots in the quiet office.

Belinda snatched her gloves off the counter. "I'm trying to be nice," she snapped. "I didn't want your heart broken again, like it was last time." Her smile dripped maliciousness. "Everyone knows my stepmother just about ruined your life."

Oh, Lord. There were times when living in a small town was a distinct disadvantage. "Thank you, Belinda, for being so considerate of my welfare," I said sweetly. "Shirley has certainly raised you right."

I thought she was going to lunge over the wooden partition and tear my heart out through my throat. "Don't you dare compare me to that bitch." With one last flounce of her hair, she jerked open the door and made an exit worthy of a Hollywood starlet.

Amelia and I exchanged a glance and burst out laughing at the same time. Even so, I felt a pang. Jealousy? Could it be? Why should it bother me if some leggy, tall, slender, young, babe-o-matic chick wrangled JT McCord into bed? He didn't mean anything to me. He wasn't writing romantic personal ads to me. Heck, they were probably from Otis Sloan to his wife, Veronica. They didn't mean a thing. And JT didn't mean a damn thing to—

The office door opened and JT came out, laughing at something Ike was saying. I swear my heart stopped for a second. JT was so handsome, young, and carefree. He made me feel young just to see him. He met my gaze. His eyes softened, taking on that hazy, sensual quality I remembered so well.

"Are you going to tell him?" Amelia asked next to me.

I jerked my attention away from JT and shook my head. "Nah. Let him be surprised."

"I don't know, Molly. According to your cards, it might be a wise idea to—" She broke off when JT joined us, smiling at me with such mischief that I automatically checked my sweater to make sure I was properly buttoned.

"What?" I asked warily.

He shook his head. "Nothing. Got a minute?"

"Sure." I led the way to my desk. JT settled in the chair next to it. I graciously set my M&M tray on the cleared space where Amelia's cards had recently foretold my fate.

"I see you still sort them by color," he said, spinning the little lazy Susan. He examined the labels I'd printed and stuck on the tray. "What's this mean?" He pointed to the green slot and the label printed in tiny letters:

Saturn: F
Quietude: Endurance: Healing
Harmony: Stability

I sighed. Nobody understood the symbolic lore of colors. "Each rainbow color is associated with a musical note, a planet, and an emotion or aura," I explained. I spun the tray and plucked out two yellow M&Ms. "Whenever I need a special boost, I choose the right color or musical note." I crunched down on the candy. "Yellow— Wisdom, intelligence, vibrancy."

He gave me an odd look. "You can't carry a tune in a bucket, what do you know about musical notes?"

I frowned. Trust him to remember that about me. "Okay, so maybe the musical part isn't important. But it's useful to know what colors I should eat to get the right effect."

JT spun the tray, reading the labels. "Where'd you get the other colors? Pink and dark blue and black—those aren't regular ones, are they?"

"Yolanda gave me a package for my birthday. You can order them online now. You can even get ones that are custom printed."

"Hmm." He paused, then took two blue M&Ms, regarding them carefully before popping them in his mouth. I knew what that label said:

Venus: G
True blue: Devotion: Tranquility
Relaxation: Importance

"Was that Belinda Devlin out here?" he asked, running a finger under the piles of paper on my desk and peeking at what he found.

I slapped his hand. "Yep. She dropped by for a chat."

"She's changed a lot," he commented, ignoring my slap and craning his neck to gaze at my computer screen. "Last I saw her she had braces and pigtails."

I grinned, thinking of my recent conversation with the diva in question. "She has indeed changed a lot." I shot Amelia a warning glance. "Now, about that fire at my place—what's the deal?"

JT leaned back and stretched out his legs. He was wearing dark pants and polished black boots. His legs were impossibly long. I mimicked his pose, tipping back in my chair and putting my stockinged feet up on the desk.

"When did you buy that padlock?" He was watching me with a single-minded intensity that was unnerving. I longed for chocolate, but restrained myself. Now that he knew the Molly Code, he might be able to interpret my emotions.

"I didn't buy it. I inherited it. I think my dad used it. Or maybe Donny—you remember Donny, right?"

"Of course I remember Don," JT said. "He and I were best friends. Sounds like he's doing real good for himself in Texas."

"You've been in touch with my brother?" This was news to me.

"Hmm." JT spun my M&M tray, considering the various labels. "We've stayed in touch. Yep, sounds like Don is doing okay." He selected a white one and dropped it in his mouth.

White. It stood for purity and strength of character. It wasn't associated with any musical note because it wasn't a color but a non-color. What did that choice mean? And what did that comment mean—he and Don had stayed in touch? I filed these nuggets of information away for later thought. "So what about the padlock?" I demanded, picking up my M&M pencil and drumming it on the desk.

JT plucked an indigo M&M from the tray *(Uranus: musical A: loyalty; perseverance; high aspirations).* "It was a new padlock." He chewed the candy, his eyes never leaving my face.

"What?" My feet hit the floor with a thud and I almost pitched over my desk. "What do you mean, it was new?" I leaned forward and groped for an orange M&M *(Sun: musical D: Bravery: energy: warmth).*

"Yep. Brand new—probably never been used." He regarded the M&M tray, then his gaze shifted to me. I felt impaled by his black eyes. "No wonder you didn't know the combination." He watched as I processed his words, then nodded when he saw the understanding in my face. "Who's got it in for you, Molly?" he asked in a soft, low voice.

"But—" I was struggling to think. "Would the smoke have killed me?" I was suddenly aware of a vast quiet around us. Ike and Amelia were standing at Ike's desk, not trying to hide their eavesdropping. I waved them over. "Would it, JT?"

He picked up my hand, running his fingers over my

bones. My hand was so small and fragile in his. I was sick at the thought that I might have been—I looked up at him.

JT squeezed my hand. "It might have. Who has it in for you, Molly?"

"I don't know." I sagged in my chair. He still held my hand. It felt good—his hands were big and callused. I felt sort of safe with him there. "I mean, besides the women who are hot for you, that is."

"What?" He dropped my hand.

"You'd better be careful. The Devlin women have got you in their gun sights." I spun my tray and selected two pinks, the color of innocence.

"Hell, one of them is married and the other is a child." He sounded grumpy about my announcement, not flattered.

"That hasn't stopped most men that I know of," I said, remembering Sam's philandering.

"Did Sam leave you anything?" Ike asked, leaning on Amelia's desk. "Anything somebody might want or think is important?"

I straightened up in surprise. "Nothing of value. It's been five years—why would somebody care about it now?"

"Because until now we didn't know Sam had been murdered," JT said.

"Huh?" This required yellows. My brain wasn't functioning.

"Look at it this way," Amelia said, hand-shuffling her cards, another nervous habit. "Perhaps something happened five years ago that appeared innocent. But now that we've found Sam—or, rather, now that Melvin found Sam—whatever that thing is might not appear so innocent anymore." She smiled tentatively at JT, who nodded.

"Exactly. So tell me, Molly. Did Sam leave anything for you?"

"I divorced him *in absentia*," I said as I tried to sort through my thoughts. "I boxed up everything from his office downtown and stuck it up in the den. Tommy Axelrod was going to charge me rent otherwise. He had the lease on Sam's real estate office."

"What kinds of things did you box up?" JT asked. But

even as he spoke, a small alarm chime sounded from his suit coat. "Damn." He pulled out a Palm gadget and pressed some buttons. "I've got a meeting I've got to get to." He took another blue M&M from my tray. "I'd like to come out and go through those boxes," he said as he stood up. "And I'd rather you weren't out at the farmhouse alone."

"I could ask Yolanda to stay with me," I said, standing also.

He made an exasperated noise. "That wasn't exactly what I had in mind. An eighty-year-old woman isn't much protection."

"You think I need protection?" I asked, sticking my hands in the back pockets of my jeans and following him to the door. Ike and Amelia trailed behind me.

"I don't know. But I'd feel better if I could see what Sam left you. Maybe that will give me an idea." He checked the Palm thing again. "Can I stop by tonight?"

"I suppose you could after—"

"Good. I'll drop by at six or so. I'll bring a pizza, how's that?" I opened my mouth to protest and he popped the blue M&M in. "Do you still love sausage and mushroom?"

"JT, I don't know if—"

"Okay. I'll see you tonight, Molly." He smiled at us all and was gone before I could continue to protest.

Amelia waved her Tarot cards. "What did I tell you?"

Chapter 6

I wasn't sure I wanted JT to 'drop by' my house that night. I resolved to check with Yolanda to see if she could 'drop by' as well. Maybe she'd be a buffer between Super Cop and me. She had Yoga classes on Tuesday mornings, so I scribbled a reminder to call her later. I submerged myself in my Springsteen CD collection while helping Amelia with the Community News. At noon, I bundled up in my outdoor duds and headed to the Tangle Butte Country Club to handle the Social Beat for the day.

The Country Club was far more egalitarian than the name implied. It was a bit pricey to join, but almost half the town belonged. Most had a social membership, allowing them to golf once a month and play unlimited pinochle or bridge with their cronies in the Starlight Lounge in the clubhouse. A few of TB's wealthier citizens had full memberships—unlimited golf and social privileges.

Sam and I had had a full membership. It was a tax write-off for him because entertaining was part of his job as a realtor. After he absconded, I kept the membership. I enjoyed golfing in the Ladies' League, playing Winter Whist in the off-season and hanging out at the Starlight Lounge during football and basketball season, when the University of Minnesota Gophers had center stage on the big-screen TV.

Today, the thirty ladies of the Festive Fling

Committee were meeting in the Starlight, brunching and drinking mimosas as they finalized the plans for *the* big winter event in Tangle Butte. The Fling took place at the start of basketball season and was a kick-off for Christmas. The Spring Spree was the May equivalent, celebrating the end of school and the start of summer. In between was the Valentine's Day Massacre, two days of parties and fun.

As always, the Fling would be held on the weekend after Thanksgiving. There was a bonfire and basketball game on Friday, parade and cookout on Saturday afternoon, a dance on Saturday night, and the Kiwanis brunch on Sunday to wrap things up. In addition, the Fling Scavenger Hunt would take place during the entire week after Thanksgiving.

Despite its name, the Starlight Lounge was a bright, cheery space above the main clubhouse bar, with pale yellow tablecloths and lace-sprigged curtains. When I slipped in at the back of the room, I glimpsed the Three Witches of Langford, Delbert's daughters, sitting near the front, all matronly and proper in their dark skirts, twin-set sweaters, and Monet jewelry. Claudia, the oldest, spied me and whispered something to Janet and Sharon, her sisters. They shot me malevolent glances, then ostentatiously ignored me.

I sat at an empty table at the rear of the big room. Several of Tangle Butte's Elite smiled in greeting. About an equal number gave me the frosty shoulder. The remaining Ladies Who Lunched were focused on Shirley Corcoran McCord Pritchard Devlin, who was standing at a podium in front, expounding.

Shirley was my age and we'd grown up together. Her father had been a Big Name in construction while my dad had been a gentleman farmer and banker. All through our youth, Shirley and I had fought each other for class offices, boys, prizes, and awards. We even had one knock-down-drag-out fistfight over JT that was often discussed over beers down at the Tip Top Tap.

As I sat in the sun-drenched room, I tried to examine Shirley without the bias of our shared history. She was still beautiful, looking like that Food Network Sandra Lee person with all the blonde hair, lithe figure, and noticeable bosoms. Her sense of style was unerring, her parties were legendary, and her appetite for sex insatiable, or so rumor had it.

I was a Shetland pony to her thoroughbred, small and solid with unmemorable tits and hair that had a mind of its own. My sexual appetite was more discriminating, my sense of style was functional, and my idea of throwing a party was to buy pre-packaged food, then tap a keg of beer. Shirley excelled effortlessly at everything I didn't particularly care about, but which I had a sneaking suspicion I should care about. She'd always made me feel outmoded, outgunned, and outclassed.

Until today, that is. As I slouched in a folding chair at the back of the room in my faded jeans and JC Penney sweater, I realized that Shirley appeared tired and worn out, the way I often thought I looked. Today there were telltale lines around her eyes and mouth, plus some slackening around her chin that the expensive cashmere sweater she wore couldn't hide. Her blonde hair looked brittle and her blush was a little too pink. Yep, Shirley was showing her years today, that's for sure.

Of course, she was also the tiniest bit drunk. The others in the room were careful not to notice Shirley's occasional slurred word or the blank stare she got when she blacked out on what to say. Her speech was mercifully short, followed by Patty Thompson, who bounced to her feet and launched into a glowing description of what the decorating committee had planned for the Festive Fling dance to be held at the high school gym a week from Saturday.

Shirley wove her way through the tables to an empty chair at a table near me. But when she saw me, she changed course, landing heavily on the chair next to mine. I smiled politely and insincerely, then focused on my note taking.

"I got JT once and I'll do it again," she whispered, her voice magically carrying in the quiet room.

I didn't raise my head, but I did swivel my eyes so I could check her out. She leaned on one hand, elbow propped on the table, glaring at me. Up close, I could see the makeup she'd ladled on and the artful way she'd made her eyes seem bright and bigger.

"Did you hear me?" she whispered loudly.

I sighed and put down my pen. Several ladies at the nearby table glanced at us. I decided to go for the Business Approach. "I'm working, Shirley. We can chat when Patty is done."

"We can talk now," Shirley insisted.

I checked the front of the room. Patty was gamely carrying on, but you could tell no one was listening to her. Everyone's ears were tuned in to the conversation at the back of the room. A few ladies were leaning back so precariously, I wondered how they kept their balance.

I stood up. "Nice talking with you. I'll give Patty a call later to get an update on the Fling planning." I left, betting on surprise and drunkenness to keep Shirley in her chair.

I lost my bet. Shirley lurched to her feet and followed, catching up to me outside the room. "Did you hear what I said?" she demanded. We were standing in a small hallway, the door to the Starlight at our backs. To the right was a French door leading to the wrap-around balcony. Straight ahead was a staircase that led down to the main bar. Angling off to the left was the entry foyer, which led to the outside entrance. Our voices echoed in the small space. I could imagine all those Ladies Who Lunched, their ears getting enormous as they tried to eavesdrop. Hell, a few were probably pressed against the door, listening.

"I heard what you said." I stuffed my notepad into the ancient leather purse that housed my M&M supply, wallet, pens, Game Boy, Ipod, and other essentials of modern life. "I swear, between you and Belinda, JT is going to be one busy guy."

"Belinda?" Shirley slurred the word. I revised my estimate of her drunkenness. She'd been acting sober before. She wasn't acting now. I wondered how many mimosas she'd sucked down. "What's that slut got to do with it?"

"My, my. Such an uncharitable thing to say about your step-daughter." I leaned against the French door leading to the balcony. Even with my jacket on, I could feel the bitterly cold wind whip against the glass.

"She's Mark's daughter. She's no daughter of mine." Shirley swayed nearer to me. "You heard what I said. I got JT once and I can do it again. So don't even bother."

"Why does everyone assume I want JT McCord back in my life?" This was starting to piss me off. Ike assumed I was interested in My Lost Love, Amelia was seeing JT and me as Beauty and the Beast, and Belinda was determined to keep JT and me apart. Now Shirley was tossing her hat in the ring. "I've gotten along fine without JT for almost twenty years. I suspect I can limp into old age without him."

Shirley's heavy-lashed eyes narrowed. "You're lying."

I opened my mouth to blast her, but she didn't give me the chance.

"You fucked up your life when JT left you, marrying Delbert like that on the rebound then marrying Sam—Sam Ferris, of all people!" She made what was supposed to be a derisive noise, but which came out sounding like a Melvin-the-pig snort. "He slept with every woman in town under the age of fifty before and after he slept with you. What kind of a woman are you that you can't keep a man in your bed?"

Now that comment did piss me off, mainly because I'd had that thought rattling around in my brain, off and on, for two decades. I hated to hear Shirley Corcoran, of all people, give voice to my deepest fear. "At least I don't lay for the troops," I snapped. "I can see where Belinda gets her morals. Her mother would never have raised a child to act that way. Isabel had more class than that."

"Why you—" Shirley lunged at me.

I dodged her easily, reaching next to me to open the door in one quick move. Before she knew what was happening, Shirley was sliding out onto the balcony, knee deep in snow. When she'd gone a few feet, I slammed the door and locked it.

Her stylish pumps were no match for the ice that had accumulated over a couple of freezes and thaws. Shirley went down with much windmilling of the arms, landing with a solid, jarring thump in one of the big urns that used to hold mums in warmer days. I gave her a jaunty wave and turned to leave.

Only to find her husband, my attorney, watching me

from the top step of the stairway that led to the downstairs bar, martini in hand. I belatedly remembered that the Kiwanis met for Tuesday lunch at the Club in the main dining room on the first floor. Pained disbelief flashed in his eyes before his expression changed to one of mild reproof. "Molly, are you beating up my wife again?"

I laughed shakily. "She wanted a rematch. I'm sorry, Mark."

He peered through the French doors, where Shirley was struggling out of the urn, her chocolate brown suede skirt all tangled and her beige sweater askew. Several emotions flickered across his face in quick succession: surprise, amusement, pity, anger, and, to my surprise, bemused affection.

I engaged my mouth before my brain, an unfortunate habit. "Why did you marry her, Mark? She's so different from Isabel. She's—"

His face drew shut. I imagined this was what he looked like in court when he had to hide what he felt so the judge or jury wouldn't suspect his client was really a lying son of a bitch. "Love's an odd thing, Molly. You of all people should know that." He smiled briefly, for an instant reminding me of that laughing boy who'd been a football and basketball star, Homecoming King, and Most Likely To Succeed. Then the mask came down again as he moved past me, presumably to rescue his floundering wife, who was skating unsteadily on the slippery deck. "Excuse me."

I decided to get while the getting was good. I raced down the short entry hall to the front door. As I got there, I saw Sue Anne Williams, nee Rinderhoff, going through a doorway that led to the kitchen. I'd forgotten that Sue Anne was a waitress at the Club. Remembering my note to myself to talk to Bobbi Jo's sister, I followed.

I caught up to her in front of the grill where Charlie Johannsen was scraping down the grease. He grinned at me. "Hey, there, Molly. What you doing here?"

Charlie was two years older than me. He was a few cards short of a 52-card deck, but he fried a mean burger. "Just trying to find Sue Anne, is she—" I spied my quarry by the big fridge on the other side of the kitchen. "I see her."

He waved his paddle at me as I wove through the crowded space. "Sue Anne," I called out. "Do you have a minute?"

She turned, leveling a look of such hatred at me that I stopped, almost tipping over a tray of pie slices obviously poised for delivery to the Fling Committee in the Starlight Lounge. "You!" she said with such malevolence that I almost ducked.

I peeked behind me, wondering if another 'you' was there. Nope, she meant me. "What's wrong? I just wanted to ask you about Bobbi Jo, did you hear—"

"Of course I heard," she said, jerking a big bowl of whipped cream out of the fridge. "Everybody's talking about how Bobbi Jo is buried out there at your house, too. What did you do to her, Molly? Did you kill her, too? Did you kill her later that night? After you killed Sam, did you kill my baby sister?"

"What?" I grabbed my purse and raised it as she barreled toward me. I dodged her, pressing against the wall when she jerked a rack of kitchen implements toward her. I breathed a sigh of relief when she bypassed the knives and went for the spoons. "I didn't kill anybody," I said. "For heaven's sake, I have an alibi. Several of them, actually."

She paused in the act of whipped-cream-scooping. Like Bobbi Jo, Sue Anne was short, voluptuous, and bleached blonde. Her blue uniform was tight across her chest and I spied a flash of industrial strength white bra in between the strained buttons. The skirt was too short, revealing heavy thighs, sturdy calves, and outlining what Sam would have called 'generous pushin' cushions.' He always liked a woman with a big butt. I'd been a disappointment in that category. And probably in others as well, but I didn't dwell on that thought.

"What do you mean, you've got an alibi?" She over-served one slice of pie, burying it under a mound of whipped cream. One of the ladies in the Starlight would be happy.

"A bunch of people went home with me after the Flower Show and the hole was already filled in," I said, then wondered why I was bothering to explain myself to her. "And before that I was judging the dahlias, so I couldn't have killed him."

Her eyes widened in surprise. "But Bobbi Jo told me she saw—"

"What?" This was news to me. Sue Anne always said that she hadn't seen Bobbi Jo since Sam disappeared. I'd asked her several times, trying to get a bead on where the lovers had vanished—with my money.

Sue Anne slathered more whipped cream, inundating the pie slices. "Nothing. It's just suspicious that his body was there and now—"

"Wait a minute." I moved forward, prepared to intercept the spoon if needed. "You talked to Bobbi Jo that night? You told me you didn't talk to her."

More pie slices disappeared under snowy mounds. "She called me," Sue Anne said sullenly. "Late that night. She was scared. She said she saw somebody at your house and she had to leave town. I figured she meant that you found her and Sam, so they both were leaving." Sue Anne glanced at me and must have been reassured by what she saw. She continued her dolloping. "When I found out Sam was dead, I started to wonder. What if she was killed because of who she saw? She's never called me since then. Wouldn't she have called me?"

"Did you tell the police about this?" I sidled out of her way as she maneuvered around the tray, her spoon dipping and distributing with a hypnotic rhythm.

Sue Anne made a rude noise. "The police didn't really investigate, did they, Molly?"

I considered it. She was right. I'd duly reported Sam as 'missing' so I could file for spousal abandonment and divorce. No one had searched for him. He'd left a note, saying he was leaving. He'd taken some clothes and my money then vanished.

Wait a minute. His car and money—where were those things? The police had filed a report and I suppose it went out to other departments, but to be honest, I hadn't wanted him back so I didn't follow up on it. What about Sam's car, the money, his clothes—had anyone checked for those since his body was found? I needed to talk to JT about that.

"I gotta get these served," Sue Anne said, putting the whipped cream bowl and spoon into the nearby sink. She paused, wiping her hands on a somewhat grimy towel. "If they find her—if she is dead—they'll tell me, won't they?"

She was so upset that I tried to assure her. "Of course. But I think she's fine. She must be. Why would anyone want to hurt her?"

Sue Anne brushed a stiff curl of overly blonde hair out of her face and hefted the tray up, balancing it on her upturned palm. "Who would want to hurt Sam?" She swept past me and out of the kitchen.

Good question. I followed her into the entry foyer, starting toward the front door, but my exit was blocked. Claudia Langford stood there, hands on her hips, glaring at me. "We need to talk, Margaret."

"No, we don't." I didn't want to deal with a Witch of Langford, not today. I had enough to worry about without dealing with Delbert's progeny. I tried to move past her solid, matronly bulk.

She stepped in front of me. "You owe us some money."

I took a long, steadying breath. The Tasteless Trio were older than me and had hated me for marrying their father. I could understand their animosity at the time, but Delbert had been dead for twenty years—couldn't they let bygones be bygones? They claimed that I'd coerced Delbert into deeding me his shares of Microsoft, Xerox, and Shell Oil. In fact, they'd been more than willing to let me have the stock in exchange for the cash in Delbert's estate. I hadn't contested their contesting of the will and had escaped town after Delbert died, heartbroken over his death, JT's defection, and the unending hatred of Delbert's children.

Through judicious investing, I'd parlayed the stocks into a nice income for myself. That, combined with my royalties from my books, allowed me to work for peanuts at the Tangle Butte Daily Tribune and, at the age of forty-five, be semi-retired.

The Three Witches never forgave me, claiming I owed them a portion of my stock portfolio. Their husbands, all local businessmen, stayed out of the fight, but the rest of the town took sides. My brother Donny said there was a betting pool on the outcome down at the Tip Top and I was leading the book. I think this attested more to a universal dislike of the Witches rather than a belief in my legal case.

"Claudia, I don't owe you shit," I snapped, trying to move past her.

She grabbed my arm. "Now you just wait a minute."

I shrugged her off. She staggered. "What do you think you're doing?" Her voice echoed in the hall. "I'll have you charged with assault."

Someone grabbed me from behind. I struggled in their grip. "Let go of me," I demanded, trying to see who had me.

"Do I have to arrest you, Molly?"

I twisted and peered up into JT's face. "Oh, for heaven's sake, let me go."

"There she is!"

We all turned. Shirley was striding down the hall, her skirt dirty, her hair a tangled mess, and minus one shoe. She pointed a hand at me. "She attacked me." Then she leaned against the wall and began to cry. Amazingly, her makeup remained impeccable. She must have spray-painted it on.

Mark was behind her, martini glass still in hand. He shrugged apologetically.

"Oh, this is awkward," I said.

"No kidding," JT said. "Two charges of assault in one day. That's a record even for you, Molly. Come on."

Before I could protest, he had me out the door.

Chapter 7

"I was speaking at the Kiwanis lunch when all hell broke loose," JT said.

"All hell, he says." I chose a pink M&M, the color of innocence. We were sitting at my desk in the TBTrib. "You haven't seen hell."

"I was married to Shirley. Believe me, I've seen hell."

A few minutes earlier, JT had stuffed me into Augie and tailgated me back to town in his squad car, not giving me a chance to bolt. When we got to the office, I'd flung off my jacket, kicked off my shoes and stormed to my desk, prepared to read him the riot act. Instead we were sitting there, sipping coffee and eating M&Ms. I don't know how he did it.

He selected a green M&M and sat back. "Why did you beat up Shirley again?"

"I did not beat her up," I protested. "She accosted me, yelling at me in a public place. I figured a visit to a snow bank would do her some good."

"She says you almost broke her ankle."

"Me?" This required several pink M&Ms. "It's not my fault she wears pizza shoes."

"Pizza shoes?"

"You know, the kind that have toes shaped like pizza wedges." I glanced at my own round-toed L.L. Bean mukluks, shedding snow in the corner. "Besides, she was drunk and couldn't balance on her stilettos."

"I don't know why you and Shirley keep coming to blows."

"What do you mean? We've only had one other fight before and that was about—" I shut my mouth, realizing what I'd almost said. I'm sure JT had heard about that catfight years ago, but I saw no need to remind him. "Anyway, I didn't want to fight with her. But she said something that pissed me off, so I thought it was best that she step outside."

He regarded me quizzically. "You were mad so you made her go outside? Using that reasoning, why didn't you make Claudia Langford Whitney sit out on the lake and freeze to death?"

"Claudia is totally out of line," I said, pointing my pencil at him. "She and the other Witches demanded some of my money."

"Wasn't it Delbert's money?" he asked, spinning my M&M Susan.

I wasn't fooled. I'd seen the alert, predatory look in JT's deep dark eyes. "For your information, Delbert tried to give me money, but the Three Witches contested the will. All I got was stock."

Ike, sitting nearby, laughed. "Just stock, she says."

I shot him a reproving glance. He made a great show of staring at his computer screen. "Good stock, I'll grant you," I said.

"Hmm?" JT plucked a yellow M&M and crunched down.

"Very good stock," I conceded. "It's not my fault Claudia and her witchy sisters got greedy and took the cash. Nobody knew back then that Microsoft would do so well. I was taking a gamble when I gave away all that cash."

"So you took the stock and ran." He raised his eyes, staring at me from under his long, dark lashes. I felt pinned by his gaze, seeing accusation, hurt, and bewilderment there.

I was getting tired of being everybody's punching bag. "Well, first you took Shirley and ran," I said, making my voice as cold as I could. "Then yes, I married Delbert when he took pity on me and my—" I almost said 'broken heart'. I stopped myself in time. "Pity on my situation.

Two weeks later he died of cancer and yes, I took the stock and ran. I didn't want to stay in town to watch you and Shirley live in wedded bliss, not after you and I dated for almost seven years before you married that bitch."

You could have heard a pin drop in the office. JT's hand hung suspended over my M&Ms. Ike was staring at us, Amelia was gaping from her spot at the counter and Dan Bailey, our high school sports editor, was grinning at me from behind his computer monitor across the room, his bright burgundy hair fuzzing around his head like antennae.

I grabbed a red M&M, which probably matched the color on my face. I was beyond caring. JT and I had dirty laundry to get out in the open. It didn't matter to me who heard. Hell, everybody in town knew about it anyway. "So don't act so high and mighty with me," I said. "You got what you wanted—a society wife and the money and position that went with her."

He withdrew his hand and sat back in his chair. "Stuff like that was important to me then. I was only twenty-nine."

"So?" I turned to my computer screen. "I was twenty-five. I wasn't stupid."

"I was."

He said it so softly I almost didn't hear him. He stood. "Try not to assault anybody else today, okay?" His voice sounded strained despite the light words. "I'll come by tonight and we—"

"I'll have Sam's things ready for you," I said. "You can take them with you."

He was watching me, but I ignored him by staring blindly at the prose on my computer. "I'll see you later," he finally said.

I didn't turn my head until I was sure the front door had closed behind him. Then I groped blindly for an M&M, unsurprised when I snagged four browns, which so precisely matched my mood. I gulped them down, then ventured a glance at the other people around me. No one would meet my eyes.

I spent the rest of the day making calls, writing up my stories, and editing Amelia's lengthy prose for the Community News column. It was almost five o'clock before I finished. As I was leaving, Ike said, "You might want to read that feature story I wrote about JT."

"Why? Does it need editing?"

Ike pushed away from his desk and crossed the room to me, watching as I struggled into my coat. He held out a sheaf of papers and I automatically took them. "Just read it, Molly. And honey—" He paused. I was surprised. It wasn't like Ike to be so sappy. "Don't hold the past against JT."

"I can't forget it, Ike." He looked hurt and I wanted to curse myself. Today appeared to be my day for tromping on people. "I'm sorry. I shouldn't take it out on you."

"I didn't say forget it, Molly." He put an arm around me and gave me a brisk hug. "I think you should forgive, though." He held up a hand when I tried to speak. "Think about it."

"Are you in cahoots with my mother? She said the same thing." I stuffed the papers into my bag. "I'll think about it," I said grudgingly. "I'll see you tomorrow." We'd have a short day on Wednesday because there would be a meager paper on Thanksgiving Thursday.

"Think about what I said." He smiled at me. "And drive carefully."

I emerged from the office to a snowy world. A couple of inches had fallen and the wind was kicking up. I brushed off Augie and arrived home as fast as the slick streets would allow. I considered calling Yolanda and asking her to drop by, then decided against it. I didn't want her driving on the snowy dark roads just to protect me from JT McCord. When I got to the house, I fed Mr. T, then trudged up to the spare room, where I'd put the three boxes of files and junk I'd harvested from Sam's office years before. I considered them, then considered the steep steps. I decided to let JT handle them.

I went back downstairs and took out the news story Ike had handed me. I skimmed it, picking out surprising details. JT had a Master's Degree in Criminal Justice and had held the position of Confidential Investigator for the Office of the Chief Medical Examiner in Kansas City, where he investigated homicide crime scenes in the metro area. After that, he'd been assigned to the Chief Prosecutor's office, investigating drugs and organized crime.

I was surprised. When I'd known him, JT's greatest ambition was to be a construction boss like old man Corcoran, Shirley's dad. He'd taken college coursework in criminal justice and business administration. I remember him saying he wanted to go into police work, but there wasn't any money there. JT had always felt the need to achieve. His father had been hard-working but poor, and his mother had been a cleaning lady. His half-Indian heritage was something he didn't talk about. His parents died when he was in college, and JT had struggled to stay in school, working construction the summer to pay for tuition.

The final paragraph made me sit up straighter.

It was while working undercover during a government sting operation that Chief McCord was gravely wounded, almost losing his life in a gun battle that left two other police officers dead. Chief McCord spent almost a year in and out of hospitals, undergoing surgery and rehabilitation therapy. "After that," Chief McCord said, "I had a different outlook on life. I think that's why I decided to come back home. There are more important things in life than money and a career. It took something like that injury to show me what I've been missing."

JT had been hurt. The knowledge shook me. For some reason, I hadn't thought of him being in the line of fire. I'd figured him for some desk guy, filling out forms. But he'd carried a gun, shot at people, and been shot. What kind of surgery did he have? I petted Mr. T, who'd taken over my lap, and stared down at the words on the page.

JT had almost died.

I wasn't sure how I felt about that. I'd put him into my past for so long and now here he was, in my present. But he'd almost been permanently erased from my past. It was scary, but weird. I didn't have time to further examine my feelings. Just as I finished reading, headlights shone in the driveway.

I pushed T off my lap and struggled to my feet. I decided to take advantage of JT's presence. I grabbed my jacket and tugged it on as he knocked on the back door.

"Hey, come with me to the barn," I said, taking the

flashlight from the hook.

"As inviting as that sounds, it's too cold to hang out in the barn." He was holding a pizza box and something else, something long and cylindrical.

"I want you to help me check on that cat." I started to brush by him.

"Can I set this down first?"

"Oh. Sure." I stepped aside as he walked past me into the kitchen. He soon came back and we went outside, the motion lights coming on to show the way. "I think she's staying in the barn, but she keeps moving around. I just want to peek inside."

We stopped by his pickup and he took a flashlight from the tool chest in the back. He was wearing jeans again, and a black leather jacket with the collar pulled up. I could see the top of a turtleneck sweater under the jacket. When we got to the barn door, he started to pull it open, but I stopped him. "Doesn't work," I said, leading the way to the small side door. "I need to get new hardware and fix it."

"Don't you have anybody to help out around here?" he asked, shining his light on the ground.

"Nope. I lease out the fields, but nobody needs the barn. I'd like to get a horse or maybe a few sheep, but I haven't gotten around to it." I pushed open the small side door. "Be quiet now, I don't want to scare her if she's in here."

"Yes, ma'am."

This had never been a full-fledged farm. Daddy had built the barn more to house machinery and our ponies when we were growing up. There were six stalls, three on each side, with a half-loft overhead. I shone the light into the stalls one by one, JT following behind me, adding his light to mine.

"There she is," he said, his light bobbing into the corner of the far stall. He kept the beam above the upended cardboard box stuffed with towels I'd put in the corner.

I glimpsed the glow of eyes and small, squirming bodies near the white body of the mother. "Is she okay?" I whispered, peering closer.

JT knelt down. "I think she's fine," he said, his voice

soothing and gentle. "Let us get closer, honey, come on," he crooned. "Let us see the babies." He inched forward, still crouched and keeping the light shining above the box, providing illumination without a glare. "Stay back there, Molly. Best we don't crowd her."

I did as he said, using my flashlight to shine on the trampled hay around the box. JT stopped a couple of feet away, still speaking in that low, gentle voice. The cat watched him, her eyes alert but unafraid. The little bodies made mewing, whimpering noises. JT soon started to edge back, not standing up until he was outside the stall, next to me.

"Five kittens," he said. "They're a week old, maybe a bit more. I don't think their eyes are open yet, but it's hard to tell. We should come out here in the daylight and check them, make sure they're okay." I looked at him in surprise and he saw it. "What?"

"Most men would say to just drown 'em and be done with it."

JT stared back at the stall. "Never give up on life," he said softly.

"I'll put her food and water dishes out here and—" He shook his head. "Why not?" I demanded. "She needs the food. You saw how thin she is."

"That'll just draw the coons. Let me check the barn in the daylight and make sure the coons can't get in here. Maybe I can make her a nesting box, too."

I stopped and turned to stare at him. "Why?"

His face was partially in shadow, so it was impossible to interpret his expression. "Because I want to help."

"Why?" I wasn't asking why he wanted to help and he knew it.

His eyes changed, softening like they had when he'd gazed at the mama cat and her kittens. "Because I'm sorry, Molly. For everything."

"Everything?" I asked. My heart was hammering so loud I could barely hear. The moment I'd been dreading for months had finally arrived.

"No," he whispered. "I'm not sorry for loving you."

We held each other's gaze for a long, long moment. I didn't know what to say. I wanted to scream at him. I wanted more words. I wanted more apologies. I wanted to cry.

Instead I turned and left the barn.

I heard him behind me, closing the door, then I heard his footsteps as they crunched on the gravel. I fled into the house, trembling from the cold and the contact with a ghost from my past. When I got inside, I dumped my coat and boots in the little mudroom and went into the kitchen. The pizza sat on the kitchen table next to a small tube of flowers—daisies, my favorite. I went to the far cupboard and pulled it open.

He came in behind me. I heard him scrape his boots on the mat, then felt the cold air on my back as he entered the room. "Molly, I want to—"

"Sam's things are upstairs," I said, not turning around. "Don's old room, second door from the top of the stairs. You can take them with you if you want."

I held my breath, wondering what he would do. When he went through the doorway to the hallway, I wasn't sure if I was disappointed or relieved. I turned on the oven and put the pizza in, then found a vase from the hall cupboard. When he came downstairs carrying one of the boxes, I felt ready to face him.

"Are you sure it's okay if I take it?" he asked, hefting the box.

I nodded. "I've gone through the papers. It's mostly real estate stuff, from his office. He had a few personal papers but I've read those, when I filed for divorce."

JT hesitated, then left. I heard him stack the box in the mudroom, then he went upstairs twice more, returning with the other boxes. When he finished, he came into the kitchen. He hadn't taken off his coat.

I leaned against the counter and regarded him. "You still haven't told me what they found out about the fire," I commented.

He jammed his hands deep into the jacket pockets. The high collar of the turtleneck accented the hard, chiseled lines of his face and his five o'clock shadow, a mix of gray and black stubble on his cheeks. Everything about him was black and white, from his black denims to his white sweater to his black jacket, black eyes and white hair.

I realized suddenly that JT had always been a

black/white person, evaluating his friends and lovers with a cool, assessing attitude that ranked us all in terms of what we could do for him. That's why he'd dumped me in favor of Shirley—she could help him attain that elusive something he'd always wanted. It wasn't enough to just love me. He's always wanted more. JT wanted to belong, and by attaching himself to Shirley, he was admitted to a world that had always denied him. I felt as though I'd unraveled an intricate piece of a puzzle, but I wasn't sure what it meant.

"The grill was smoldering for at least twenty minutes or more before I got here," he said, leaning against the opposite counter.

I stowed my philosophical thoughts for a later time, then pulled the pizza out of the oven and set it on the kitchen table. JT looked a question at me and I gestured. "Take off your coat."

He took the pizza cutter I handed him, slicing the pizza while I got out the beer and glasses. Then he shrugged out of his coat and sat down, taking a bite of his slice before saying, "The grill was put against the north side of the building. We had a good north wind last night, so the fumes would be sure to get under the floorboards."

"It was so smoky, though," I said. "It wasn't just a regular fire."

"Nope. It was damp."

I nodded. The smoke had been biting, making my eyes sting long after I'd gotten away from the fumes. "So if it was going for twenty minutes, how—"

He sipped some beer. "The way I figure is this. Somebody was planning on setting your shed on fire and had it smoldering to start after your party broke up." He gave me a reproving glance. "Your Mr. Sex party."

"But no one would know that I'd go outside," I pointed out, deciding to ignore his little rebuke. "The most I might do is walk outside with the girls when they're going to their cars."

"And what if you'd smelled smoke? What if you saw a fire out there?"

I nibbled on a slice of pizza and considered it. Before I could speak, he said, "Who else knew there was a pregnant cat around?"

"What's the cat ..." My voice trailed off as I realized what he was saying. Anyone who knew me would know I'd worry about the stray cat on my property. They'd know I'd try to rescue the cat if she was in trouble.

"Who knew about the cat, Molly? And about the grill?"

"Geez, I don't know. Most of Mr. Sex's Ladies, I suppose. I've been trying to find homes for the upcoming kittens. Somebody even donated a recipe for some kind of herbal poison, to make the coons sick and leave the cat alone. And they all knew how sick poor Cassie was. I remember talking to Peggy and some others about it. I said how I'd have to get the grill out to dig the grave."

JT nodded. "So a lot of folks knew."

"But it still doesn't make sense."

"Think about it," he said, taking another slice of pizza. "Somebody decides they want to lure you out. They know you've got a cat you're keeping an eye on. So they start a slow fire, figuring you might come outside to check on the cat and smell the smoke. Even if you don't, they'll just start the shed on fire, knowing the fire would draw you out."

"And then what? So they've got me out of the house? What's that mean?"

JT glanced toward the mudroom and the boxes stacked there. "I think there's something in Sam's things that somebody wants to see. And they wanted you out of the way to find it."

"I'm gone all day, JT. Anybody could just come in here and go through stuff—" He was shaking his head. "What?"

"Your neighbor, the pig."

"My neighbor ..." I glanced at my living room and the big window there, which faced the farm fields and Mrs. Dalworthy's house, just beyond the windbreak of trees.

"She's always home," JT said, finishing his beer. "She's retired. If she sees a car in the drive and you're not home, she'd notice. She might not call the police, but she'd call you, mention it to you. No, the best time to get in here is at night, when no one would notice somebody parking down the road and coming across the fields." Unspoken, but hanging in the air between us was 'with you out of the way.'

"So does that mean I have to be on the lookout every night from now on?" I glanced at the mudroom door, which had a flimsy chain lock.

"It wouldn't hurt to be more alert," he said, pushing back from the table. "But I made it known in town that I was taking Sam's papers back with me. I doubt you'll be bothered." He stood up, taking his empty beer glass to the sink. "I'll go through those boxes as soon as I can. I've got several meetings tomorrow, but I'll get to them tomorrow night or Thursday."

"That's Thanksgiving," I said, watching him put on his coat. "Don't you get a day off?"

"No family in town anymore." He settled the coat on his shoulders. "It's just another day for me. I've got no plans."

"Well, if I wasn't a suspect in a murder investigation, I'd invite you to join us," I said. "But that would be a conflict of interest."

"Really? You've learned to cook since I knew you?"

I stuck my tongue out at him. "I can cook a turkey and stuffing. I have a regular group that comes out. Yolanda makes the green bean casserole, Ike brings pie, Amelia makes the cranberry jell-o mold, Kathy brings the potatoes, and Paula brings the wine. So there."

"Sounds like a real feast. And since you're not a suspect, I accept."

"Huh?"

His glance flickered to the daisies, which I'd set on the sideboard in their vase. "I'll make sure to bring something for the hostess. Thanks, Molly." He went out through the mudroom, calling back over his shoulder, "Lock up behind me. I'll see you on Thursday."

I heard the door open and close. I sat there, staring at the pizza remains. The door opened again. "Molly? Lock the damn door."

I jumped to my feet and went to the mudroom. JT was standing in the doorway. "Are you sure you should come to dinner? I mean, won't it seem odd if—"

"It's fine. We'll take care of your cat when I come out." He bent over and kissed me on the cheek. "See you." Then he vanished into the darkness.

I closed the door behind him. What the hell was going on? Had JT truly apologized to me tonight? Was he really sorry about—

"Margaret Olivia Lawson, lock the door," he demanded, his voice loud on the stoop outside.

I did.

Chapter 8

Wednesday turned out to be chaos. Before leaving the house I verified that the turkey I'd purchased for our feast was, indeed, thawing; that the cat was okay in the barn; that my china and silver was presentable; and that I had all the ingredients I needed for stuffing. By seven-thirty in the morning, I was heading to town.

It had snowed again and the roads were slick. I inched my way along, thankful to have Augie, who was built like a small tank. At the office, Ike and I had to tear up the front page and re-set it several times to accommodate a story about a fire in a downtown office building and a multi-car accident on the bypass highway that circled the town. We took our first break at lunch, when Amelia dashed over to the Brew 'n' Chew and got us take-out sandwiches, which we ate at our desks while she read our Tarot cards for the day.

"Strength," she said, tapping Little Bo Peep.

I gulped down my egg salad sandwich on Wonder Bread. "Why do I have Little Bo Peep in my future?" I asked, proofing the fire story one more time, trying to eliminate enough words to make room for an article on the clock tower repair coming up. "And what's that one? It looks like kids flying."

Amelia tapped each card in turn. "Strength—Little Bo Peep—means you need to take charge of your life. The six of pentacles indicates that one good turn deserves another. You need to return a favor. The Fool—the Scarecrow—means that you should be happy with your choices. The six of cups—that's Peter Pan and Wendy—shows an opportunity for you to correct a past wrong. And the Page of Swords—"

She hesitated, her long, plain face worried. "It's a telescope," I pointed out. "Am I supposed to watch something?" I eyed my computer screen again, seeing a few redundant words in paragraph six that might give me the space I needed.

"It means there's a spy among us."

"Oy. Any idea what this spy looks like?" I rearranged some prose and sat back, satisfied. I had the space I needed.

"He's young and quite innocent appearing."

Her voice sounded tremulous. I glanced at her and was surprised to see real concern in her pale hazel eyes. "Hey, thanks," I said as sincerely as I could. "I'll be on my toes. It's good to have a warning about stuff like that."

She smiled, looking relieved. Amelia really believed her cards and I had to admit, her advice was often right on. She scooped up her deck to proceed to Ike's desk, where he was talking on the phone. I went back to my page layout. Ike hung up the phone and called over, "We need to change page four, the Shop 'n' Save special on Diet-Rite Cola has to be put on hold. The truck carrying the cola got stranded down in Iowa and all the cans froze."

"Yikes." I visualized a semi-truck full of exploding pop cans. What a mess. I flipped my computer's virtual newspaper page to four and examined the full-page ad. The Diet-Rite Cola ad was smack in the middle. "What goes in its place?"

"Helen Lundberg is coming over now to help you set the copy." Ike absently cut the cards for Amelia and went back to his computer screen.

Helen was a Mr. Sex Lady whom I'd worked with before when similar crises had arisen. With her in charge, I could relax. I looked up as the chime over the door sounded, but it wasn't Helen coming in, it was Chuck Anderson, Charlene's husband. He was a short, round man with pale skin and a bright red nose, undoubtedly from the cold whipping down the streets outside. Chuck was one of those unfortunate males who, at eighteen, acted thirty and who at thirty was just non-descript. He'd probably fade out of sight by the time he was sixty.

"Hey there, Molly, just the person I needed to see." He pulled off his gloves and blew warm air on his plump fingers.

I joined him at the counter. "What's up? Did you find my money?" This was a running joke with us, since he was the junior banker who had tried to help me track down the money Sam had taken years ago. We'd finally concluded that my ten grand was long gone, but we still joked about it now and then.

His eyes opened wide in shocked surprise. I patted his coat-clad arm in reassurance. "It's a joke, Chuck, don't worry." I suppose with Sam turning up like he did, Chuck was surprised I could joke. I had to remember to play the part of grieving spouse. I frowned and tried to look woebegone.

This placated him. Now that I considered it, Chuck always appeared to be worried. It probably came of handling money. It seemed to me that people who cared about making money often looked worried.

"It's about Sam," he said in a low voice, glancing past me. I could feel Ike and Amelia a few feet away, probably trying to act like they weren't eavesdropping like crazy. I moved to the end of the counter and Chuck followed my lead.

"What about him? You heard they found the body, I suppose."

He nodded, his thinning pale blonde hair wisping around his shiny pate. "Charlene told me. I was wondering—do you have any of his old real estate papers? He handled the sale on our house six years ago and a question has come up for our taxes. Charlene said that you might still have some of Sam's files and things."

"I do have his papers, but I don't really have them, if you know what I mean. I gave it all to Chief McCord. He wanted to check Sam's stuff."

Chuck's face paled so fast I was afraid he'd pass out on his feet. The first thought that floated through my brain was, *'Did Chuck do something illegal when he sold that house?'* Then I dismissed the thought. Chuck didn't have an illegal bone in his body. It was probably just some stupid form that was needed to dot a government 'i' somewhere. I hurried to reassure him before he keeled over. "I can check with JT and see if he can get me the—"

"No, no, that's okay," Chuck said. He still looked worried, though.

"It's no problem. I'll be seeing JT tomorrow for Thanksgiving and can ask him then." The front door opened again and Helen Lundberg, a short fireplug of a woman came in brushing snow off her bright pink jacket. "I'll be with you in a minute, Helen." She passed through the drop-gate and went to stand with Ike. Chuck pulled on his gloves. His hands were trembling, which made the job tough. "Do you want me to check with JT?" I asked.

"No, that's okay. I would need to read through the files anyway. I know what the form looks like but it's hard to describe to somebody."

"Well, if JT finds a folder with your name on it, I'll ask him to set it aside."

Chuck nodded distractedly. "That's fine. Thanks for trying, Molly." He left, his old man's face creased with thought.

I scribbled a note to myself to talk to JT about Sam's files, then turned to the problem of the Shop 'n' Save layout. It took us an hour to get that nailed down, then put the paper to bed for the day and send it off to Mankato for printing.

As soon as we wrapped up, I hurried home, wanting to check the barn cat while it was still light outside. She was curled up in her corner nest composed of old sweatshirts and blankets. In the filtered light coming through the cracks in the barn, I could see the five little bundles that squirmed next to her. I put out fresh water and piled some cat food nearby that I'd gotten from the veterinarian for nursing mothers. The cat gobbled it down with one eye on me the whole time. Then I refilled the dishes outside and put some more cheap-o cat food down the drive by the garage, hoping to distract any coons that might be around. It was the best I could do until I could figure out a better solution.

I called Mark Devlin when I got into the house but he wasn't in his office. I assumed that meant I wasn't going to be charged with assault, so I promptly put the whole Shirley-in-the-snow incident out of my mind. I spent the evening prepping for Thanksgiving—cleaning the china, ironing the linen, setting the table, cutting up stuffing ingredients. Before I knew it, ten o'clock was chiming and I was dropping into bed. I slept badly, waking whenever I heard a noise outside, thinking a coon was attacking the poor cat or someone was trying to break in to attack me. When I got up the next day, I felt groggy and disoriented until I'd consumed three cups of coffee.

My guests arrived early. I didn't expect anyone until noon, but at eleven, JT's truck was pulling into the drive. Thank God I'd already changed into clean jeans and my nice pink fake cashmere sweater, purchased at Bert's Lady's Fashions on Main Street at the yearly sales the previous February. I assessed JT as he helped Yolanda down from the truck. Today he wore faded blue jeans, his black leather jacket and a powder blue sweater. There was a big blocky object in the bed of the truck. I wondered what that was.

He assisted Yolanda up the stairs, which I found amusing. Since her hip replacement eight years earlier, she could run rings around me, but she made a good show of acting her age around men who could give her a helping hand. JT had a wicker basket slung over his arm that I knew held Yolanda's famous green bean casserole. He also carried another small box, gift-wrapped in bright pink paper. I opened the door to them just as Ike and Amelia pulled in behind JT in Ike's pristine Chevy SUV.

"You kids are early," I said chidingly, taking the basket from JT.

"Have some chores to do out in the barn," JT said. He helped Yolanda remove her coat, then handed me the other package. By then Amelia and Ike had come in, bringing with them a gust of cold air. We got them unwrapped, as Ike called it, then I turned my attention to the present JT had given me.

"What's this for?" I asked, rattling the six-inch-square box.

"For asking an orphan over to your house on Thanksgiving day," he said, pulling a pair of canvas work gloves out of his coat pocket and slapping them against his thigh. "But I plan to earn my meal."

"What?"

"I made a cathouse for your girl out in the barn," he said, his dark eyes laughing at me. He gestured to the package I still held. "Go ahead. Open it."

I peeled off the pink paper, then opened the small cardboard box it revealed. Inside was a beautiful dark burgundy fiber basket with an intricate interlinked design worked into the side in yellow and pale blue. It was filled with blue M&Ms. "It's beautiful, JT," I said in awe. It had a jaunty little lid with a dark blue string holding it to the basket. The basket felt soft in my hands but it was solid and sat without wobbling when I put it down.

"My grandmother made that," he said. "She used to make baskets all the time. I thought you might like it."

"You didn't need to bring me anything." I wasn't sure what to say. The gift was so nice and so personal. I felt awkward taking it.

"I know I didn't have to." He glanced at Ike and nodded to the outside door. "But I wanted to. We'll go get that cathouse set up. Save some turkey for us." Then he and Ike vanished out the door before I could say anything else.

"What are they doing?" I asked, peeking out the mudroom windows to see Ike and JT getting into JT's truck.

Yolanda spoke from the kitchen. "He made some kind of shelter for your outdoor cat. He said he was going to get it put in, then he was going to fix that barn door. Sounds to me like JT wants to make himself useful around here for you."

I looked to heaven, hoping for divine intervention like a lightning strike aimed at my mother. None was forthcoming. I took the little basket into the living room, putting it in a spot of honor on my coffee table. It was beautiful and it exactly matched the dark burgundy of my sofa. I rejoined the ladies in the kitchen, where Yolanda was bent over the open oven door, inspecting the turkey, and Amelia was making room for her cranberry salad in the overcrowded fridge. Kathy Fahr and Paula Belkin soon joined us and our party was complete.

I'd been sponsoring this Thanksgiving lunch since I'd returned to Tangle Butte eight years earlier. We'd have lunch, then folks would help me put up my Christmas decorations. It had become a yearly ritual, just like the Christmas Eve party at Ike's house, the Easter dinner at Amelia's, the Fourth of July picnic at Kathy's, the Memorial Day party at Yolanda's and the Labor Day party at Paula's. Yolanda, Paula and Ike were all widows or widower, and Kathy and Amelia had never wed, so we were all family-less on those holidays. I had come to anticipate and enjoy these celebrations together.

The women bustled around the kitchen, getting in each other's way while laughing and talking. Wine flowed freely and soon we were all hashing over the latest news of the day—the car accident out on the bypass, the fire in town, the fire at my house and, of course, Sam turning up under my living room window.

"I think it's somehow fitting that Sam should bring you and JT back together again," Paula said, as she unrolled the crescent rolls and got them ready for baking.

"We're not back together." I examined the meat thermometer stuck into the turkey. God forbid I should kill anyone with my cooking. I nodded with satisfaction. It was perfect. I hauled the monster out of the stove and manhandled it onto the serving tray nearby. Kathy moved into place to begin the gravy prep.

"You would be if you'd let him get close enough," Yolanda said. She was dressed in her harvest gold sweater, black pants and gold lame pumps. Chunky gold bangles bobbled from her ears. Her black hair, showing just a few threads of white, was curled into tiny ringlets. She and Amelia sat at the kitchen table, where Yolanda was cutting the homemade mincemeat pie Ike had brought.

"It's just nostalgia." I went out onto the stoop and peered down the drive at the barn, where JT's truck was sitting. He and Ike were emerging from the newly fixed door, which was slid back on its hinges. "He fixed that door. That was nice of him. And perfect timing." I waved to them. JT waved back before getting into the truck.

"What do you mean, nostalgia?" Paula asked.

"He's in love with the past." I had thought about this

most of the morning and this made sense to me. "He doesn't love the me I am now. He's in love with his memories of the past. Let's face it, everybody is kind of in love with their past."

Paula straightened up from the stove. "That's what marriage is all about, isn't it?" she asked, glancing at Yolanda then at me. "When you marry somebody, you stay in love with the person you married but you also fall in love with the person you're with now. Love isn't a fixed point in time. It's always changing."

I heard the truck doors slamming outside. "But he doesn't even know who I am now. How could he be in love with me?"

Yolanda said, "You're right. You haven't given him a chance. Who knows, once he gets to know who you are now, he may run screaming in the other direction."

"Gee, thanks Mom, for that little vote of confidence."

She shrugged. "It shouldn't matter to you. You're not interested in him, right?" Her shrewd green eyes watched me, then shifted to the back door when JT and Ike walked in.

JT smiled at me as he shucked off his jacket and tossed down his leather gloves. "Got your girl all settled. She'll be safe out there from now on." He ran a hand over his cropped hair, then walked into the kitchen, sniffing. "Smells good in here. I didn't believe you could do it, but maybe you can cook, Molly. I'll have to taste it to believe it, though."

I was tongue-tied with sudden infatuation. He was very masculine, so tall and broad-shouldered with his face red from the cold and his hair tousled from working outside, the white curls clipped short but springy. I wanted to wrap my arms around him and hug him, just to feel all that male body against mine.

"You just wait," I managed to say, then I went back into the kitchen, my face flaming with color. Yolanda and Kathy exchanged a smug look but I ignored them, not anxious to examine what I was feeling.

JT fit right in with our group, joking with folks as we ate, then helping me decorate the fireplace mantle, bookcases, and windows. I've always had pets, so have never had a Christmas tree, but I always find plenty of other spots to display my Christmas bangles. JT was impressed with my M&M ornament collection, which I'd been collecting for years and which numbered in the dozens. We lined them up in the windows from oldest to newest, setting them carefully onto the sills high above Mr. T's elderly paws. And JT provided the height when it came to stringing my M&M Christmas lights above the fireplace and in the china cabinet.

My brother Don called as we were decorating. He and his family usually came for a visit in the summer, when travel weather was somewhat predictable. He and JT had a long chat, which I covertly tried to overhear, but Yolanda circumvented me by coercing me into the kitchen to dish out Ike's pie. I wasn't able to shake free in time to pick up any juicy gossip. We ended the afternoon with coffee and pie in the living room. I was feeling drowsy with turkey-drug and good cheer, not to mention the several glasses of wine I'd consumed.

"I was wondering how much you remember about the flower show that day Sam disappeared," JT said.

He was stretched out on the other side of the couch from me. We were sharing a hassock, his long legs almost drooping over the end while mine were comfortably propped up on the edge. The other guests were on the other couch, the love seat, and in armchairs. JT's gift to me was in the center of the coffee table, like a magical pot sitting next to my *Northern Gardener* magazine and the latest copy of *Writer's Digest*.

"Flower show?" I sipped coffee, willing my brain cells to work.

"I know it's been a long time, but I'd like to put together a time line of what happened that day." JT glanced at Yolanda. "Did you go to the show?"

She nodded. "I've volunteered every year for the past twenty years or more. If I recall correctly, I accepted entries that morning at the main building, then I helped set up displays in the barn. It was hot that day. I remember that. I was afraid the flower arrangements would wilt before they got judged."

I nodded sleepily. "It was one of those Indian summer days. It's really stuck in my mind, because when I found Sam and Bobbi Jo in the shed, I remember thinking it was so hot in there, how could they stand it?"

"Shed?" JT's coffee cup paused on the way to his mouth.

"The shed out at the fairgrounds that the Garden Club used to store supplies—you know, potting soil, tools, stuff like that."

"Insecticide?" he asked.

Something in his voice made me sit up a bit. "Yeah. Why?"

"Were you at the flower show all day?"

I heard something again in his voice, an insistent quality that bothered me. "I was there from about seven in the morning," I said. "I was in charge of the show that year. Shirley was Garden Club President, but she didn't do shit." I frowned at my coffee. "Typical of her, she always delegated everything so other people ended up doing all the work. Anyway, I had to be there from seven in the morning until dark every day of the show. It was a long week of preparation, then the show, all capped off by Sam pulling his little stunt, then leaving." I leaned back on the couch. JT was staring into his coffee cup, his long face thoughtful. "What's up, JT?"

"Can someone verify that you were at the show all day and that you didn't see Sam?" He turned to stare at me. I was surprised by the intent, somber look.

"I can," Amelia said immediately.

"Me, too," Paula confirmed. "We were on the committee with Molly. We all spent each day of the show out at the fairgrounds."

"Do you know who Sam had lunch with that day?"

"Lunch?" I struggled to think back to a day five years previously, but soon gave up. "I have no idea, JT. Let's see, it was a Friday. The Garden Show always went from Thursday to Sunday, and Sam left—" I revised myself, "—Sam disappeared on Friday. I figured he'd just taken a room at the motel, since I didn't think he'd leave town on a weekend." I saw JT's puzzled expression. "Sam was a realtor, he was always showing houses on the weekend. After our fight, I figured he'd go to a motel, then maybe come back, pack up more thoroughly, and move out." I sipped my coffee, remembering JT's original question. "Lunch?"

JT nodded. "I've got his Day Planner from that year. I've read through it, but he must have used abbreviations for his clients or something. He's got a notation in his calendar, but I can't figure out who he was meeting that morning at eleven."

"Why is that important?" Ike asked.

JT stared down at his hands. I followed his gaze, seeing the rough chapped skin and the big knobby knuckles. He stared at me. There was something assessing in his gaze, as though he was trying to make up his mind about a decision he had to make.

"What is it, JT?" I asked.

"Sam didn't die from the pitchfork," he said. "He was poisoned."

Chapter 9

The first thing I thought was, *I don't want to hear about poisoning right after eating Thanksgiving turkey.* Then my brain clicked into gear.

"Poisoned? But you said he was pitchforked to death." I took a handful of blue M&Ms from the basket JT had brought, needing the chocolate jolt. Blue was not the best color to kick-start my thought processes, but it would have to do in a pinch.

"I said we found the pitchfork," JT corrected me. "This is confidential, you know."

"Confidential?" I struggled to straighten in righteous indignation, but turkey and inertia kept me pinned on the couch. "You've got three reporters in the room. It's a little late to—"

"That's fine," Ike said. Since he was my editor, I couldn't quibble, but I shot him a reproving glance. He deftly sidestepped it. "Must have been a poison that was somewhat slow-acting," he said, his forehead creased in thought.

"Poisoned?" Yolanda asked. "Was it a contact poison or ingested? How did they know he'd been poisoned after all this time? Wouldn't it have leached out of the body? I mean, I presume there's been some decay after all this time."

Kathy took a tiny bite of pie. "It wouldn't necessarily leach out, Landie. Some poisons settle in the organs, especially if it's had a chance to traverse the digestive tract."

"Or if it left a distinctive appearance on the mouth or gums," Paula pointed out. "Some poisons can discolor the gums. I imagine that would remain, even after all this time. That was on one of those CSI shows."

JT's gaze moved from Paul to Ike, Yolanda, and finally to me. "CSI?" he asked in what I thought was a strangled sort of voice.

I picked up the conversation. "JT was asking about the gardening supplies, so that must mean it's used in horticulture." I started running through ideas in my head. "We don't keep any Class Three pesticides in that shed, so it couldn't be nicotine or anything like that. Bob Durham keeps those locked up in the shed under the grandstand. He's the only one of us with a Class Three Pesticide license."

"It had to be ingested," Amelia pointed out. "JT was asking about lunch and who Sam might have met."

We all nodded. That made sense. "So if Sam had it in lunch, it had to be something that tasted okay. Otherwise he'd have noticed and—" I stopped when I saw the astonished expression on JT's face. "What? I write murder mysteries, remember? Where do you think I bounce my ideas?" I gestured to the elderly people all sitting in my living room. "These are some of the finest murder minds in the country."

"If Sam was poisoned, it must not have affected him too badly," Ike said, obviously thinking out loud. "I mean, he and Bobbi Jo were going at it in the shed. It must not have been a drug that affected his performance, if you know what I mean."

"You're sure they were—" JT stopped, a dark flush on his high cheekbones. "I mean, you're sure they were having—"

"I caught them, JT," I said flatly. "Pants down around their ankles, part A in part B. Trust me, whatever poison it was, it didn't affect his performance."

"Okay, that's good to know. I wasn't sure if you were sure." I couldn't quite interpret the emotion in JT's eyes. Was it amusement? Jealousy? Envy? "We're not sure what the poison was. You mentioned someone in your group told you about something that could make the coons sick?"

"That was probably me," Paula said. "We used to put out leftovers laced with Ex-Lax."

"Or me," Kathy said. "My father used to put ipecac in cakes, bake them and put them in the trash. The coons got sick and left the trash alone after that. You had to do it four or five times a year, but they always got the hint. Coons may not be the brightest bulb on the Christmas tree, but they learn after a while."

JT eyed them both warily. "There were signs Sam was sick before he died."

I made a face. "I'm not sure I want to talk about this after eating a big dinner." I thought about Sam on that last day I'd seen him. Bobbi Jo had been stretched out on a bench with her skirt around her waist. Sam was on top, his pants down but still wearing his shirt. I remember how funny he'd looked. A woman doesn't see a man's butt during sex, but it really is a funny sight. Sam had been so proud of his physique and that he still retained his solid, muscular form even after too many martini lunches, desserts and late night meals. Sam loved his sweets. But I still remembered his jiggling butt as he and Bobbi Jo panted on that bench.

"Poor Sam," I said. JT was watching me and I met his gaze. "No, he didn't look sick when I saw him. That was about one or one-thirty, I think."

"No," Amelia said. "No, the dahlias are always one of the last classes to be judged, don't you remember? It was probably more like three or three-thirty." She smiled at JT. "I always need a bit of a pick-me-up in the afternoon, and I'd just gone to the refreshment tent when I heard Molly shouting at Sam."

I remembered now. I'd had a busy morning and wanted to relax over lunch. But somebody called in sick and I had to—"Janet Langford," I said. "She called in sick. She was supposed to judge the roses but she didn't show. I had to find somebody to take her place, that old witch. I think she did it on purpose, to make me look bad. Those Langfords were always in cahoots with Shirley. I'd just gotten the roses started when somebody told me I was needed at the shed. I was due to judge the dahlias and didn't really have time, but—"

"Who told you?" JT asked.

I grabbed his little M&M basket and plunked it on the couch to be more conveniently at hand. "Hell, I don't remember, JT. It was a lifetime ago." I curled up on the couch, tucking my legs to one side so I could turn and face him. "There were people talking to me all the time. I had to run the show and judge a couple of categories. I was so busy, I barely had time to think."

"But somebody told you to go to the shed?" he asked. Our hands met at the M&Ms. I withdrew mine hastily but he just smiled, taking out a blue M&M and popping it in his mouth.

"I think so. I remember being told there was a problem, something about vandalism. Of course, there wasn't a problem—there was just Sam and Bobbi Jo in that shed. I thought later how I would never have known about Sam if somebody hadn't told me to go there. But I really didn't stop to consider it. I was so pissed off at him. It was the third time I'd caught him messing around. I was just so disappointed and—" I stopped, not sure how to articulate what I'd felt. I shook my head. "It was a long time ago."

JT put his arm on the back of the couch, tapping impatiently with one finger in a quick, staccato rhythm. "So somebody wanted you to find him."

"Or maybe somebody just wanted him to leave the Garden Show," Yolanda pointed out. "Let's face it, this is a small town. Everybody would know that if he were found with Bobbi Jo, then Molly would read him the riot act. We all know how Molly is. She wouldn't stay quiet about that. He'd leave the show. There's no way he'd hang around."

Ike nodded. "Let's say somebody poisoned him, but wasn't expecting him to be with a bunch of people, in public."

"I had something like that in my second book. I made it up," I said defensively, glancing at JT. He just gestured for me to continue. "It had to do with the timing of the death. My killer didn't want to be anywhere near the victim when he died. How long did Sam's poison take to work?"

JT shook his head. "Not sure. We're still waiting for

test results. He may have vomited, though. And maybe had a seizure." He hesitated, then said, "We think he was sick and probably would have died of the poison, but somebody else stabbed him first. We're not sure what exactly killed him."

"Oh, dear," Paula murmured. "Poor Sam. He certainly wasn't a lovable man, but he didn't deserve that."

I felt awful. For years I'd thought Sam had been having the time of his life, screwing Bobbi Jo on some warm, sandy beach somewhere. Now to find out that he might have suffered—might have been alone and sick. All these years, I'd been sort of relieved that he'd presented me with such a clear-cut way to get him out of my life. He and I had argued interminably for a month or more, both knowing that our marriage was over and neither wanting to make the move to end it officially. Finding him with Bobbi Jo had given me grounds for justifiable divorce. I felt guilty now to have been so relieved at the time.

"Good Lord," Yolanda said. "Who hated Sam so much they killed him twice?"

I blinked widely. She was right. JT stood up, setting down his coffee cup. "That's a good question, Landie. From what I can gather, Molly didn't hate him enough to kill him and neither did any of the husbands who caught him messing with their wives."

I peered up at JT. "Wives?"

"Why don't we go out to the barn and check on that cat?" he said.

"What do you mean, JT? Was Sam—"

"Go with John, dear," Yolanda said. "He obviously wants to chat with you in private. Don't be obtuse."

"Oh, for heaven's sake." Grumbling, I got to my feet and followed JT into the kitchen. We put on our coats and he took down the big flashlight before we went out into the sharp cold. "Was Sam messing around with someone other than Bobbi Jo?" I demanded as soon as we left the house.

JT took my hand. I was so surprised, I didn't know what to say. We hurried down the frozen drive to the barn. "Yeah, we think he was. I've had Bucky tracking down the people that we're sure of from Sam's datebook. I think maybe Sam and Shirley had something going for a while." JT hunched his shoulders into his jacket as the biting west wind hit us. "There were a couple of other women he had noted in his book."

"Jesus!" I was so mad I wanted to stomp. "Am I so bad in bed that he couldn't be satisfied with me?" The surprised expression on JT's face made me laugh. "Think about it, JT. Sam had all these women on the side. It must mean I'm lousy in bed."

He shook his head, releasing my hand to pull open the newly fixed barn door. "Sam was a man who just liked women, Molly. It had nothing to do with you. Trust me."

I gave a bitter little laugh. "Right."

He blocked the doorway, turning to stare down at me. "You can trust me on that," he said in a low, even voice. "I may have done something stupid by leaving you and going with Shirley, but it had nothing to do with you, Molly. Believe me. It had everything to do with me, not with you."

I brushed by him. "That's bullshit and you know it."

He grabbed my arm, pulling me to a stop. "Listen to me. I married Shirley because I thought she could give me something important—I thought she could help me be a different person. You loved me just the way I was, but Shirley wanted to make me better. Or at least that's what I thought." He shook my arm a bit, drawing me nearer to him. "She married me to get back at Mark and at her father."

"Mark? Mark was married to Isabel and—"

"She and Mark dated in college, then he up and married Isabel. I suspect his father pressured him into that. Shirley never got over him, and her father never let her forget it. Her old man just about went ballistic. He wanted her to marry well, so what does she do—she turns around and marries a half-breed construction worker on one of her father's crews." JT gave a bitter laugh. "She told her father and me she was pregnant. He wasn't going to kick her out. By the time he and I found out she'd lied, she and I were married." JT's face appeared hard in the half-light of the torch. "Mark was the one love of her life. I know."

I was stunned. I'd never suspected any of this. If it

was true, then... What a monumental waste of love and life they'd all endured.

"A year and a half later, she divorced me and married Calvin Pritchard. Three years after that, Mark's wife died, but Shirley was stuck with Calvin for another seven years before he died and she could marry Mark." JT shook his head, his dark eyes haunted and sad.

"But Mark's cheating on her now," I protested. "I know he is."

"I don't know if he is or not," JT said, his voice brusque and harsh. "But I do know that Shirley's using me to make him jealous. She told me as much." He turned and disappeared into the inky darkness of the barn.

"What?" I hurried after the bobbing beam of the flashlight.

"She told me," he said over his shoulder. "Said she wanted to make Mark jealous and knew that I was the way to do it. I told her to just talk to him, find out what's going on." JT made an indecipherable noise. "I told her it was probably just a guy thing. A man gets older and starts to worry about things like—"

"Like what?" I asked.

He stopped so suddenly I almost ran him down. He turned. I realized we were just inches apart. "A man worries if he's got it any more, that's what." He put the flashlight on an upturned box. "A man worries if he can interest a woman. Someone like you."

"What?"

His hands slid down my arms to my waist, then went around me. It felt like the most natural thing in the world for me to put my arms around JT's neck and let him help me stand on my tiptoes. I raised my face to his.

"You heard me," he said. He lowered his face.

When his lips touched mine, I felt as though I'd tumbled back in a rabbit hole of time. I was twenty-five again and this was a man whom I knew intimately and very, very well. There was no hesitation, no uncertainty and no worry—there was just passion, desire, and need, a shocking flaring of nerve endings that I'd thought were dormant. I felt the long length of him press against me, felt him move between my legs. I remembered in aching detail what it felt like to hold him between my thighs as he entered me, filling me the way no man ever had before or since. I dug my fingers into his shoulders, tearing my lips away.

"John, don't," I said. "Don't do this."

"Why not?" He nuzzled into my neck, his beard rasping me. Then his hand moved under my sweater and closed on my breast, thumbing the nipple through my bra. I involuntarily arched against him, and he laughed softly, his breath hot on my throat. "Oh, Molly, there's never been anyone in my life like you. Why shouldn't we?"

A tiny thread of sanity was returning to my brain. "John, you can't just come back to town like this and jump into my life."

JT moved closer. I felt his erection, insistent, pressing into me. Part of me wanted to take him in my hands. Another part wanted to run away. It had been years since I'd been a woman, reacting to a man. I wasn't sure what to do. I wasn't sure what I wanted to do.

He stared down at me, his face all angles and planes in the erratic light. "I came back because of you. You know I did."

I edged backward. He reluctantly released my breast, but kept his hands on my hips, preventing me from moving too far away from him. "What did you think would happen?" My voice was shaking but I couldn't help it. I wasn't sure if I wanted to cry or hit him. "Did you think you'd just move here and I'd fall into your arms? Damn it, John. I made a good life for myself here. I was fine. I was just fine without you."

His eyes were dark pools in the shadows of the barn. "I know. I don't know what I was thinking. I guess maybe I wasn't thinking." He shook his head. "Molly, after I was wounded a few years ago, I lay in that hospital bed and looked back on my life. None of it made any sense. None of it made sense because you weren't there to share it with me. That's when I knew I had to come here. I had to—I had to at least try." He ran a hand through my hair, cupping my face in his palm. "I was hoping, Molly." He kissed me gently.

I wanted to weep. I never expected this. I had honestly thought I'd go to my grave and never have to see JT McCord or face the feelings he'd raised in me ever again. I didn't want to face those feelings. I didn't want to be alive again. I didn't want to be a woman again. I wanted to be safe in my life that I'd made for myself and never open myself up to pain again.

"Molly, just give it a chance, please. Don't let what happened between us interfere with what might happen for us in the future. I hurt you and I'm sorry for that, more than you can know. But I've paid for it, too, Molly. Don't make me keep paying."

I stared up at him, trapped by the beseeching in his eyes. "I'll try, John. But I'm not sure about all this. I never wanted—"

He put two fingers against my lips. "Just try," he whispered. "Please."

I nodded, unable to speak past the lump in my throat. He stared into my eyes, then he nodded once, abruptly. "Come on." He picked up the flashlight. I followed, numb with surprise and glad I didn't have to immediately face the emotions he was forcing to the surface. I'd deal with that all some other day.

He shone the light into the corner where the cat had been. Now a tall wooden box faced the wall, a couple of small porthole-windows facing out into the barn. "I made sure the barn is secure," he said. "The coons can't get in. I put a couple of openings on the side of the box and it's two levels inside. I think she wanted to move the kittens higher. There's a spot there where you can put the food." He gestured with the flashlight.

I was impressed. "Thank you," I whispered. I cleared my throat. "You must have worked all night on that."

He stared into the corner. I could see two eyes glinting in the reflected light, peering out at us from one of the little windows. "I like cats. I never thought I could admit to that before—you know how it is, guys are supposed to like dogs and cats are just a waste of time. But I've always liked cats." He glanced down at me. "I may take a couple of the kittens off your hands when you're ready."

"Sure." I was breathless with shock, my mind reeling.

He led the way out of the barn, making sure the door was closed behind us. "Just feed her every day and I think she'll be fine. I got a good look at the kittens and they seem okay. They're all moving around and making noise."

"Thank you. I appreciate it." I covertly wiped the tears off my face, hoping he'd attribute them to the biting wind.

He started to walk back toward the house and I fell into step with him. "I'm going to be out of town for a couple of days. I just wanted you to know."

"Oh?" I tried to appear nonchalant. "Police business?"

He nodded. "I've got a lead on Sam's car. Now that we know he didn't leave town, I'd like to find Bobbi Jo." His eyes swept my back yard and the area near the garage. "We did what checking we could, but somebody took Sam's car and went to Minneapolis. It's a cold trail, but I'd like to follow it."

"Bobbi Jo was alive," I said, suddenly remembering my conversation with Sue Anne. "She called her sister that night. I talked to Sue Anne the other day—the day I assaulted everybody at the Country Club." I rolled my eyes in exasperation and he grinned. "Sue Anne said that Bobbi Jo called her that night. The police never talked to her because we all figured Bobbi Jo and Sam had left town. But if Bobbi Jo called—"

JT nodded. "I'd planned to check with Sue Anne. I'll do that before I leave town." We stopped by his truck. I glanced at the stoop and saw Yolanda poised and ready to descend. "Looks like it's time to go," he said. "I'll call you when I get back, tell you what I found out."

"Good. I'd appreciate that." I hesitated. "Thanks, JT. For the cat and for—" For what? For coming back and trying to sweep me off my feet? For disrupting my life? I wasn't sure. I think my confusion must have shown in my eyes.

He leaned down. "Just give me a chance, honey," he murmured. He kissed me, one hand caressing my face. Then he turned to my mother and offered his arm. I watched as he got her bundled into his truck. He paused by the driver's door. Then he smiled and got up into the cab, waving out the window as they drove away.

I watched until they'd made the turn at the end of the lane and vanished from sight. Then I went inside, a thousand emotions shooting through me like the icy wind that blew down the drive.

Chapter 10

Black Friday, that traditional Day After Thanksgiving Shopping Orgy, is a low-key affair in Tangle Butte. Some people splurge and drive to Mankato or Albert Lea for their consumer fix. Others really splurge and drive to Minneapolis and the gargantuan Mall of America. Since I view shopping as a chore, not an avocation, I stay in Tangle Butte.

I followed my usual agenda on the Friday after Thanksgiving. I stopped by the office and did a couple of hours of work. Then I went to the Dollar Store and bought Mr. T a new catnip mouse for Christmas. I went to Bert's Lady's Fashions, where I found a bracelet for Yolanda. I got a book for Paula and one for Amelia at the Tangled Pages Used Book Store and Bakery Shop. My last stop for the day was Bill's Hardware Store, where I browsed for an Ike present but did not buy. I decided to save the video store, two drug stores, two clothing stores, other dollar store, gift shop, and Antique Emporium for another day.

Amelia pounced on me as soon as I re-entered the office, and I endured my Tarot predictions for the day *(beware the stranger; Love's course does not run smooth; the fulfillment of your dreams is close at hand)*. I was relieved she hadn't predicted imminent marriage or love sweeping me off my feet. I was still unsettled by having JT McCord in my life. I needed time to get accustomed to the idea.

We were wrapping up the paper for the afternoon when Mark Devlin called. "Can you drop by the office on your way home? A legal matter has come up and we need to talk."

I immediately thought of the Shirley Assault at the Country Club. I knew that bitch wouldn't let me off without making a fuss. "Sure," I said in resignation. "I'll be there in a few minutes." I grabbed my handbag.

Ike glanced up from the story he was editing. "Problems?"

"Shirley is probably going to have me arrested for assault."

"Well, let me know if she does, I've got room in the Police Reports column for it."

"Gee, thanks for the concern about my potential legal problems."

"Nothing personal," Ike said with a laugh. "I'll save the space for you just in case."

I waved a goodbye and went out, walking the two blocks to Mark's office next to Baxter's Drugstore. In ten minutes, I was sitting in front of his desk, a cup of coffee in hand and watching as he sorted through an impressive pile of papers in front of him.

I assessed him with new understanding, based on what JT had told me. Somehow, I'd always assumed he and Shirley married because they were so alike—both part of the social scene in Tangle Butte, both somewhat well-off and expected to be leaders in the community. I hadn't considered that love—long-term love at that—might have had anything to do with it. It made it harder to dislike Shirley if I thought of her pining for Mark all these years.

I realized he was watching me with a quizzical look. He must have asked me a question. I said the first thing that popped into my mind, an unfortunate habit of mine. "I'm so glad I never slept with you, Mark. I think you make a better friend than a lover."

He sat back, obviously surprised. "What made you think of that?"

My ears heated with embarrassment. "I'm sorry. It's just that having JT back in town has made me think about a lot of things—things I haven't thought about for a long time."

He peered down at the papers on the desk, his bright blue eyes thoughtful. He was such a handsome man with his tawny gold hair and his rugged Robert Redford looks. He and Shirley were a perfect match, both tall, well-dressed, and ironed to perfection. "I know what you mean," he said, still not meeting my eyes. "Shirley and I had a long talk last night." He finally raised his gaze and I met it squarely. "I'm glad, too, Molly. You're right. You're a good friend."

I felt as though something momentous was almost being said, just below the surface. I also knew it would never be verbalized more. So I nodded and said in a light voice, "In that case, I hope you'll protect me from your wife. I suppose that's why I'm here. She wants to sue me, right? I swear, Mark, it was... " I searched for the right word. "...unplanned."

"Nope, it's not Shirley." He smiled, pulling a piece of paper from the stack in front of him. "It's about Sam, actually."

"Sam? Now what? I swear, he's causing more trouble dead than he ever caused alive." Then I realized how that sounded and grimaced. "You know what I mean."

He grinned. "Yeah. Here's some more trouble." He slid the paper across the desk to me.

I picked it up. It was a copy of my divorce proceedings. "So?"

"Your divorce is null and void." He barreled on when I tried to talk. "You're a widow."

"Huh? You must be wrong, I divorced him."

"But he was dead." Mark pulled over an impressively huge leather-bound book and opened it to a page marked with a sticky note. "You became a widow the day he died." He tapped the opened book. "It says so right here. That means we need to probate his will and settle his estate."

"What estate?" I leaned forward. "When I divorced him, all of his accounts and things were frozen, weren't they?"

Mark nodded. "Exactly. Now we have to unfreeze them. Don't forget the Hunt land deal. You can go forward with that."

"Whoa. I'd forgotten about that." Years ago, Sam had

obtained land from Jacob Hunt, Charlene Anderson's father. A developer had expressed an interest in the property because it was near Point Park, a popular spot that saw a lot of use, winter and summer. Sam had started negotiations with the developer, but Charlene's family had blocked him, saying that Sam got the land under false pretenses. They'd wrangled about it in court for a while, then Sam was awarded title. I'd heard from the development group when Sam left town or, rather, when we thought he'd left town. But I couldn't help them. I wasn't legal owner of the property.

"So I can sell that land?" I asked. I remembered Chuck Anderson's request to go through Sam's papers. Did that have anything to do with the land near Point Park?

"We'll have to get a death certificate and official time and cause of death, but yes, eventually I think you could. You and Sam made wills when you got married. I took the liberty of checking when I heard Sam was found." Mark shuffled some more papers on his desk, finally sliding another stapled sheaf toward me.

I recognized the page of dense, legal mumbo-jumbo. Sam and I had, indeed, made wills. I'd changed mine when he vanished, splitting my 'estate,' such as it was, between my nieces and nephews.

"And since you're a widow..." he said.

I looked up at him in inquiry.

"You should plan a Memorial Service. It's sort of expected, you know."

"Aw, shit. You're right." I flopped back in the chair.

Mark tapped a pencil on the desk. "You could set Yolanda loose on it," he suggested. "She'd love planning something like that."

I cheered up at the thought. "You're right. She loves doing stuff like that." I shuffled through the pages on the desk. "Is there anything I have to do to make this all happen?"

"No, I'll get the paperwork started. I'll have to contact the coroner and get the legal forms, so it's not going to happen right away." He cleared his throat. "There is one other thing."

"Hmm?" I tore my thoughts away from the bizarre

idea of a Memorial Service for Sam.

"It's the Langfords."

"Oh, Lord, now what?"

He leaned forward and I automatically leaned forward, too. "This is strictly on the QT, okay? Rumor only."

I nodded.

"Now that Sam's body turned up they're considered exhuming Delbert and..."

I sat back, stunned. "What?" I almost shouted it.

He pressed his hand down in a 'shut up' motion. "I heard, and this is just between me and you, that they talked to one of my colleagues in town. They wanted to know if there were grounds to have Delbert exhumed and checked for poison."

"He was dying of cancer!" I was so mad I was stuttering. "For heaven's sake, the poor man had terminal—"

"I know, I know. To make a long story short, my colleague, who shall remain nameless, essentially laughed them out of his office, in a very polite way. He pointed out that any poison probably wouldn't have remained in the body after twenty years, that there were no grounds for an exhumation, and that if you wanted to, you could counter-sue, claiming harassment." Mark tapped the papers on his desk. "They might demand that you settle out of court."

"I won't," I said flatly. "No way. Those witches aren't getting any of my money."

He grinned. "I figured you'd say that. I told my colleague as much. I told him that if he wanted a long and expensive court battle with little chance of getting a fee at the end, he could go ahead and sue." Mark leaned back. "I think you'll be okay. But keep an eye out for them, okay? This business with Sam has got a lot of people heated up."

I couldn't believe it. The Witches of Langford weren't giving up. How could someone as sweet as Delbert have had such lousy kids? I stood up. "Thanks, Mark."

He stood up, too. "Thank you, Molly." I must have appeared surprised, because he added, "I think seeing how you and JT are together again has made Shirley realize a lot of things. I don't know, somehow she and I have managed to talk more in the last week than we have in the last few years. I think it's because of how JT feels about you."

I didn't know what to say. "JT and I aren't—I mean, you know, we aren't—"

He smiled, escorting me to the door. "Maybe not. But maybe you will be. Who knows?" Then he frowned. "Although I should warn you..."

"What?"

He looked embarrassed. "It's kind of complicated, but Belinda ... well, I think she wants to try to get JT interested in her just to spite Shirley. She and Shirley don't get along. Belinda has this idea that..." He stopped, a dark flush coloring his face. "Anyway, Belinda's gone up to Minneapolis to shop for the weekend. I wouldn't put it past her to ask JT to the dance when she gets back. You might want to ask him yourself, first." He smiled weakly and shrugged, as though to say *Women—who can figure them?*

Good heavens, this was a surreal conversation. The Festive Fling dance would be held in a week and was the social event of the winter season in Tangle Butte. I was on duty that night as photographer for the paper, since Dan, our regular photographer, was nominated for King of the Fling. I wasn't sure if I should invite JT or not. I decided to do a Scarlett and think about it tomorrow. "Thanks for the warning, Mark," I said inanely. "And thanks for reminding about my widowly duties." I escaped his office, my head spinning.

I called Mom when I got home and enlisted her help in planning a Memorial Service for Sam. She was intrigued by the fact I was a widow, as I knew she'd be. Knowing her, I could expect a new black wardrobe to appear on my doorstep by Monday morning. I put the entire planning into her manicured and capable hands.

I was distracted all weekend. I couldn't settle down to anything. The manuscript I was working on felt stale. Luckily, my editor wasn't holding her breath waiting for it, so I could afford to let it lie fallow for another week or so. I tried writing Christmas cards, but gave up after doing two. I spent a weepy half hour putting flowers on Cassie's grave and visiting the other pets in my memories.

The only bright spot during the entire time was that the mother cat let me get close enough to view the babies, who now had their eyes open and were moving around.

I helped Jake on Sunday get the Monday paper ready, and by Sunday night, I felt drained with the effort of avoiding thinking about JT. It was almost a relief to discuss Yolanda's plans for Sam's service, which we did at length until the topic was thoroughly beaten into the ground. I couldn't sleep that night, haunted by thoughts of Sam, JT, and possible changes in my future. Did I want JT in my life? I didn't know. I didn't enjoy change in my life. I was a Minnesotan, and we don't adapt well to change. I hid my head under the pillow and decided not to decide. It was the easiest thing to do.

When Melvin awakened me at dawn with his foray into my yard, I was happy to leave my sleepless bed and chase him away. Anger beat that awful, at-loose-ends feeling. I went next door and had a pre-dawn chat with Mrs. Dalworthy, my elderly neighbor and owner of Melvin. She was honestly perplexed by why and how Melvin kept getting out of his comfortable bedroom in the entryway off her kitchen. In the end I promised to come over later and check her door arrangements, since Melvin obviously had figured out a means of escape. I went home to survey the damage and prepare for a new work week.

I decided to stop at the vet's on the way to work. Maybe Dr. Swanson would have a reason for Melvin wanting to escape his warm bed to come dig up my flowers. Doc and I had a pleasant chat and he promised to find me some info about pot-bellied pigs. Then I went to the police station, just to put this latest misbehavior on file in case it was needed in the future.

I swear, I wasn't really checking to see if JT was back in town. That had nothing to do with it.

The station house was attached to the City Hall downtown. I went inside where Janice Carlson sat behind a counter which, like at the newspaper, separated the public from the work that went on inside. Unlike the newspaper, though, there was a wall behind her. It hid the doings of the police station from prying eyes like mine. A single doorway in the wall was open, showing me some desks and offices beyond. I suppose one of those offices belonged to JT.

I explained what had happened and Janice filled out a bunch of forms. I was just getting ready to leave when one of those far office doors opened and Belinda Devlin emerged, standing in the doorway and talking to someone in the office. Then she crossed the room of desks and must have gone to another doorway I didn't see. She came out into the lobby just as I was pulling on my mittens.

Her cheeks were bright pink and there was a jaunty sparkle in her eyes. I don't know how to describe it, but she looked like a woman who had just gotten a surprise. She slid on her leather coat, covering her large boobs in the tight sweater that so clearly revealed her erect nipples. "Molly," she said with a cheeriness I usually ascribe to an over-indulgence in booze. "You're out bright and early on this Monday."

"So are you." I glanced through the center doorway and saw JT emerging from the office that Belinda had just come out of. Even at this distance, I could see his face was flushed. He was wearing a uniform today, black pants and gray shirt with a lot of badges and insignia on it. As I watched, he straightened his necktie, then took something Bucky handed him and went back into the office.

Belinda followed my gaze. "I just wanted to stop and thank JT for the weekend," she said as she tugged on her gloves. She started toward the front door.

I was pulled along like a magnet had me in its tow. "Weekend?" I managed to ask.

She nodded, her bronze/blonde hair dancing in pretty waves. "I ran into him when I was shopping in the Twin Cities. We had drinks." She held the door for me as I stumbled out onto the sidewalk. "It was so nice to meet up with somebody I knew. And JT is so much fun to be with. But of course, you know about that. Well, I can tell you, he hasn't changed."

The low, sultry tone in her voice told me that they'd had more than drinks. "I thought you used to live in the Cities," I said, struggling to find a topic of conversation. "Didn't you meet up with friends there?"

She glanced back over her shoulder at the front door of the City Hall, then she smiled. I swear, she looked like a cat licking cream off her face. "Yes, I did." The dreamy quality of her voice almost made me retch.

"Well, that's nice," I babbled. "I've got to get to work. See you later." I managed to walk woodenly away.

"What's the deadline for those Teasers?" she called after me.

"Noon today." I fumbled open Augie's door.

"Good." She smiled again at the police station. "I want to make sure to put one in for tomorrow's paper."

Now I *knew* I'd be sick. I jammed the key into the ignition, my guts churning and my mind whirling. She may as well have come out and said, 'Oh, by the way, I spent the weekend in bed with JT, so there.'

Calm down, I told myself. *Just because Belinda acts that way, it doesn't mean anything happened. Just calm down. JT wouldn't lie to me. He wouldn't do anything that stupid.*

Would he?

Because of the morning's events with Melvin and the police, I was late getting to work. We were so busy that no one noticed how I was acting. Even Amelia, who dutifully read my cards *(beware of making rash choices; trust your instincts; take care of yourself first today)* didn't notice how distracted I was. It wasn't until Ike was setting the page for the Teasers that he looked closely at me.

"Got your Tuesday Teaser here," he said.

Something in his tone alerted me. "What's it say?"

He gestured me to his screen and pointed. I wheeled over and saw *Do you want me to wait forever? I've told you how I feel. Now it's your turn. Your Lost Love.*

"Hmm." I wheeled back, wondering if Ike saw my trembling hands. "Sounds like an ultimatum. I guess that lady in his life had better fish or cut bait."

Ike snorted. "Got another new one today, too."

My stomach clenched. I was expecting this. "Really?"

"From Belinda." He peered at his screen. *"Thanks for the weekend. Hoping for many more. B."*

Amelia, Dan, and Ike all gazed at me with alert, curious eyes. "How about that?" I managed to mumble.

I grabbed a handful of M&Ms. It didn't matter what color they were.

Nothing would help.

Chapter 11

I don't remember much about the rest of Monday. It passed in a fog, full of little voices in my head. Did he or didn't he?

That's what it all boiled down to.

Did he?

Didn't he?

He had in the past, but was this a new JT?

Even the distraction of Community News didn't help. Amelia was agonizing over how to phrase a social faux pas that had occurred. It appeared that Susie Hunt, Joe Hunt's ex-sister-in-law, had indeed come to town and expected to stay at Joe's house. Joe had flat-out told her no. She'd told her ex-husband Jimmy (Joe's brother) that Joe had refused her shelter. Jimmy promptly pitched a fit and refused to come to Thanksgiving dinner at Joe's house. Consequently, Joe and his wife were stuck with six empty place settings and a bunch of leftover food.

"They must be sleeping together again," Ike said as I packed up to leave for the day.

"Who?" I demanded, rounding on him like a duck on a June bug.

He eyed me closely. "Susie Hunt and Jimmy. Who'd you think I meant?"

"Nothing." I downed three red M&Ms, hoping for some vitality. Unlucky for me, I got Yolanda instead. She came in the office as I was leaving.

"I've got Sam's memorial service all planned for tomorrow. It starts at ten-thirty at the Johnson-Strayer Funeral Home. The church ladies will make the coffee afterwards. I ordered a sheet cake from the Tangled Page for treats." She peered over the counter at Ike. "Did you get that announcement in for me?"

He nodded. "It's in today's paper, right next to the announcement for the Scavenger Hunt. Although I still say you didn't need to put in an official notice, all you had to do was tell Peggy over at the Brew 'n' Chew and everybody in town would know."

Yolanda shrugged, her stylish faux leopard coat and hat making her appear twenty years younger than I felt at the moment. "One has to follow the social niceties at a time like this. Regardless of what we think of Sam, he deserves our time and effort." She caught my glum expression. "What are you doing, practicing to be the grieving widow?"

"No one would believe it," I said. "I'm just tired. I didn't sleep well last night."

"I heard Belinda put an ad in the paper, thanking JT for their so-called date." Yolanda said this with elaborate nonchalance, which didn't fool me. I caught a glimpse of the interest in her sharp green eyes.

I tried to wrestle my curiosity to the ground but failed miserably. "What date?"

"Oh, didn't you hear?" She examined the polish on one bright pink nail and made a little face of disgust. "Belinda is claiming she and JT had a hot date up in the Cities."

How did my mother do it? I worked in a newspaper office but I couldn't match her for gossip. "Where did you hear that?" I sidled toward the door, hoping to lure her out before the rest of the office got involved in the discussion.

"Marcia Bennett is in my bridge club. Her daughter, Sarah, is friends with Belinda. Sarah lives in the Cities. Sarah and Belinda went shopping on Friday. And on Saturday Belinda had to cancel their afternoon shopping because she had a date with JT." Mom gazed expectantly at me, as did everyone else in the room.

"How nice for them," I snapped.

"It's probably nothing," Mom said. "You know how Belinda likes to set a fox in the henhouse. That girl is always up to pranks."

Everyone in the office nodded. I felt relieved. She was right.

"Of course, Sarah did say as how Belinda didn't get home until late on Saturday. Really until early on Sunday."

My spirits plummeted again.

"That doesn't mean she was with JT the whole time," Ike pointed out.

My spirits rose.

"That's true," Yolanda agreed. "I'm sure JT will explain it all when you talk to him."

My spirits dropped. "I don't know when that will be."

"Oh."

That little word spoke volumes. I decided to leave before my spirits did any more flip-flopping. "I'll see you tomorrow at the service," I said, making a lunge for the door and the escape that beckoned to me.

"Wear something nice, dear," Yolanda admonished. "He was your husband."

"Will do." I bolted out the door but not before I heard her say, 'So Ike, what did you hear? I heard that JT and Belinda...' I longed to go back and listen in but knew I didn't dare. My roller-coaster feelings couldn't take it.

This felt like twenty years ago. Substitute 'Shirley' for 'Belinda' and I was a twenty-five-year-old waitress in love with a construction worker and itching to get married, settle down and have babies. Well, okay, forget the 'married and have babies' bit now. At my age, the baby thing wasn't an option I wanted to consider. But I could never forget the humiliating moment when I realized JT and Shirley were An Item. I felt like that all over again, a jolt of past grief and anger and fear, all rolled into one.

I drove home, trying to convince myself that nothing had happened during the past weekend that I need concern myself about. The weather reflected my feelings. A dense fog hung over everything, so it felt like I was driving in a cloud. Damn JT had come back into my life and now I felt like I was floundering.

I wandered around the house, heating up leftovers that I ended up giving to Mr. T. I flopped in a chair and munched blue M&Ms, staring gloomily out the window as the day darkened. When the phone rang I almost jumped out of my skin.

It was Charlene. I leaned my head wearily against the chair back. I was in no mood to deal with Charlene and her damn tax papers. Thank God she got right to the point. "Molly, I know that Chuck talked to you about this. I don't think he told you how important it is. Did you have a chance to talk to JT about Sam's papers?"

I had totally blanked out about it. I was trying to make up some suitable lie when she said, "I realize it might be awkward for you to talk to him right now, but I was hoping maybe he'd brought the papers back to you. We really need to check them for that tax matter."

Awkward? Good Lord, was it all over town? I felt a headache start to blossom behind my right eye, a sure sign either of a sinus problem or a brain aneurysm waiting to happen. "I didn't have a chance," I said. "JT was out of town and what with the holiday and all ..."

"I know, it's been so busy. We had everybody over here. Twenty-eight people, can you believe it?" She laughed nervously. I could imagine her walking around her immaculate kitchen with the phone pressed to her ear as she watched some perfect cake baking in the oven. Charlene was Susie Homemaker, reincarnated and living in Tangle Butte, Minnesota. She had probably learned her alphabet by reading a Betty Crocker cookbook and her math by using measuring cups and spoons. "Do you think you could call him? It's so important. We have to get it by the end of the year and there's a lot of paperwork to fill out."

"I don't have JT's phone number." I was relieved to have a legitimate excuse. "I'm sure I'll see him tomorrow sometime. I'll ask him then. Or I'll call at the station." By tomorrow I'd be ready to face him, I told myself. I just needed some time.

There was a long pause. "I read that you're having a service for Sam." Charlene's voice sounded tremulous. I wondered if she was one of those women who cried at all funerals and weddings. She probably was. It fit with the

Susie Homemaker image. "That's nice."

Nice? I had no idea what this service would entail. My socially conscious mother had planned it. But knowing Yolanda, the service would be appropriate, unsentimental, and to the point. She'd planned Daddy's funeral, her parents', my younger sister's, her sister's, and her brother's. Mom could easily handle a service for a philandering husband whom we thought was 'ex' but had now found out was 'late'.

"It seemed like the least I could do," I mumbled guiltily.

"I'll make sure to be there," she promised. "And maybe we can talk to JT together afterward."

Oh, Lord. She was like a dog after a bone. "Sure, Charlene. We'll do that. See you tomorrow." I hung up the phone, but it rang again almost immediately.

It was JT. My heart almost stopped when I heard his voice. "I got a lead on Sam's car. It was found in a small town outside the Twin Cities five years ago," he said. "Now it's sort of a suburb. It's a place called Lawson's Corners."

"That's good. I guess." I was thinking furiously, trying to tiptoe around the questions I wanted to ask. "Did it take long to track down?"

"No, not too bad. Most of Friday and part of Saturday."

Part of Saturday. What did that mean? "So you came back on Saturday night?" I asked, hoping I sounded casual and not like I was angling for information.

There was a pause. "No, I came back on Sunday. I had some things to do on Saturday. I wasn't able to trace the driver of the car. It was found abandoned in a gas station in that little town. A bus comes through town and the police figured whoever was driving the car got on the bus. I'm still trying to track it down, though."

"That's nice. I mean, it's good that you found it." What kind of things was he doing on Saturday? Damn it, I wanted to know. "So was it busy in the Cities? I mean, did you go shopping?"

He paused. "Are you listening to what I'm saying?"

"Of course I am." I chewed on an already ragged fingernail.

There was another long pause. "Yeah, I had to do some shopping. Listen, I read about Sam's service tomorrow. I thought I'd attend if that's okay with you."

What kind of shopping? Were he and Belinda out and about? Damn it, this bugged me. "Sure, it's a free country. You didn't know Sam, though, did you? He moved to town after you left, I thought."

JT chuckled. "I'm a cop, Molly. Remember? Sam was murdered."

He waited expectantly. My poor brain was definitely fogged. It made no sense. "Well, whatever," I said.

"Are you okay?"

"Of course I am," I snapped. "I'm just a bit stressed, I'm burying my husband tomorrow."

"You're not really burying him, Molly. His body hasn't been released yet and—"

"You know what I mean. And why did you and Belinda meet in Minneapolis?" I stared in horror at Mr. T, who was lying on his back, snoring. Where the hell did those words come from? What space alien had put them in my mouth?

"What?" His voice was definitely cautious.

"Belinda said that you and she spent the weekend together." A minor lie, I decided. It was just a slight stretching of the truth. I was damn well justified. "I saw you and her together at the police station this morning. She said that she'd met you in the Cities."

I waited for his reply, barely able to breathe.

"What did she say?"

Shit. I was in a bind. It wasn't so much what she said. It was how she said it. And I knew what that would sound like. "She said you met for drinks."

"We did. She called my hotel and said she wanted to talk."

"Talk? She called you?" My voice had risen a notch and I struggled to control it. "How did she know where you were staying?"

There was another ominous pause. "I don't know. Why are you so upset?"

"I'm not upset." My voice cracked and I gave up on pretense. "Okay, I am. She said—I mean, she implied—that you and she—" I gulped. "You know. That you and she—"

"Did you believe her?" His voice was low and almost angry. I recognized that tone of voice. I'd heard it a time or two before.

Oh, no. No no no. He was going to make this into a trust thing. Damn him. Before I could reply, he said, "Do you remember what we talked about on Thursday, Molly? Do you remember talking to me in the barn?"

"Of course I do. But Belinda—"

"Did you believe her?"

What could I say? I struggled to find something, *anything*, to fill the awkward void. He did it for me.

"I guess that answers my question. Are you ever going to trust me again, Molly? Are you always going to hold the past against me?"

"Damn it, that's not fair, JT!" Tears were starting to slide down my cheeks. I rubbed my nose with my sleeve, not sure if it was anger or grief that was swamping me. "You've been back in town for one week and you walk into my life, acting like I'm supposed to believe everything you say."

"We loved each other once," he said, his voice harsh. "Doesn't that count for something?"

"That was a long time ago. I've loved other men since then. Why do you think it's all going to be the same as it was?" I wiped at my face again, praying the inevitable hiccups would stay away for at least a few more minutes.

There was a long pause. "I suppose you're right. I suppose it was stupid of me to come here and hope that I might still mean something to you."

"That's not what I said."

"It's what you meant though, isn't it?"

I remembered the latest Tuesday Teaser. *Do you want me to wait forever? I've told you how I feel. Now it's your turn.* "I don't know, JT." I struggled to put my thoughts into some semblance of order. "I just need a chance to get used to this. I never thought I'd see you again and all of a sudden you show up on my doorstep."

There was such a long pause that I thought we'd been disconnected. "I understand, Molly. I'll see you tomorrow."

"JT, don't. You don't understand, it's—"

He'd hung up.

That's when I really did start crying.

I alternately cried and dozed all night. Yolanda called me early in the morning and gave me precise instructions on what to wear, thank God. I followed her directions to the letter, grateful not to have to use my poor over-worked brain.

Disjointed thoughts, jumbled feelings, words never spoken, emotions not articulated—all bounced around in my head, making me dizzy and nauseous. My red-rimmed eyes and pale face helped strengthen the image of grieving widow when I went to the office. Ike and Amelia tiptoed around me as I stared at my computer screen, last night's phone conversation with JT hammering in my mind. At ten o'clock, Yolanda came to get me, tucked me into her VW Bug, and we drove to the funeral home. If she noticed my pallor and blotched complexion, she wisely didn't comment.

The number of people who attended surprised me. I'd forgotten how popular Sam had been. I think perhaps everyone was relieved to find he hadn't been the jerk we'd all thought he was. Several men from his golf group stood up to talk, as did people from the real estate office where he worked. Their anecdotes and stories made me remember why I'd married Sam in the first place—he'd had a boyish, engaging charm that made everything he did seem fun. Sam was the Tom Sawyer who fooled the other boys into doing his work for him. No one could stay mad at him for long, even me. I found myself missing him, adding to the melancholy of my day.

Those thoughts led me once again to wonder who might have killed him. Murder was such a vicious, awful thing. Who could have hated him so much they'd want to poison him—and then stab him, presumably to make sure he was dead? The poisoning indicated that somebody had planned it. And the pitchfork—that made no sense. The consequences of murder were far worse than anything Sam might have done to someone. Why would someone take that risk?

I glimpsed JT in the last row of the room wearing his uniform, looking official. The next time I spied him was after the service finished. We all moved to the next room in the funeral home for coffee and the sheet cake provided by the Tangled Page Used Book and Bakery Shoppe. JT and Mark Devlin were in one corner with their backs to the crowd, talking. Yolanda and I were in the Chairs of Honor, front and center, where folks could come by, shake our hands, and murmur to us. It was a bit awkward, of course, because most people had already given me condolences when they thought Sam was an adulterous bastard and left me high and dry. There was a lot of backpedaling going on in the back room of the funeral home.

I finally managed to break free of my throne and mingle, anxious to get up and move. To my surprise, Shirley left the group of women she was chatting with to intercept me. I watched her warily as she approached.

She was different today. Maybe it was the dark dress and low-heeled pumps, but she was a bit more demure, a bit...classier. Her hair was twisted into a subdued knot on the top of her head without the flirtatious wisps floating around. To my surprise, I realized that she was looking, and acting, her age. My age.

"I don't know what to say, Molly." She shrugged. "I can't say I'm sorry Sam is gone, because I think it's the best thing for you. But I'm sorry he's dead. He was a nice guy. He didn't deserve to be murdered."

I was surprised. It wasn't like Shirley to be so open. "I know," I confessed in a low voice. "It's all very weird."

She sipped her coffee, checking the crowd over its rim. "Are things okay with you and JT?" She sounded truly concerned.

"Why are you asking? The last time we talked, you were warning me away from him."

Her eyes zoomed in on something. I followed her gaze and saw Mark watching us, a small smile on his face. "The last time we talked, I was stupid." Then she turned her attention back to me. "Molly, I'm the last person in the world to be giving out advice about love and relationships, but I'm going to do it anyway. If we're lucky in this world, we find one special person we can love. Sometimes we can't always live easily with them, but it's worth it when you try. Don't blow this with JT. He's always loved you. It used to drive me crazy when we were married." She blew out a long breath. "I could never measure up to you in his mind. I swear it always felt like I was doing battle with a ghost."

She glanced across the room. JT had gone and Mark was working his way through the crowd to us. "Take the chance you're given, Molly. Don't waste it."

Charlene Anderson was beyond Mark, moving toward me at a determined clip. "Oh, damn. I promised Charlene something."

Shirley turned, watching as Charlene nudged aside some people. "I heard she and Chuck are having trouble," she said in a low voice. "Financial problems as well as ..." She shrugged then smiled at Mark. "Ready to go?"

He nodded, then said to me, "I'm glad you did this, Molly. It gives us all a chance to apologize to Sam."

I smiled, for the first time that day feeling cheered. "You're right, Mark. I guess it did. This is closure in a way. Do you know if JT is still around? Charlene and I need to talk to him."

"He was just leaving. You can catch him if you hurry."

I nodded and gestured to Charlene to follow me. I moved as quickly as politeness would allow through the ebbing crowd to the door. I caught a glimpse of JT near the front door, talking to someone, then he started outside. He turned, glancing back and I waved to him. He hesitated and for a minute he smiled, his face relaxed and happy.

Then his eyes cooled and he was a polite stranger, waiting for me to talk to him. I paused and Charlene barreled into me, almost pushing me into JT's chest. "I'm glad I caught you," I said. "Charlene needs to go through Sam's papers. Can I get them back?"

His gaze shifted from me to Charlene, his dark eyes revealing nothing. "I'm not done with them yet."

Poor Charlene looked so scared, I was afraid she'd drop over. "But can't we—" she asked, nervously twisting her hands.

"No." He turned away.

"JT." I put a hand on his arm to stop him.

He stared down at it, then at me. "What?"

I wasn't sure what to say. "I'm sorry," I blurted.

For an instant, the hard lines of his face softened. "So am I," he whispered.

Then he walked away.

Chapter 12

I felt as though someone had punched me. Luckily I was at my husband's funeral, so nobody expected me to act coherent. Charlene murmured something and drifted away. Gradually the rest of the people left, too. Finally it was just Ike, Yolanda, and me. I struggled into my cloth dress cape, bone tired and brain dead.

"Why don't you take a day off?" Ike suggested, holding out his arm to Yolanda to help her down the front steps.

We emerged from the funeral home into the glare of sun on snow. I fumbled my sunglasses out of my purse, glad to have the chance to cover my eyes from the alert prying gaze of my boss, He Who Sees All and my mother, She Who Knows All.

"Oh, no. That wouldn't be right. I'll just come by and do some editing." The thought of going home alone was unbearably depressing. "Besides, I need to get a start on the Scavenger Hunt clues. I haven't even read them." I tried to make my voice light and cheery, but I doubt if I succeeded. It felt like lead weights were attached to my shoulders, pulling me down. God, what a day—I'd listened to my adulterous late husband praised, seen a complete personality reversal in my greatest enemy, and been given the cold shoulder by the love of my life. I was afraid to find out what else could happen.

Yolanda left us at her car, then Ike and I went to the

office. Amelia fussed around me when we got there, explaining once again that she just couldn't 'manage' funeral homes. "They give me the chills," she said apologetically for perhaps the fourth time. "I can't stand it, the thought of all those bodies that have been stacked in there and—"

I held up a hand. "It's okay. How about my cards? We haven't read my cards yet today."

My distraction worked. She pulled out the Tarot cards, I dutifully cut them, and she proceeded to interpret the signs for me. Mercifully, there were no Lovers. There was, however, Puss In Boots *(trust your inner voice)*, Humpty Dumpty *(disaster at hand)*, the Fairy Godmother *(take control of your life)*, good old Sleeping Beauty, a.k.a. Death *(great changes coming)*, Little Miss Muffet *(you owe yourself some R&R)* and the Ugly Duckling *(swallow your pride and ask for help)*. "You need some relaxation, dear," Amelia summed up. "Something to take your mind off your troubles."

I pulled over a copy of yesterday's paper and opened it. "And here's just the thing." A scavenger hunt was held every year for the Festive Fling. It started on the Monday after Thanksgiving and ran until Saturday night, at the Fling Formal, where the King of the Fling would award the prize for most items found. Every day, ten more items were listed in the paper for a grand total of fifty clues. People could scavenge independently or, like those of us in the office, form teams.

I examined Monday's list. As always, it was mix of ludicrously easy and ridiculously hard. I grudgingly admired the committee who, year after year, came up with these things.

> *1. A murder mystery novel with red on the cover and the word 'dire' inside*
> *2. A black whisker from a cat or dog*
> *3. A report card from Tangle Butte Senior High, between 1965 and 1970*
> *4. The growing leaf of an outdoor plant with the Latin name of the plant*
> *5. A used bullet*
> *6. A wishbone*

7. *An out-of-state business card*
8. *A raccoon's footprint*
9. *A dance program from the Festive Fling,*
   pre-WWII
10. *A mulberry*

I ticked through the list. "Bullets?" I asked no one in particular. "Do the police have a target range or something?"

"Deer season," Ike said from his desk. "It doesn't specify what caliber. We got that covered."

He was right. I'd forgotten about hunting season. The land around my house was posted, but hunters could and did hunt along the river in the park about a quarter of a mile behind the house. "I can get the raccoon footprint," I said. "And I think I still have the wishbone."

"I've got the business card," Amelia said, rummaging in her purse. "But no plants are growing now, are they? Isn't everything blown off the trees? Where will we find a leaf?" She extracted the card and put it on the spare desk, which was always designated as our 'Hunt' desk.

"I've got an idea about that," I said. "I need to check my *Dirr's Guide to Trees and Shrubs.*" Dirr's was the Bible of the horticulture industry.

"I may have the old dance program," Ike said. "Did you see this story?" He pointed to something on his monitor.

I wheeled over to him, peering over his shoulder. He'd worn his Sunday suit in honor of Sam's memorial service and it smelled faintly of English Leather. *Widow demands audit of inheritance.* "What about it?" I asked, wheeling back to my desk and selecting a green M&M to give me that feeling of youth. I needed it.

"Are you going to have Sam's estate audited?" Ike asked.

"Why would I?" I chewed the M&M, willing youthful energy to infuse my body. Nothing was happening. I added two yellows to the mix.

"It says in this story that the lawyer who drew up the will was under suspicion for embezzlement from his clients." Ike tapped the monitor, then looked at me.

My hand paused in the act of plucking up two more

yellows. "Mark?" I grabbed two yellows, a red, and a green. I needed a bright mix.

"All I'm saying is, it might not hurt to get the bank involved. They have auditors that come in every year. They could probably point you to an independent audit group. It might be a good idea to check Sam's estate."

I chewed thoughtfully. I was saved from answering by my ringing phone. It was Charlene. I sighed. I should have known she wouldn't let me off so easily. She apologized profusely, but got right to the point. "I know how distraught you are about Sam, Molly, so I took the liberty of calling the police station and talking to JT personally."

I spun my M&M tray, noting that I needed to refill my yellows. I'd hit *the wisdom, cheerfulness*, and *vibrancy* quotient hard in the last week. "That's fine, Charlene. I don't mean to put you off, but I've just had a lot of other things on my plate." To prove it, I took one candy from each color slot and put them on the paper plate that had held my morning bagel.

"Oh, I know. But Chief McCord said he hadn't found any folders in Sam's real estate papers that had our name on them. I just know if I could go through them, I might find what we need. I'm just sure of it. Maybe it's stored in a different folder. Did you give JT everything?"

I rubbed my forehead. "Okay, I'll talk to JT. I'm sure I'll have Sam's things back by this weekend at the latest." I had a sudden thought. "Maybe the information was on Sam's computer."

"His computer?" Charlene's voice sounded a bit loud. "You didn't say he had a computer. Do you still have it?"

"No, I gave it to Yolanda when Sam took off. It was a laptop and she wanted to log on to the Internet." I laughed, remembering the effort it took to get Yolanda to use a mouse. Now she was inseparable from salon.com, shopzilla.com and banterist.com. In fact, I suspected Yolanda was making a tidy profit on Ebay selling the overly-cute collectibles we kids had given her over the years. It seemed like every few months another of her Department 56 Snowbabies was gone from the curio cabinet in her house and Yolanda was wearing new shoes purchased from zappos.com.

"Yolanda has it? Do you think I could get it? Maybe our information is there."

Charlene definitely sounded stressed. I hated to disappoint her. "Sorry, I formatted the hard disk and reinstalled the software."

"Oh."

Her voice was depressed and weary. I tried to soften the blow. "I did make backups, though. I wasn't sure if Sam might come back or not. I didn't back up everything, but I copied a bunch of his files and put them on a CD. It's at home someplace. Tell you what I'll do, I'll dig it out and skim through it. If I find any real estate files on there, I'll copy them for you."

"Thanks so much, Molly. I really appreciate it. If I can help, just let me know."

I wasn't sure what was in those files, so I didn't want anybody else reading them. Although after all this time, it probably didn't matter. "No problem. I'll call you if I find anything."

"Thanks. You don't know what this means to me."

"Oh, hey, Charlene? Maybe you could help me." I glanced at Ike. "Do you know of any auditors? I mean, does Chuck know of an auditing firm?"

There was a long pause. "I'm not sure. I can ask him. Can I ask why, Molly?"

"Oh, I thought—" I hesitated, not anxious to impugn Mark's reputation. "There were some things that Mom came across when she was cleaning out some of Dad's papers. I thought I'd have an auditor look at them." The story was weak, but it was the best I could come up with. "Could you ask Chuck?"

"Sure. Glad to help."

I hung up, feeling marginally better about the day. At least something might go right for someone. Then I looked up at the door as the bell chimed and JT walked in.

Or maybe not. He glanced at me. "Do you have a minute?"

"Sure." I sat back in my chair, but he just stood at the counter, staring at me.

Ike cleared his throat. "You folks can use the back office if you'd like."

JT nodded once. "Thanks, Ike." He came through the

drop gate and went past me into the office he and Ike had used the other day. I got up and followed, glancing back over one shoulder at Amelia, who gave me a consoling wave. I went into the small ten-by-ten office and closed the door behind me.

Two chairs and a desk occupied the space. JT had taken one of the chairs. I sat down next to him. He stared down at the floor, bent over with his elbows on his thighs and his hands clasped between his legs. His uniform was immaculately pressed and clean. I wondered if he sent them out for ironing or if he did it himself, at home.

Then he turned his head and looked at me. All mundane thoughts fled. I'd never seen such sadness in someone's eyes that wasn't caused by a loved one's death. JT was desperate, his black eyes like deep pools of misery. Then he straightened up and the mask settled back into place. "We've got a line on the poison that killed Sam."

"Oh. Good. I guess." I waited, not sure if I was expected to comment further. When he didn't speak, I prompted, "Was it easily traceable?"

He shook his head. I resisted the desire to touch his arm. He looked so tired. "We're still not quite sure what it is, but it appears to be organic. It's not a chemical. Traces of it were still in the intestine, so we think it was ingested. I'd like you to go through his appointment book. If we can figure out who he was meeting that day, we might be able to track his movements. Somebody must have given him something that made him sick."

"But he wasn't sick," I said, confused. "I told you, he was fine."

"Sick later on that day," he corrected. He pulled a small book out of his coat pocket and handed it to me. I opened it, recognizing Sam's distinctive angular scrawl. "I'd like you to check it, tell me if you remember anything. I'm hitting a wall on this case."

He sounded frustrated. "Of course I'll help." He stood up. That's when I did touch his hand. "JT, don't be mad at me, please."

He looked down at me. For a minute, his eyes softened. "I'm not mad. I guess I'm just... I don't know. I guess hearing folks talk about Sam today made me realize some things."

I stood up, too. "Like what?"

"Like you had a good life here and maybe you miss him. Like maybe you don't need anybody in your life." He moved to the door.

"I never said that, JT." The quiet tone in my voice stopped him in his tracks, his hand on the doorknob. "I said I was confused. I said I needed some time." I took a deep breath, remembering the Fairy Godmother card. I decided to take the plunge. "Are you going to the dance on Saturday with anyone?"

He glanced over his shoulder at me. "Do you mean Belinda?"

Damn the man. Trust him to hit the bulls-eye in one. "Anyone?" I repeated.

He shook his head.

"How about going with me? I have to work, but I don't have to take pictures all night." I moved across the small space to stand next to him.

His hand clenched on the knob. Then he released it and turned. "Are you sure?"

I moved closer. We were just inches apart. "I'm sure for Saturday night," I whispered. "And maybe Sunday morning." I saw the hope flare in his eyes. "I said maybe, JT," I cautioned.

He bent to me. "I'll take it." His lips hovered over mine, then he kissed me. "I'll take anything I can get." He smiled, his dimples deep in his cheeks. Those dark, impenetrable eyes warmed. "Thanks for giving me a chance."

"Damn it, JT, you don't give me a choice." I held up the date book. "I'll go through this and report back to you tomorrow."

"Thanks." He paused again. "For everything." Then he opened the door and stepped out, nearly running down Amelia, who was hovering nearby. He smiled at her and she nearly swooned. Then he went out the front door.

"A date," she said, her voice breathless. "Oh, that's so nice."

I rolled my eyes in exasperation. "People my age don't date," I said, going to my desk and my restorative M&Ms. "We go out."

"Whatever." She waved a hand. "We'll have to do a

full reading of the cards to make sure you're prepared."

"I've got a few days," I pointed out. "Let's not panic yet."

Amelia nodded, her pale hair bobbing. "I'll consult my books. We may want to do the Celtic spread in order to get the most detail." She hurried to her desk and the cache of Tarot books stored there. "Or better yet, the Clarification spread. Yes. That would be best."

"Now that your social life is back on track, do you have time to help me with the paper?" Ike asked tartly.

So much for taking the day off. I wheeled over to him and we started editing. I was grateful for the distraction. JT's intensity was overwhelming. I wasn't accustomed to having a man pay so much attention to me. It was unnerving.

When I got home that night, I exchanged my dress slacks and sweater for my reliable old sweatpants and shirt. I visited Barn Cat and got her fed, verifying that the kittens were indeed still there and moving around. Then Mr. T and I dined, him with his half of a can of Tuna Feast, while I munched a bag of microwave popcorn. We settled on the couch in the living room and I pulled out Sam's date book.

It felt odd to read those entries from so long ago. I recognized some of them. My birthday was circled with a notation: *MOL, dinner, Hoyt's.* I remembered that fancy dinner at the restaurant in Mankato. He'd put a big heart next to the time, which I thought was cute.

I leafed ahead to summer, trying to remember the exact dates of the show that year. The date book was full of appointments, usually with just initials noted: CH, CA, SM all occurred with regular frequency along with others such as JK 1345 or DP 984. I puzzled over those for a second, then realized the numbers were probably the street addresses of homes Sam had been showing. He was one of the four full-time realtors in the county, and he'd always been out showing houses—or so he said.

The phone rang and I picked up.

"Hi, this is Susie Hunt."

I propped myself up a bit straighter on the overstuffed arm of the couch. "Susie Hunt? I'm not sure—" Then I remembered. She was the adulterous in-law that

Amelia had been struggling to write about in the paper.

"Listen, there's something I think someone should know. I wasn't sure who to tell."

"Uh, okay. But, do you know me? I mean, isn't there—"

"Joe was working at your house the day your husband died."

This conversation was making no sense at all. "Joe? Do you mean Joe Hunt?"

She laughed mirthlessly. "Yeah, Joe Hunt. My ex-brother-in-law."

Oh, oh. This sounded like a bitter woman to me. "I'm pretty sure you're wrong," I said, hoping to calm her down. "I think it was Jimmy who was at the house."

"Jimmy was with me. Sam wasn't feeling good and told Jimmy to leave early. Jimmy wanted to finish the job and bitched about it when he got home."

I grappled with this explanation. "But the job got done. The septic tank was covered when I got home and the sign-off sheet was there."

"Jimmy didn't do it," she stated. "I just thought you should know. What you do with the information is up to you."

"But if it wasn't Jimmy then who—"

She'd hung up. I replaced the phone. All this time, I figured Jimmy Hunt had come back and covered up the septic system, the way he'd promised. But Susie Hunt was saying it was Joe at the house. Why would Jimmy—or Joe—lie about that? I went upstairs and rifled through my file drawers in the office, searching for the bill from Jimmy Hunt's Construction. I'd just found it when the phone rang again. I picked up the extension, walking to the window with the phone to peer out at the dark woods behind the house.

"Molly, I hate to bother you, but this is Chuck Anderson."

Lordie, would I ever get away from the crazy Anderson family? "Hey, Chuck. I suppose Charlene told you about Sam's computer, right? I'm just putting that CD in my purse right now." A small lie, I figured. I put down the folder with the house bills. Sam's old desk was on the other side of the room. I pulled open the top drawer and prepared to root around.

"I appreciate it. This will save us a lot of money if we can—"

The phone went dead. There wasn't a dial tone or anything. It just stopped working. I checked the charging base, but the red light was still on, which meant it was getting power. I put the receiver back into the base unit. As I did, I glanced outside and saw the motion light come on over the barn. It was a black night out, with no moon, but I could have sworn someone was walking through the edge of darkness cast by the light and shadow.

I moved to the other window, which faced more fully onto the drive. As I did, the light came on over the garage. This time I was sure there was a shadow there—a tall shadow that was not a raccoon.

Fear hit me hard. Somebody was in my yard and my phone didn't work. This was like a bad Alfred Hitchcock movie. I was a mile outside of town and the only protection I had was a fourteen-year-old overweight neutered tomcat.

I stepped away from the window and raced down the stairs to the dark kitchen. My bag was lying where I'd dropped it. I fumbled inside and pulled out my cell phone, normally just used for long distance calls. I opened it with shaking hands.

The kitchen door started to open.

Oh, shit. I panicked. I raced back the way I came, through the dining room toward the back door that led to the seldom-used back stoop on the south side of the house. Mr. T watched me curiously from the couch in the living room. I considered pausing to pick him up, but decided a struggling cat would probably be a liability. I wished him a silent *good luck*, pulled open the door and stepped out into the night.

Cold assaulted me. I was wearing sweatpants, a sweatshirt and my old felt clogs. I sank into snow up to my knees, piled there by the wind. I bit back a curse and edged around the side of the house. That was when I realized I still had the cell phone in my hand. I turned on the phone, punching in the first number on my speed dial.

"Hello?"

Damn. I'd called Mom. "Call the police," I whispered.

"Something's happening."

Yolanda hesitated just a second. "Molly? What's going on?"

I heard a door open and slam shut behind me. I inched around the side of the house. "I don't know, but there's somebody here. Call the police."

"Why didn't you call them?"

"It's a long story, Mom. Just call the damn police." I closed the phone. Pressing against the house, I edged along the west side, which faced the barn in the distance. The motion light had gone out and the drive was just a snowy ribbon in the meager moonlight. I considered making a break for the garage, but decided it would be safer to aim for the windbreak and the relative safety of the trees. If I stuck to the trees that bordered my back yard, I could cross the drive near the barn and head for the woods behind it.

I took a long, deep breath, trying to still my shivering. I began to inch forward, sticking close to the lilacs that bordered the yard, hoping for a bit of cover. One step forward, then another. I hazarded a glance to my right, at the side of the house that faced the garage. The kitchen was brightly lit. Someone had gone inside and turned on the light.

I took another step forward. Something hit me so hard I spun, losing my footing on the snowy ground. I fell backward, toward the dormant herb garden and the azalea bushes that Melvin had tried to uproot in one of his first forays into my yard. I did a crazy two-step dance, struggling to keep from falling into the sharp, spiny bushes. I wasn't aware of pain but I was aware of a blinding, stunning heat that radiated out from my right arm, encompassing my entire chest.

I stared down and saw the blood, glistening black in the pale moonlight.

Chapter 13

My arm was covered with blood. The gray sweatshirt material was soaking it up like a sponge. It was the only part of me that felt warm. Everyplace else was cold. I tried moving my shoulder and almost passed out from the pain.

That's when I realized I was lying in the snow. I'd fallen down. A piece of wood was pressing against my face. I peered around groggily. I'd fallen under the lilac bushes, at the far end of the yard. I must have staggered toward them and landed in the debris under the thick bushes. Dead leaves, stems, and something sharp were gouging me in the neck.

There were noises. Someone was shouting. I saw lights. I wanted to move but I couldn't. I felt a marvelous lassitude, like slow molasses was holding me down. I was cold but it didn't really matter. It wasn't a shaking cold. It was more of a summer-day-that-feels-good cold. I nestled into my snowy cocoon.

"My God, John. What's going on?"

That was Yolanda. I could hear her as loud as if she was standing right next to me. I tried to open my eyes, but it was too much effort. My eyelids did flutter, though.

"That's blood. John, what's happening?"

She sounded panicked. I hoped someone was with her. Yolanda didn't panic easily, but when she did, it was memorable.

"Landie, step back. Let the paramedics work."

JT sounded calm. I decided not to worry about anything if he wasn't worried. I felt something on my face, something warm. "Honey, open your eyes."

Oh, that was JT. I recognized his voice. He sounded very sexy, like if I opened my eyes I'd see some big male surprise. I remembered when he used to call me *Honey* in that tone of voice. It made the cold in my bones start to evaporate. I struggled with my heavy eyelids but they just wouldn't obey.

"Molly, honey. Open your eyes for me." His lips were tickling my ear. I shivered.

It was one of the hardest things I'd ever done in my life but I managed to pry open my eyes. JT was near me, his face just inches away. There was panic in his eyes. *Hello*, I tried to say. But nothing came out, just a gurgling croak.

JT must have seen the confusion on my face. He smoothed back my hair. "It's all right. We're here now. But you have to stay with us. You have to stay conscious."

Someone was crying with loud, gulping sobs.

"'kay," I mumbled.

He smiled. "Good." His eyes flickered to the side. I followed his gaze, far slower. A man in a heavy winter coat was kneeling in the snow next to me. I was on JT's lap. He was sitting in the snow and I was laying half-on, half-off his knees.

"Cold," I croaked.

He nodded. "I know you're cold. It's okay. We got here fast. They'll get you warmed up in no time."

"You're cold." I pushed my head against the arm that held me. "Cold butt," I whispered.

He looked like he wanted to cry. His face went so tender it just about broke my heart. "You'll have to warm it up for me," he whispered, bending down and putting a kiss on my forehead.

"'kay." My eyelids started to close of their own free will. He shook me.

"Stay with us, Molly."

"You bet."

****

I was on something hard. It swayed back and forth,

127

back and forth. Lights were flickering and there was a loud noise, a wailing like a hurt animal.

"Barn cat?" I mumbled.

"We're going to the hospital."

"Who's hurt?" I tried to peer around, but I couldn't move my head.

"You're hurt, Molly."

JT's face moved into sight. He was sitting next to me. He was moving back and forth, too. He was wearing jeans and a sweater that were splattered and stained. His face was pale in the flickering light and I could see his beard. It was dark on his cheeks.

"Cat?" I mumbled.

"Everything's fine."

"Check the cats." I swiveled my eyes because I couldn't move my head. A bunch of tubes and machines were all around me. "Were they hurt?"

"I'll have Bucky check," JT promised.

"Mr. T, too," I whispered.

"We'll check."

"Was it a hunter?"

"Who?" His attention focused in on me so sharply I could almost feel it. He leaned over me, staring down.

"The man outside."

"I'm not sure." He squeezed my hand. "What did he look like?"

"Couldn't see him clearly," I whispered. My throat hurt all of a sudden. I started to shiver, which caused pain to radiate down my shoulder. "It hurts." I twitched, anxious to stop the pain, to stop the shivering.

He put a gentle hand across my middle where I lay. "Don't move. They've got an IV line going in you. You don't want to shake it loose."

I was still shivering. "I'm cold." He leaned over and tugged something up around me. I felt a bit warmer. I put my arm around his arm, tugging him closer. "Don't leave me, John."

"Never."

****

"She's my baby girl. I already lost one daughter when she was just a toddler and I'm not losing another one now, not to some crazy man with a gun. I don't know how you feel about her anymore, John. You used to love her, but maybe you're just toying with her. Maybe you're just playing with her heart. I don't care about that. You're still a cop. Hell, you're the damn Chief of Police. You're supposed to protect people. I'm telling you, John Thomas McCord, if you don't do something to catch the murdering son of a bitch who did this, I'll shoot you myself after I kill the man who shot my baby."

Well, heavens. Yolanda was having a royal fit. I had my eyes closed and I could hear her shouting. It sounded like she was at least a few feet away, but I could hear her clear as a bell.

"I may be an old woman, but even I know that she shouldn't have been left out at the farm all alone. You should have had someone with her. You should have—"

I tuned the voice out. I knew Mom well. She had another minute or two of anger left in her, then she'd collapse and cry a lot. I hoped someone would catch her when she fell apart.

I opened my eyes.

White, white, white, white.

Boring. I closed my eyes. There wasn't anything to see.

"How many fingers?"

My eyes flew open. Three meaty black fingers were waving in front of my face.

"Three." I started to close my eyes.

"Keep your eyes open. Look at me." A black man with a round face and bald head was peering down at me.

"Who are you?"

"Your doctor."

"Nah. We don't have any black doctors in town."

He grinned at me, a sudden flash of white in his dark face. "You're in Mankato."

"Oh." This made sense for some reason. I heard footsteps. JT suddenly was standing by my bed. I squinted at him. "Did Yolanda beat you up?"

He smiled. "She tried. Now she's beating up Mark Devlin. He drove her here, along with Amelia, Ike, and Shirley."

"Sounds like fun. I wish I could have heard that car ride." I was starting to feel very tired. And something hurt. I had an overall pain that moved in waves, up and down my body. It was the sort of pain that left you breathless and clenched, waiting for the next wave to strike you. "I think I got shot."

"Yeah, I think you did." He was leaning over what I now saw was my bed. That explained all the white. "Did you see who it was?"

"No." I turned my head as a rattling noise entered the room. It was another bed, this one on wheels. "Am I going someplace?"

"Surgery."

"What?"

He took my hand. "Just something minor. I'll be there when you wake up."

I was starting to drift off. I wanted to stay awake, but I think they must have given me something. I was falling slowly, inexorably, asleep. "John?"

"Yes, Molly?"

"I love you."

I didn't hear his reply.

****

I woke up several times, but not completely. It was more like turning over, opening my eyes, then going back to sleep. Except it wasn't sleep. I was conscious that time was passing, but I wasn't sure how much.

When I became fully aware, it was nighttime. A black rectangle with small pinpoints of light filled one wall. I assumed that was a window and a city—Mankato?—outside. A light was shining over a chair.

JT was sitting there, reading from a pile of papers and making notes. The light cast half of his face into shadow, emphasizing his high cheekbones and the hard, angular lines of his face. He appeared very tired, the skin stretched tight around his eyes, which looked puffy. His hair was mussed, too, standing up in little licks. He'd changed clothes and didn't wear the stained sweater. He wore black jeans and a black and white bulky turtleneck. It looked warm and comfortable, with a homey appearance that surprised me. JT was usually so very fashion conscious, but the sweater seemed old and hand-made.

"Doing your homework?" I croaked.

His head snapped up so fast I almost heard it. "Hey there." He dropped the papers on the floor and was at my side in a second. "You've been sleeping a while."

"When is it?" I glanced around the room. Several vases of flowers were on a table and a small whiteboard was on the wall at the foot of my bed. I peered at it, confused. "Wednesday?" I asked, reading the word on the whiteboard. "Really?"

"It's Thursday morning." He leaned on the bed, staring down at me. His hands twitched, then he touched my upper arm. "You had surgery on Tuesday night. The doctor said it takes a while to come out of the anesthesia completely."

"Wow. I've never been in a hospital before." I wiggled, trying to sit up. I was wearing something faded and soft. It wasn't my usual sleep T-shirt, but some kind of gown thing. It was loose and fluttery. JT touched some controls and the head of the bed started to rise up. Another bed was across the room, but it was empty. "Where's Mom?"

"She's at the hotel. We've been taking turns being here."

I reached for the glass of water and he got it for me, holding the straw so I could drink. It tasted great. My mouth had a dry, cottony feel to it.

"What happened?"

He set the glass down, then smoothed back my hair. I wondered what I looked like. Probably awful, I decided. I guess it didn't matter. He didn't seem to notice.

"We can talk about it later," he said. "You're still tired."

I shook my head. "What happened?"

He glanced at the papers he'd set aside. "You were shot. The bullet went in your arm, just missed the artery and nicked the bone. You were lucky."

His voice was harsh and unsteady. I took his hand and squeezed it. "How so?"

He inhaled a deep, ragged breath. "If you'd been turned just a bit more it would have hit your heart or your lungs. As it is, you'll probably be released on Friday, Saturday at the latest." He smiled shakily at me.

The last twenty-four hours were evident in his puffy eyes, the lines of strain around his mouth and the unsteady way he stood. "Was it a hunter?"

He shook his head. The cop started to return to his eyes. As much as I appreciated his concern, I was glad to see the professional come back. "It was hunting caliber, but I don't think it was a hunter. We found tracks that did come up behind the barn, from the park, but your land was posted. Hell, your land has always been posted, even when your parents lived there. Everyone knows where your house is. You're at least a quarter mile from the river, maybe more." He ran a hand over his hair and I smiled. That explained all the little spiky bits that stood up. "I didn't think anyone would attack you. I thought that because I had Sam's papers, you'd be okay."

I heard the guilt in his voice. "You couldn't have known."

"I should have known. I've been in law enforcement for twenty years. I should have known. I didn't take the fire seriously enough. I over-reacted."

"Huh?" My brain was still foggy. He didn't make sense.

"I discounted my worry because of how I feel about you. I thought it would look bad if I had someone with you, protecting you." His voice shook with anger—anger at himself. "I thought I was worried because I cared. But I should have paid attention to my gut. I knew you were in trouble, Molly, and I didn't protect you."

It made a sort of sense to me, but I was so tired I wasn't sure. What I was sure of was that he felt responsible. "John, it's not your fault. I just wish I knew why all of a sudden it happened. I've been out there alone all this time. Why did somebody decide now to attack me?"

My words distracted him, but not the way I planned. He leaned over me, one arm propped over my head on the bed and his other hand stroking my face. "You called me John," he whispered. "You never used to call me John unless we were in bed together."

What a time to remember that. He was right, though. I patted the mattress. "Well, come on. I've got a bed right here."

He smiled, his eyes soft and tender as he bent over me. "I'll take you up on that offer, but someplace a little less public, okay?" He kissed me, slowly and carefully.

I felt warm and toasty when he finally straightened up. I wanted to put my arms around his neck and pull him into bed with me, but I was just too tired. I think he saw that in my eyes because he tugged my blanket up. "Sleep some more, okay? I'll come back and see you tomorrow." He touched my face, his eyes suddenly bright. "I was afraid I'd lost you, Molly. I was so scared."

I did try to hold up my arms then, but the pain stopped me—the pain and a stiff bandage on my shoulder. He enfolded me in a gentle hug. I could feel the solid thud of his heart against my ear and felt him snuffle into my hair, his breath warm. "I won't let you off the hook that easy," I whispered. "We're going to the dance on Saturday. You're my date."

He croaked out a laugh. "Yeah, I almost forgot."

"Oh, now that hurts." I pushed him away. "You forgot we had a date?"

He settled me on the bed. "I've been a bit distracted." He kissed me again, a lingering caress, then moved back. "I'll stay here until you fall asleep. We'll make sure you're never alone. The nurses are keeping an eye out for you."

I nodded. I felt deliciously warm and safe. The dull throbbing pain in my shoulder was bearable, I decided. It was okay as long as he was there. "John?"

"Hmm?"

I snuggled into the covers, peeking over their edge at him. "I meant it, I think."

"What?" Then his eyes showed me he understood. He smiled, dimples creasing his cheeks. "Really?"

I nodded and fell asleep.

Chapter 14

I was released from the hospital on Friday afternoon. The stay in the hospital was a good experience. It convinced me I didn't like hospitals, I wasn't a good patient, and I didn't like being bed-ridden. When I finally bade the place good-bye, it was with a sense of giddy relief.

Mark came to pick me up with Mom in tow. I was surprised, but Mom said that Mark had insisted. I was a bit disappointed that JT didn't do it, but I knew he had to work and probably didn't have the time. I wondered if I'd see him soon.

To my surprise, there was a welcoming committee at the farmhouse. Ike and Amelia were waiting for me, along with two young men from the high school. "Guards," Ike said as they all gathered around me in the kitchen. "JT set it up. We've had somebody out here since you went in the hospital and there'll be three boys sleeping downstairs here at night until they catch whoever did this. Dan Bailey is coming over after the basketball game. And your mom, Amelia, and Mr. Sex's Ladies are going to take turns staying with you, too. Don't you worry. We've got you covered."

Well, that certainly put the kibosh on any romantic plans I might have fostered. But then again, I wasn't up to any romance, not yet, at least. My arm and shoulder hurt like hell and I was still taking pain pills three times a day that alternately knocked me out or left me woozy.

My fridge was stuffed full of donated food and we dined well that night. Afterwards, the grownups sat in the living room while my guards sat in the kitchen and played Texas Hold 'em with Dad's old cardboard poker chips. Mr. T and I took one of the couches. My portly tuxedo monster appeared none the worse for the excitement or my absence, but he was more affectionate than usual. I assumed that would wear off with time. I nibbled on M&Ms, glad to be home but anxious to have my life back to normal.

"Won't happen too soon," Ike said when I mentioned this. "JT is busting his—" He cleared his throat. "JT is working hard to find out what's going on, but it's tough."

Everyone looked at me. "I told you. I didn't see who it was. And I've got no idea why someone would attack me. Unless it's one of the Langfords."

"What? What do those old biddies have to do with this?" Yolanda asked.

"Mark said they were thinking of suing me for Delbert's wrongful death."

I don't remember the last time I saw my mother so angry. "Why those ..." She took a long, deep breath. "I think it's time I had a little talk with Sharon Langford."

Ike shifted in his chair. "Landie, now, calm down. You don't—"

Yolanda got that narrow-eyed, calculating expression that I recognized from childhood. This was her *I saw what you did and I know who you are* look. "I know a few things about the Langford sisters that I may have to make known if they don't finally back off."

I stared at her in astonishment. "Blackmail? You've got blackmail dirt on the Langfords?"

She gave me a haughty glance. "Suffice it to say, I know where Janice Langford went one summer after she and Tommy Slocum dated all year in high school so hot and heavy. And I know someone who mentioned how chummy Claudia had been with her old college roommate—a female college roommate. They were apparently very, very chummy."

Amelia and I both gaped at her. Ike looked uncomfortable. "You knew about this?" I asked him when

I could find my voice again.

He shrugged. "News gets around." He smiled sheepishly.

"I'll handle this," Yolanda said with a finality that told me I didn't need to argue.

"You must know where all the bodies are buried." I winced. "Bad choice of words. But I doubt even the Langfords would take a shot at me. And why would anyone else? I don't know anything about Sam's—" I suddenly remembered that odd phone call from Susie Hunt. In all the excitement, I'd forgotten it.

"What?" Yolanda demanded, seeing the perplexed expression on my face.

"I just remembered something."

"Hold on to that thought," Ike interrupted. "JT said he was coming out right about now. No use telling us twice."

I picked up the TBTrib, sitting on the coffee table. "Okay. It's probably nothing anyway." I opened the paper and noticed the last Scavenger Hunt list. "Damn, I've missed the hunt. What do we need from our list? Maybe I can still help."

Amelia rummaged in her Sears imitation Coach bag, finally pulling out a notepad. "We're doing okay, but I still need that plant leaf and the raccoon print from Monday. We got most of the rest except for the hand auger, the folding yardstick, the potted grass, the 1937 Christmas card and the silver cuff link. Oh, and the *Ladies Home Journal* from the 1950s and a copy of *Reader's Digest* with a Billy Graham article. Dan came through with the autographed hockey puck, the fencing sword, and the 1960s science textbook."

"Fencing sword? Where did Danny find a sword?"

"They had some at the school, for PhysEd class and for school plays," Ike said with a smug smile. "They aren't sharp swords, of course, but according to the rules they're good enough. I'll tell you, it's a good thing we've got an in with the teenagers. I was told some scavenger teams had to merge because there were only twenty swords to be had in town, and that includes some Civil War relics found in attics."

"I've probably got the tools out in the shed," I said. "A

bunch of Dad's old tools are still out there." I made as though to sit up.

"Don't you move," Yolanda said. "We've got boys sitting in the kitchen who can be your legs. I'll have 'em go out and check. They should check that cat, too. JT's been keeping an eye on her and it's about time for her dinner." She left the room and I heard her talking to my guards. We soon heard scraping chairs and doors opening.

"JT's been watching the cat?" I settled back into my afghan, happy not to stir.

"He's come out every day, twice a day," Amelia said, pulling out her ever-present deck of Tarot cards. "He said he can pick up the kittens now. He said he wants dibs on the black one." She smiled when she said this, as though begging me to ask why.

I obliged. "Why the black one?"

"He said she reminded him of you." She shuffled the cards on top of the end table next to her. "All pretty and tiny with that soft black hair."

Ike waggled his eyebrows at me. "That sounds serious to me."

I burrowed deeper into afghan and cat warmth. "Don't count your romances before they're hatched." I gestured to the bookcase that lined the stairway. "Get my Dirr's for me, would you, from that bottom shelf? It's the big green book on the end there. I can check that plant I'm thinking about." Headlights shone in the drive. "The cat man is here."

Ike handed me the thousand-page plant Bible as Yolanda and JT walked into the living room. He must have shed his coat in the mudroom because he was wearing black jeans and a black plaid flannel shirt. My heart sort of stuttered. The jeans were the tiniest bit tight and the shirt fit very well. He looked yummy.

He smiled when he saw me, propped up on the couch with fourteen pounds of cat on my legs and a couple of pounds of book on my lap. "You're looking good, Molly."

I wasn't and I knew it. My hair was a flyaway mess, I wasn't wearing makeup and I was dressed in old jeans and a sweatshirt. But I appreciated the compliment. "Back at you, JT," I said. "Do you need any supper? Half the town brought over a casserole."

"Maybe later." He peered over my shoulder at the open book in my lap, his hand gently touching my neck as he did so. I shivered at the contact. "What's that?"

"Scavenger hunt clue," I said, flipping to the 'R' section of the book. "Here it is. I wasn't sure how to spell it. *Rhododendron canadense*. I've got one in the back yard, right near the herb garden." I dog-eared the page to mark it.

"So?" Ike asked, watching JT as he picked up Mr. T and sat on the couch near my feet. Mr. T took over JT's lap, rumbling out a purr that was loud enough to be heard in town.

"Rhododendrons are evergreens," I said.

"And?" JT prompted, giving Mr. T a back massage that appeared to be downright fun. I wondered if I could get one of those sometime.

I shook the thought aside. "We need the leaf from a plant growing outside. There are no deciduous plants still growing outside." I saw their blank expressions. "Deciduous equals 'plants that lose their leaves'. Rhodos are evergreen but they don't have needles, like pine trees, they have leaves. Evergreen means they don't lose their leaves. They're an odd species that way. So tomorrow morning I'll go out and take a leaf from my *Rhododendron canadense* and, voila, we'll have a growing leaf." I tapped the Dirr, sitting on my lap. "I wanted to verify the Latin spelling." Something else about rhododendrons was whirring around in my brain like a buzzing insect that wouldn't sit still. There was some little fact I couldn't quite remember, something from a horticulture class about rhodos.

"I'm not surprised the president of the Garden Club would know all that." JT stroked Mr. T, who showed his appreciation by going boneless and limp.

I snorted. "I barely got the presidency. I just about had to arm wrestle Shirley for it. Although why Charlene didn't want it, I don't know. She's our real flower expert. She's got a botany degree. I think we can count on her team having a rhodo leaf, too."

"I don't think she's playing," Ike said. "Or if she is, I'm not sure what team she's on. She dropped in the office the other day to see you and seemed surprised to see our

Scavenger Hunt results on the spare desk."

"I guess the Hunt isn't a big deal for some folks like it is for others." I set the Dirr on the floor as a reminder to me to do more research into it later. I nudged JT with my foot. "Any luck on finding out what happened the other night?"

"Not much. I found tire prints out in the park and footprints in the snow, behind the barn. It looks like he followed Melvin's path."

"That damn pig," I muttered. "That reminds me, I told Mrs. Dalworthy I'd check her door and see if I can figure out how Melvin gets out."

JT slid his hand over my foot, stilling it. "I already checked when we backtracked the footprints. Melvin was able to nudge the latch with his nose and the door is lightweight so he could push it open. I fixed that."

"Thanks, JT." I was pleased to think I'd have no more pig incursions.

"We've taken impressions of the prints and checked for fingerprints in the kitchen and out on the stoop."

"How long was I out there?" I asked. "I'm hazy on the details. Did he have time to run back to his car before you guys got here?"

JT squeezed my prodding foot. I twitched, expecting to feel tickled, but instead he started a gentle massage. My socked foot easily fit in one hand, and he ran his thumb over the instep. I almost melted from the delicious sensation.

"You'd passed out. He probably heard the sirens coming down the road and took off." JT's hand tightened on my foot, then he began the massage again. "Good thing you had your cell phone with you."

I'd thought about that in the hospital. If I hadn't managed to call Mom, would I even be alive now? I met his eyes and saw that knowledge there. "Yeah," I said, my voice shaky. "Good thing I did."

His hand tightened again on my foot, remembered pain darkening his eyes. "Tell me again exactly what happened. You said you were upstairs and the phone rang."

"That's what I just remembered," I said. "I went upstairs because Susie Hunt called."

"Susie Hunt? Jimmy's slutty ex-wife? Joe Hunt's ex-lover and adulterous ex-sister-in-law?" Yolanda asked.

"Ex-lover?" Amelia squeaked.

"Didn't you know? That's why she and Jimmy got divorced. Susie slept with Joe and Joe bragged about it to Jimmy." Yolanda stated this as a matter of proven fact, like 'the earth is round' or 'Pastor Svenson gives the most boring sermons.'

Pieces of a puzzle fell into place. "So that's why she's got it in for Joe." I described the phone call I'd gotten on Tuesday. "I went upstairs to check the construction bill. I thought maybe I was wrong. But it was Jimmy's signature on the sign-off sheet. Or what I thought was Jimmy's signature. While I was up there, the phone rang again."

"Do you have caller ID on that phone?" JT asked.

"Nope, it's just a cheap-o plug-in I got at the hardware store. Anyway, I knew who it was." I made a face. "It was Chuck Anderson. He still needs those damn real estate papers. I told Charlene I'd find the CD and Chuck—"

"CD?" JT's hand paused.

I wiggled my toes. He obediently resumed my foot massage. "I made a backup of Sam's files before I gave Mom his laptop. I was searching for it when the phone went dead." I glanced at the phone on the end table.

"Somebody cut the wires. We got that fixed," JT said, his mind obviously miles away. "You said you were talking to Chuck Anderson?"

I tried to reconstruct the moment in my mind. "Yeah. I was talking to Chuck and the phone died. I looked outside. That's when the motion light came on."

"Why now?" Amelia asked. "What's changed? Why would someone attack you now? You've been out here alone all this time—why now?"

"What happened on Tuesday?" JT asked.

I prodded him with my other foot and he began the massage anew. "Tuesday." I hunkered down in my blanket, struggling to think. "It seems so long ago."

"Sam's memorial service," Ike said, his voice soft. "Remember?"

Oh, man. Guilt flooded me. I'd forgotten all about

Sam. "Yeah," I said.

"Who'd you talk to that day?" JT asked.

"Everybody," I said in exasperation. "Half the town was there. I talked to you, Mark, Charlene, Shirley—everybody."

"What did you decide to do about that audit?" Ike asked.

"Audit?" Yolanda and JT asked simultaneously.

"Ike saw this article in the paper about some lawyer who embezzled money from a widow. And since Mark told me I'm a widow now and not a divorcee, Ike thought maybe I should have an audit. I suppose I should, since the Langfords are thinking about suing me for wrongful death. I may as well get all my ducks in a row. That reminds me, I wonder if Charlene asked Chuck about any independent audit firms. I'll have to check on that. And I'll probably have to deal with the Hunt land, too. That might get messy. I wonder if Charlene's family will re-contest it? Sam won that court battle, but the Hunt boys were really pissed off." I poked JT's immobile hand. "I was wondering if Charlene wanting to read Sam's stuff had anything to do with that land deal Sam made with her daddy."

"When were you planning to tell me all this?" JT asked, his voice mild. I recognized that tone of voice. That was his 'I'm on a slow burn and I might get pissed off depending on what you say in the next ten seconds' tone of voice.

I thought I had told him all of that. But now that I considered it, maybe I hadn't. I took a few M&Ms as a stalling tactic then went on the offensive. "Why should I? I mean, it's not pertinent to anything, is it?"

"Damn it, Molly. I'm trying to keep you safe and now you tell me that at least two other people may have a reason to want to hurt you."

"Two? Who?" I thought about it. "Mark? Oh, for heaven's sake, I've known Mark all my life. He didn't embezzle anything. Sam didn't have anything to embezzle. Well, he had that land but that was all, really. I think. Who else?" Then I thought about what JT had said. "What do you mean, you're trying to keep me safe? Don't get me wrong, JT, I appreciate it, but it's not your job to keep me safe, is it? Your job is to find out what happened to Sam. If we can figure out who—"

"You're damn right my job is to keep you safe," he said, dropping my foot like a hot potato. "You and every other citizen in this town."

"Me and every other citizen?" Didn't he sound righteous? For some reason, his cavalier assumption that I needed protecting pissed me off, probably because there was a grain of truth to it. I was tempted to give him a real piece of my mind, but I refrained because others were in the room. "As I recall, we had this discussion before. Things were going along just fine until we found Sam and you came back to town. I'll grant you, this may not have been the most exciting life a girl could lead but—"

"Oh, my."

Both JT and I glared at Amelia, who had cut her deck of cards and was staring in bemusement at the one face up in her hand.

"What is it?" I asked. "No, don't tell me. It's the Death card again, right?" I glanced at JT. "I always draw the Death card."

"No, it's the Knight of Rods. Such an auspicious card." Amelia smiled at us, looking like a wizened little Christmas elf in her dark green sweater with red holly berry trim. "It means that you should take a chance and be spontaneous. *Your dreams are one step away from reality if you'll just take a chance and grab them.*" She gazed from me to JT. "Truly. That's what it means. You need to be spontaneous."

I heard the mudroom door open and voices in the kitchen. I decided to use that as my chance to beat a retreat and regroup my scattered brain cells. "I'll see if the guys found those tools." I pushed aside the afghan and got up, almost tripping over Mr. T, who had hopped off JT's lap. I fled to the kitchen where Dan Bailey was just coming in, followed by his two high school friends.

"Hey, we won the basketball game," he said. "I figured I'd write up the story tonight while we're on guard duty."

The other boys, who had been introduced as Jim and Jason, showed me the ancient hand tools they'd found in the shed. "I think that's what we need," I said. "I thought

I had that stuff out there. Maybe you can show Ike, he'd probably recognize them. He's from the 'pre-power tools' era of home improvement."

"I heard that," Ike called out. "Bring those tools in here."

JT came into the kitchen. Dan nudged Jason toward the door. "Come on," he said. "Let's give them some privacy."

The two other boys shot Dan an incredulous look. "They're like, old," one said as they left the room.

Dan laughed. "Not that old."

I rolled my eyes. There was nothing like being the talk of the town. I pulled open the fridge door, but JT was behind me. He closed it, then bodily picked me up. Before I could protest I was sitting on the counter and he had me trapped, leaning on the chipped ceramic tiles with his hands on either side of my thighs.

"What part of that conversation pissed you off?" he asked, staring at me.

I tried to avoid his eyes but no matter how I tried, his dark gaze pinned me. "I don't know," I said in a small voice. "I told you, I'm just not used to having anybody watching out for me, I guess."

"It's more than that, Molly. What is it?" When I didn't answer he said, "Molly, I'm a cop. It's what I do. I'm responsible for the people in this town and you're one of them."

I shot him a quick glare. He smiled and moved closer, nudging my legs apart. He put his arms around me. "You're a very special person in this town. Very special."

I slipped my arms around his waist. He pulled me against him, bending down to kiss my ear. I shivered, then sank into his embrace. It felt so good to have him hold me like this. I felt like I was in a warm, solid cocoon. "I'm just worried, I guess," I admitted.

"About what?"

I didn't know how to explain it. I didn't know how to tell him that I was worried that if we got naked, he'd take one look at me and see all those signs of aging I'd been trying so hard to keep at bay—the not-so-soft skin, the pudgy legs, the sagging butt. I wanted to be the woman I'd been when he and I were together years ago, but I couldn't turn back time. I couldn't reverse decades of M&Ms, lack of exercise, and the inevitable wrinkles. I didn't want to see the disappointment in his eyes.

I also didn't know how to tell him I was out of practice with sex, lust and love. I think one of the reasons I married Sam was that he was so easy. He didn't require deep emotions, seductive behavior or a woman who'd try to entice him. Sam was so easy to please I could continue my life almost as though he wasn't there.

But JT was different. JT wanted commitment, love, and passion. I wasn't sure I had that in me any more.

"Molly?"

"Hmm?"

He muzzled against my neck. "I'm older, too, honey."

Damn the man. He always could read my mind.

"Molly?"

"Hmm?"

"Your dreams are a step away from reality if you'll take a chance and grab for them."

I burst out laughing. Then he kissed me and I lost all my breath. I had a hard time being a full participant because my arm was still bandaged tightly, but JT took care of that. He put a hand behind my head and another behind my back, then pulled me against him. His tongue and his hands left no doubt in my mind as to what was in store for me soon. I used my legs to pull him closer, anxious to feel his hardness press right into me. Delicious warmth started to infuse me. I realized that I may have been out of practice—but there are some things a girl never forgets, and one is the feeling of a good man ready to please her.

And I'd never forget the way JT McCord could make me feel.

"Man, you're right. I guess they aren't too old."

JT and I pulled apart. He and I both peered over his shoulder at the audience in the doorway.

Amelia shuffled her cards in her hands, smiling. "Was I right?"

Chapter 15

Your dreams are one step away from reality if you'll take a chance and grab for them.

The words echoed in my head that night as I went upstairs to bed. I slowly undressed, my mind churning. I heard voices downstairs and the sound of Yolanda moving in the guest bedroom next door. I was so used to being alone that I kept jumping when I heard the smallest noise: a quiet laugh from the kitchen, the toilet flushing in the guest bathroom, then a door closing. Mr. T and I hunkered down in our blanket and as soon as I did, the memory of JT's incendiary kiss and my equally passionate response swamped me. My body still tingled from it but my brain was trying to put on the brakes.

I didn't want to be hurt again.

That's what it boiled down to.

I'd given my heart to two men in my life—John McCord and Sam Ferris. I'll grant you, Sam wasn't the great passion of my life but I trusted him with my love and my respect.

Both men cheated on me and humiliated me in front of my family and friends.

Could I take that chance again?

Luckily, the pain pills kept me from tossing and turning all night. I slept later than usual, waking at nine to the sound of women's voices downstairs. Mr. T had deserted me, knowing there were better food opportunities elsewhere. I used the bathroom, then went to the kitchen where Peggy Calder and Paula Belkin were sitting.

"Hey there." Peggy held up a coffee mug. "Can I get you some?"

I sat at the kitchen table, which held two coffee cakes and a plate of donuts with the distinctive Brew 'n' Chew lopsided center. Three of them were adorned with melted M&Ms. "Yummy." I grabbed one from the plate, the gooey sugared kind. "Did you bring these?"

Peggy nodded. "Carl made them special for you. He said to say hello." Carl was the baker at the Brew and a high school buddy of mine. "How are you feeling today?"

A hopeful black and white face was peering up at me from under the table. I gave Mr. T a hunk of donut and tucked myself onto the worn wooden chair. "Pretty good, really. My arm itches, but I guess that means it's healing." I took the mug of coffee Paula handed me. "Are you girls my escorts today?"

"At least until noon," Peggy said. "Then we turn you over to Ike at the lunch. That is, assuming you're up to attending."

"I wouldn't dare miss it." The Festive Fling Celebrity Cookout was held on the Saturday of Fling weekend. City officials set up an outdoor grill at the city hall and took turns making brats and burgers. I couldn't wait to see JT flipping hot dogs.

After the cookout was the Festive parade, complete with floats, balloons, children in Christmas lightbulb costumes, dancing reindeer and Santa on a fire truck. Macy's Thanksgiving Day parade had nothing on the Tangle Butte Festive Stroll. Rain, snow, sleet, or shine, the cookout and parade went on.

The highlight of Fling weekend was the Festive Fling Fairyland tonight, when the high school gym would be transformed into a winter wonderland and everyone wore his or her best duds. Then tomorrow we'd have the Kiwanis pancake brunch followed by the lighting of the Christmas tree in front of the city hall and an afternoon of Christmas carols and open houses to wrap up the weekend. In Minnesota, winter starts at Halloween and ends at Easter. You need these little celebrations to keep your spirits up.

"You're lucky you had your cell phone," Peggy said, jerking my mind back to the grim realities of the day.

I patted my bathrobe pocket. "It goes with me everywhere now."

"It's a good thing you found it so quickly."

I paused with my coffee mug halfway to my mouth. "Found it?"

"Yolanda said your purse was scattered all over the kitchen table, like you were searching for your phone." Peggy tapped the table for emphasis.

"Nope. It goes in a little pocket inside my purse."

"Maybe the shooter did it." Peggy, Paula and I exchanged a look. "You'd better tell JT."

I pulled over a paper napkin and the pen from my pocket to jot a note. "You carry a pen with you?" Peggy asked.

"I'm a writer. I'm always making notes." I scrawled *JT: purse* then stuffed the napkin in my pocket with the pen.

"Lucky, too, Yolanda called JT right away," Paula said. She was stylishly dressed in dark slacks and a Christmas sweater with prancing reindeer. Her immaculately coiffed white hairstyle didn't have a strand out of place.

"She did? I thought she just called 911." I gave T the last of the donut and considered another one. Then I remembered my thickening waistline and potential upcoming romantic rendezvous and reconsidered.

"Nope. She called JT on his cell phone. He was out here in five minutes flat, or so she said." Paula sipped her coffee and regarded me with sharp hazel eyes. "Good thing he gave Yolanda his number."

"I'd guess he wants to keep tabs on you," Peggy said, giving T another bite of donut. At this rate, he'd be waddling around the house for a month.

Although Paula and Peggy were at opposite ends of the fashion spectrum, I recognized tag-team play when I saw it. "Why didn't he give me his number, then?" I asked.

"Maybe he's waiting for you to ask," Paula said with a tart tone to her honeyed voice.

"Yeah, well ..." I caught Peggy's disapproving expression. "What?"

"Don't know what you're waiting for," she said. "He's been sending you public love letters for almost two months now. What more do you want?"

I shifted my gaze to Paula. She was regarding me with a calm impassivity that offered no escape. "I'm not sure," I mumbled.

"If you're worried about being hurt again, don't be," Paula said with surety.

"No guarantees," I said, giving in to the donut craving. I'd been living on hospital food for a couple of days. Surely I was entitled to a splurge.

"There are no guarantees on anything," Peggy said. "Look at me. My jerk first husband left me with a child to raise. After Jonny graduated from high school, I figured I could relax and take it easy. Then Bill comes along and sweeps me off my feet." She laughed. "Now I'm fifty years old and having the time of my life with a sixty-year-old man. Better late than never, I say."

"But what about—" I stopped, mortified. I couldn't ask her a personal question like that.

"Sex?" She correctly read my mind and shrugged one plump shoulder. "It's great. Maybe not as great as when I was a teenager, but as you get older, you realize that it's as much intention as action, if you get my point. I've got to tell you, an older man is a sweet treat."

Paula was watching me with unnerving understanding in her eyes. "Everyone worries about that, even if you've been married for years," she said. "Let's face it. If you're married for twenty or thirty years, you'll see some changes, especially if a woman has babies. Seems to me it's all about trust—you trust the person you marry to not laugh at your body and to appreciate you even if you're not your best."

Peggy nodded. "I had the same worries. Nobody's perfect unless you're Shirley, and she has some help from her beautician and a cosmetic surgeon up in Minneapolis."

"Not," I said in disbelief.

Peggy nodded. "I heard her talking down at the Brew. She had that botox stuff done and was talking about having a boob job. But then someone heard Mark say that more than a handful was wasted, so she was putting the boobs on hold."

We all laughed. "The power of love." I stretched, then winced. My shoulder and arm hurt like crazy, but at least today I felt bruised, not broken, which was a vast improvement over how I'd felt the first couple of days.

"I still can't believe someone shot at you," Paula said, shaking her head. "What could you know—what could you have—that anyone would want to kill for?"

"I have no idea. JT and I talked about it for hours last night, going over the same things over and over. It's got to have something to do with Sam, but what?" I ran a hand through my hair and made a face. "I need to shower."

"Do you want some real breakfast?" Peggy asked, watching as I staggered to my feet.

"No, I think I'll save myself for some of JT's cooking." Then I blushed when I realized what I'd said.

"The power of love indeed," Paula said with a laugh. She waved me out of the room. "Go and get prettied up for the day."

I took a long and leisurely shower, then made my fashion choice with what passed for care with me, settling on dark jeans and my slightly-too-tight-across-the-tits pale blue polka dot turtleneck. I came downstairs into the living room and spotted my Dirr's Guide on the floor. I turned to the Rhododendron page. What was it about rhodos that bugged me? I read the description again but nothing clicked. I'd gotten a degree from a tech college in horticulture while I was in Iowa and I ran over the coursework in my mind. We'd covered a lot of topics from irrigation to construction to pest management. Pest management? Was that it?

"Ready to go?" Paula asked from the doorway.

I glanced at the old Seth Thomas clock on the mantel, surprised to see it was almost eleven. "Sure. I'm hungry."

She waggled her eyebrows. "And your man has just what you crave."

"Oh, give me a break." I dropped the Dirr back on the couch.

"He's cooking today, right?" She put an arm around

my shoulders. "Then he's got just what you need."

"I swear, this town is set on getting me hooked up with the police chief."

"Are you bragging or complaining?" She laughed at the sour glance I shot her. "Come on. Let's go see if JT has figured out who's messing with his woman."

We drove to City Hall in Paula's sedate dark green Taurus. She went inside to help the Ladies' Auxiliary with the food while Peggy and I joined the crowds going to the cookout. Four huge grills were smoking under the open-sided red-and-white striped tents at the far side of the parking lot. A sawhorse barrier demarked the grill area from the line-up area. The Santa Claus All-Star Kazoo and Tambourine Band was performing Christmas carols, providing a festive atmosphere for the crowds lining up to get their food hot off the grill.

We met Ike at the garland-festooned sawhorse that marked the entrance. After paying our five dollars to the elf guarding the gate, we took our places in the line, which moved quickly. The temp was a balmy twenty degrees with little breeze, so at least wind chill wasn't a factor. I glimpsed JT, our fire chief, mayor, city treasurer, public works director, and other assorted city officials flipping burgers, doling out hot dogs and talking with the public.

As we stood in line and chatted, I examined the crowd. Most of the town attended at least part of the festivities. I had grown up here and I knew probably eighty percent of the people here. Who would want to kill me? What kind of a secret was so big a person would want to kill somebody for it? Why had someone killed Sam? This made no sense at all in our quiet little town. Tangle Butte wasn't a hotbed of passion, greed, or power. It was a sleepy little backwater of a tributary of the Minnesota River, which in turn was a tributary of the Mississippi. We were off the beaten path and content to be so.

JT laughed at something Cholly Puckett, the city treasurer, said. I know I was prejudiced, but I thought JT was the handsomest man I'd ever seen. He wore a Santa hat pushed back on his head, a red plaid flannel shirt and dark pants with a big white apron wrapped around him that only emphasized his long, masculine body. He carefully extracted a hot dog from the grill and placed it on a little boy's plate, smiling at whatever the boy was saying, then nodding politely to the boy's mother. He was so at home there, fitting right in with everyone else.

The line shuffled forward and the crowd shifted. I lost track of JT for a minute and when I could see him again, Belinda was standing in front of him, sort of leaning over the sawhorse that separated them. She wore form-revealing powder blue ski pants, a navy sweater that looked as soft as a cloud and had a poncho-thing draped strategically to show off her bosoms to their best advantage.

"Well, my, my," Peggy murmured next to me. "No one's seen much of Belinda lately. Rumor had it she went back to Minneapolis for a little fun when JT turned her down."

"Say what?" I tore my gaze from Belinda to Peggy.

"Oh, yeah. Didn't you hear? Let's see, it must have been Wednesday morning. Yes, it was. You were in the hospital. Apparently our girl Belinda just happened to drop in to the police station to chat with the Chief. From what I hear, she invited him to the Fairyland Fling. He explained that he already had plans and would not be available then or at any time in the near future. At which point she made some very uncharitable comments about you, Molly."

"What?" My voice came out as a high-pitched squeak. Several people around us turned, probably to see if there was a mouse in the area.

Ike nodded, his hands deep in his pockets as he bounced up and down on his heels. "Oh, yeah. I heard about that, too. Belinda surely showed her stripes that time."

"Why that little—" I narrowed my eyes and shot a poisonous glare at Belinda's powder-blue butt. "What did she say?"

"Oh, you know, just how she couldn't understand why a man like JT would care for someone—let's see, how did she say it—" Ike screwed up his face in thought. "Yeah, it was something like 'with the style sense of a farm wife and the body of a fireplug.'" Ike glanced at Peggy, who nodded in confirmation. "Yeah. Something along those lines."

I eyed Belinda, who was leaning forward, saying something to JT. He nodded, his eyes intent and interested. Then he shook his head and turned back to the grill. She appeared to be waiting for him to say something more. When he didn't, she moved on, giving him a nasty glance over one shoulder.

"What did he say to all that?" I asked.

"I'll give him credit," Peggy said, admiration evident in her voice. "He said as how he was disappointed in her. He said, 'I know your mother would be unhappy to hear you talk like that, Belinda. I knew Isabel well and I think she tried to teach you better before she died.' Well, that shut up little Miss B, I can tell you."

"How did you hear all this?" I asked as our line shuffled forward. I noticed Claude Murphy and his wife, Bernice, ahead of us. She was leaning back slightly in order to catch the good gossip. The news would be all through the Catholic segment of the county in an hour and would be moving like a slow tide through town all afternoon.

"Carly Swenberg is a waitress with me at the Brew and her brother's a deputy down at the station. She said that the guys were all a bit nervous about JT coming in and taking over, but after seeing the way he's been handling things, they're feeling a bit more relaxed. I mean, really." Peggy shook her head in disgust. "To think Belinda would sneak around while you were in the hospital. No, the Chief handled it just right, I think."

Mrs. Murphy nodded in silent agreement ahead of us.

"Well, I'm surprised he has time for this," her husband said, his voice righteously loud. "After finding a dead body and having a shooting in our town, you'd think the police would have better things to do with their time than grill hot dogs."

Mrs. Murphy's cheeks flamed a bright red. Her husband was a well-known writer of letters to the editor, decrying the waste of taxpayer money on our inadequate snow plowing, appalling street repair and now apparently our shoddy police force.

He glanced over his shoulder at me. "Well, Molly, how are you? I heard what happened." He turned his gaze on JT, who was chatting with Mrs. Alcorn, the cleaning lady at the bank. "I guess your problems don't have very high priority."

If there is one thing I have a hard time stomaching, it is righteous indignation from a pompous asshole. "As the primary party involved in all the crap going on lately, I have to say that I have no complaints about how matters are being handled."

He smirked at me, looking remarkably like Don Knotts of Mayberry fame. "Of course you'd say that. After all, we know about you and Chief McCord. We know about your past...history."

"Oh, wrong thing to say," Ike muttered. "Really the wrong thing to say."

"Do you?" I demanded. "And tell me, what do you know?"

Murphy took a hesitant step back as I advanced on him. "You know. You and he are, well..." He backed up again. This brought us to the sawhorse and the grill where JT stood, watching us. "You and he are involved."

I glanced over Murphy's shoulder. JT's eyes were alert and amused. "Yeah, you might say we're involved," I conceded.

Behind Murphy's back, JT waggled his eyebrows.

"Very involved," I continued.

JT grinned.

"But that hasn't made me stupid. Even an idiot would know that a five-year-old mystery is tough to solve. And an idiot would know that an attack with no witnesses is just about impossible. And—"

"I meant to tell you, Molly," JT said, waving his barbeque spatula.

Murphy whirled and almost overbalanced, obviously unaware of his proximity to the object of our conversation.

"We got a good tire impression and boot impression from the tracks we found near your house. And we got excellent fingerprints from the door. The state crime lab is running tests for us now."

The implication was evident. An arrest was imminent. "Good," I said, stepping past Mr. Murphy, who appeared paralyzed. "But it's only what I expect." I held out my plate. JT raised a quizzical eyebrow. "Hot dog, please." I know he saw the laughter in my eyes because he was grinning when he turned to the grill.

"Hot dog coming up." He plunked a big dog down on my plate.

"Thanks, JT." I made sure my voice reflected my appreciation.

"Any time, Molly." He smiled at me, his dimples dancing. Then he turned to Mr. Murphy. "And you, sir?"

As we moved away, Ike said, "You should have just tossed JT down and jumped on him. That way, everybody would know for sure where you stand."

"Standing has nothing to do with it," Peggy said.

We hurried with the rest of the crowd toward the city hall and the tables that were set up in the council chambers where our city government met with its citizenry once a month. As we moved toward the building, Belinda paused to stare at me. I shivered at the malevolence she shot me. "Why doesn't she give it up?" I whispered.

Peggy followed my gaze. "She and Shirley have always competed. Maybe it's something to do with that."

Ike looked thoughtful. "I wonder what kind of footprint JT found."

"Why?" I opened the door for him and gestured him into the warm foyer.

"I wonder if he found a man's footprint or a woman's."

"What? It must be have been a man's, don't you—" My voice trailed away as I realized what he was implying. "Belinda?"

"She's a crack shot," he said, as we made our way through the crowd. "Mark always took her out pheasant hunting with him. And she was on the skeet team in high school."

"Oh, I can't believe that she would care that much to do something like that."

We got in line for the fixin's—potato salad, coleslaw, chips, condiments, and beans. "You weren't in town when this happened, Molly, but a few years ago Belinda got into trouble." Peggy helped me handle my plate since I was having trouble with my bandaged arm. "It was when she was in high school. She was sent away. I think it was go away or be sent to reform school, to tell the truth."

"What?" This was news to me.

"I remember that." Ike's voice sounded sad. "She was mad because her boyfriend had taken up with Polly Darland. Polly applied to some club Belinda was in and they had a hazing that got out of hand. Polly was hurt."

"Hurt?" I almost lost my tenuous hold on my plate. "How bad?"

"Polly went to the hospital. Belinda rigged some sort of gymnastics bar and Polly took a bad fall. She broke her arm and couldn't be on the cheer squad for the whole season. Belinda was sent away for a semester to some special school up in Minneapolis."

"Holy shit." I piled food automatically onto my plate and followed Ike to an empty spot at a long table near the wall. "I had no idea. Do you think JT knows?"

Ike glanced across the room where Belinda was sitting with some of TB's young society elect. Her eyes flickered to us, cool, distant and hard.

"Oh, I think you can bank on that," Ike said solemnly.

Chapter 16

The highlight of lunch was the announcement of the King of the Fling and his court. Our own Dan Bailey from the newspaper won and with much blushing on his part and hooting from his friends, he was crowned with his snowflake tiara. According to tradition, he chose his Queen, and to no one's surprise, he chose Jennifer, a pretty high school girl whom he'd been dating.

After lunch we all lined up to watch the Tangle Butte Festive Stroll. Ike took photographs for the newspaper with his new, highly prized digital camera. Children dressed as Christmas trees, Christmas lights, and elves danced along the parade route, flanking the gaily decorated tractors, ATVs, and the convertible that carried the King and his Queen. Ike made sure to get plenty of pictures of Dan and of Amelia, who rode on the Public Library float. She was dressed as the Ghost of Christmas Past, admonishing Charlie Pratt from the Sewer Department about his misspent youth as Scrooge.

Belinda and her cronies rode by on a float from the Point Park Ski Lodge, reminding me that I needed to contact that developer and see if he was still interested in Sam's land. Belinda was, I thought, a bit underdressed in a mini-skirted Alpine shepherdess outfit that made her look like a busty St. Pauli Beer girl. She tossed a handful of candy at me, which I successfully dodged. Several other business displays followed, then the high school floats, the real stars done up in chicken wire and toilet paper, trundled down the street. I recited notes into a little tape recorder about the offerings while Ike snapped pictures with the enthusiasm of a man who knows he won't have to pay for film developing.

"I'm glad to see you're feeling so good," a low voice said behind me.

I twisted and looked up into JT's face. "I'm feeling fine. I just needed a good night's sleep in my own bed, I guess."

He leaned over and whispered, "If I have my way, you won't sleep at all in a bed tonight. I'll keep you too busy to sleep."

My face got so hot it felt like snow was steaming off it. "Big promises."

His dark eyes seemed to draw me into his heart. "I'll pick you up at seven, okay?" Then he winked. "And I keep my promises." He brushed a kiss across my cheek, then was gone, vanished back into the crowd.

Ike laughed. "I guess I don't need Amelia's Tarot cards to know that there's a hot date in your future."

The parade wrapped up in mid-afternoon and I went back to the house with Yolanda and Darlene Abernathy, a Mr. Sex Lady. I napped, then prepped for my evening out, considering and discarding several wardrobe choices with help from Mom and Darlene. I finally settled on my long black skirt that was slit up the side, a black camisole and a pale lavender sateen jacket. The jacket fit over the bulky bandage on my arm and hid most of the bandage on my shoulder. I fussed with my hair, then let Darlene take over on the prep work since I was all thumbs.

"Of course you're klutzy," Darlene said as she whisked my hair up into soft little black spikes. "You're recovering from a gunshot wound. I still can't believe that. I just can't believe somebody took a shot at you."

"I wonder if JT will fingerprint everybody in town," Yolanda said from her spot on the trunk at the foot of my bed. She was sipping bourbon, watching Darlene dab powder on my face. "Although, why would he? What good will fingerprints be unless it's a known felon and his prints are in that fingerprint thing?"

"AFIS?" I asked, barely moving my lips so I wouldn't

interfere with Darlene's wielding of an eye shadow wand full of lavender. I'd researched fingerprinting for my second book and thus knew something about AFIS and fingerprint identification systems.

"He'll have to match the fingerprint to something," Darlene said. "Unless he's got a suspect." She eyed me in the mirror over my vanity table, in the corner of my bedroom. "Did he say anything about that?"

"Nope." I grabbed three red M&Ms from the crystal M&M dish on my vanity. Red, the color of love. I hoped it would be prophetic. Then headlights turned into the drive. "Looks like he's here."

"Nervous?" Yolanda asked, getting to her feet.

"Kind of," I admitted. "It's been a while since I've been on a date."

Darlene gave me a gentle shake, her hand on my good shoulder. "It's like riding a bike, honey. Some things, you just never forget."

I remembered the feel of JT as he held me in his arms, kissing me. "I know." I picked up my chic little beaded bag, which had once been Yolanda's. "Are you ladies going tonight?"

"Marv and I are going to come later," Darlene said.

Yolanda shook her head, preceding me down the stairs to the kitchen. "I'm going to pass this year, I think." Her eyes twinkled as she glanced back at me. "I'll go back to my house tonight and I won't wait up. If JT needs a babysitter for you, just call."

Heavens, I hadn't even thought about that. I wondered if he'd called off my guards for the night. It might be embarrassing to be here with him and have three high school boys walk in on us. I got my dress cape out of the hall closet as Yolanda and Darlene went ahead. I heard them greeting JT, then I walked out to join them.

I almost fell over. He was, quite simply, tall, dark and handsome. Okay, his hair wasn't dark but his suit was black with small gray threads shooting through it. He wore a dark gray shirt and black tie, all of which contrasted with his soft white hair and dark eyes. His shoulders looked about two yards wide and his legs were long and lean in his dark slacks.

He held out a box to me as I entered. "What's this?" I

opened it and saw a small corsage inside, two small white roses and a green leaf. "That's so nice."

"You're beautiful, Molly," he said in a soft voice. His eyes were moving over me and I blushed under his gaze.

Yolanda bustled over to the fridge. "And here's one for you, JT." She pulled out a cellophane-wrapped rose, slightly smaller than the one he'd given me.

"Where'd that come from?" I asked as she pinned the corsage on JT's lapel and Darlene pinned the one on me.

"Oh, I thought it might come in handy," she said, patting JT's arm as she stepped back. "We'll lock up before we leave. You kids have fun tonight. And as I told Molly, if you need me to babysit later on, you just give me a call. "

JT's eyes were crinkled with laughter. "I doubt that'll be necessary, Landie, but thanks for the offer." He stuck out his arm. "Ready?"

I took a deep breath. "You bet." We went down the steps carefully, me balancing on my black pumps and holding up my skirt with one hand. When we got to his truck, I stared with dismay at the running board. "JT, there's no way I can climb up in there."

He opened the passenger door for me. "No problem." He swept me up into his arms and before I knew what was happening, he'd slid me onto the seat of the truck. As he leaned in, one of his hands slid along my leg where my cape had dropped away. "You know I'm always glad to help a lady in distress."

He went to the driver's side and got in. As we drove out of the lane, Yolanda and Darlene got into Darlene's car. "Will we need my high school guards tonight?" I asked.

JT sighed. "I was meaning to talk to you about that. I'm not sure."

My heart plummeted. "Oh?"

He glanced at me. It was an overcast night and the moon shone fitfully between clouds. The road to town was an inky ribbon of gray between white fields that stretched into the distance on either side. "I may be making an arrest tonight. I'm just waiting for confirmation on some evidence from the state crime lab. If I do have to arrest somebody, I'm going to be busy most of the night."

"Oh. I see." I hadn't realized until that minute how much I was anticipating a night with him. "I guess that means I won't need any guards, then. If you're making an arrest, things must be under control."

"We'll see. I don't want you left alone unless I'm absolutely sure we've got the right person." His hands clenched on the steering wheel. "Somebody tried to get you twice, Molly. I'm not risking a third time."

I put a hand on his arm. "It's the same person, isn't it? I don't have two enemies, do I?"

"We'll see." He smiled. "One way or another, we'll be together, Molly. It just might not be the way we planned, that's all."

I had to be content with that. No amount of pestering on my part would make him reveal any more clues. We got to the high school and went inside, checking our outer coats with a freshman at the door. Then we went into the gym, which had been transformed into a fairy wonderland with soft lighting, small tables and chairs arranged in little arbors with fake snow on their interlaced beams, and a dance floor to one side where people swayed to the sound of Johnny Boyd's Boys, a local band. We followed the 'path,' a carpet runner, which led to a bar set up in what appeared to be a hollow tree festooned with giant paper snowflake cutouts. JT got us each a glass of punch and we meandered to a table and sat down. His eyes moved constantly, examining the crowd or watching people on the dance floor.

"Is he here?" I whispered.

"Who?"

"The person you're going to arrest." I glanced around, trying to be furtive.

He eyed me over the rim of his punch glass. "Not yet."

"Ooh. You're going to arrest him here?" I wondered where Ike and the digital camera were. We'd need a picture.

"Not if I can help it. Why don't we dance?" Before I could say 'no', he'd plucked my glass out of my fingers and was leading me out to the floor. I had a hard time raising my arm to his and he must have known because he kept his arm low. When I slipped my left hand up his side, I felt something.

"Good Lord, are you wearing a gun?" I whispered.

He steered us past Mr. and Mrs. Murphy, who glared at us. "Of course I am." He must have seen my shocked look. "Molly, I'm a cop. Did you forget that?"

"But are you always a cop? I mean, don't you ever get to go off-duty?"

He thought about it for a minute as we moved around the dance floor. "No. I'm always a cop." His hand moved caressingly along my back. I longed to move even closer to him, but I was aware of the glances we were getting as it was. I didn't want to tarnish his reputation any further. "It's not something I do, Molly. It's who I am."

Now it was my turn to think. JT was a cop. He was trained to arrest people, shoot them if needed and maybe—My hand tightened on his shoulder. Maybe be shot in turn, like he had been before. Good heavens, I hadn't really thought it through.

"It's like you, Molly. You're a writer. You're always a writer. You're not always writing, but you're a writer."

The tight knot of panic I'd felt started to subside. He was right.

"Can you live with that?" he asked, his voice intense yet soft. "Can you live with a cop?"

I met his eyes. "Yes," I whispered. "I can."

He smiled, his hand tightening over mine. "Good."

Someone tapped JT on the shoulder. We turned to find Ike, smiling at us. When JT started to move aside, Ike shook his head. "No, no, I'm not cutting in. I just wanted to hand off the camera to Molly." We all moved to one side as Ike pressed the little digital camera into my hand. "I've got to help hand out the awards for the scavenger hunt, floats and the costumes. We didn't win the hunt, by the way. The team from Ace Hardware got every thing on the list. Oh well, next year." He shrugged. "Dan already took a lot of pictures out in the parking lot when the floats were being judged, but if you could get some crowd shots, that would be great."

"Sure." I tucked the camera into my little bag, making sure Ike saw how careful I was. He breathed a sigh of relief and hurried away.

"And, of course, you're a reporter," JT said with

laughter in his voice. He gestured toward the tables at the side of the dance floor. "I can wait for you over here while you do your job."

I spied Belinda coming in with her father and Shirley. Both women were drop-dead gorgeous in low-cut dresses with high hemlines and heels. "That's okay," I said, taking his arm and tugging him along the winding path that led into the private arbors. "The crowd will be here for a while. I can pay attention to my date."

JT put an arm around my shoulder and we strolled along the path, pausing to chat now and again with someone we knew. It felt so right to be here with him. This reminded me of all those times he and I had attended parties and dances together, all those Harvest Balls and Apple Fests and Homecomings. I felt as though the intervening twenty years were the dream and this was the reality of my life, finally coming back to me. I was Sleeping Beauty waking from a long sleep with her prince at her side.

Sleeping Beauty. She was on the Death card in Amelia's Tarot deck. Damn. There was that Death card again.

I was so preoccupied with feeling happy that I didn't notice we'd come to the far side of the gym, near the door that led to the locker rooms. "Come on," JT said in a low voice. Taking my hand, he cracked open the door. We slipped through into the darkened hallway.

"Where are we going?" I asked.

"Unless they did some major remodeling, I know of a spot..." He led the way down the hall to a door at the end. Pushing it open, we ducked inside what appeared to be a storage room for discarded and broken equipment. JT flipped on the lights, revealing untidy stacks of broken hockey sticks, duct-taped baseball bats, bags of deflated soccer balls and other forlorn athletic gear.

"Here it is." He opened another door on the far side of the room, then went inside. It was a small office, barely large enough for a desk and chair. "The equipment manager always kept inventory sheets here," he said, pulling me in behind him, then reaching around to close the door and lock it with the deadbolt. His arms stayed around me as he maneuvered me to the desk. "Have a seat," he said in a low, husky voice.

I pulled up my skirt a bit and he helped me to sit up on the edge of the desk. "Don't mind if I do," I said, my heart hammering so hard I almost hiccupped.

His hands slid up my thighs, pushing my skirt with them. I felt a delicious pooling of heat start in my crotch and work its way outward, spreading like fire. I hooked my fingers in his belt loops and pulled him toward me. "I think I might have to take the law into my own hands tonight," I said.

He stepped between my legs. "I won't arrest you if you do," he said as he lowered his face to mine.

His kiss ignited something hot and urgent in me. Any residual ache from my wound was drowned by the feelings surging through me. I arched against him, anxious to have as much as I could get, as fast as I could get it. I struggled out of my jacket without breaking contact with his lips, then we separated long enough for me to peel off my camisole. He watched me, his dark eyes hungry and predatory. As soon as I'd tossed the silk top aside, he touched me, his hands sliding over my skin as they sought my bra's clasps. I shivered under his touch, my nipples enlarging to painful sensitivity.

I focused on his belt buckle, my fingers trembling as I tried to get it undone. When his lips closed on my nipple, I gave up. I sank back on the desk, leaning on my arms as he bent over me, suckling my nipples while his hand stole under my skirt. He broke off to look up at me with a crooked grin. "I was counting on this," he whispered.

"What?"

His fingers slid under the elastic leg of my panties. "You never did wear panty hose." He put a hand under my butt and lifted me, tugging at my underwear.

If I didn't get him inside me in the next few minutes, I'd probably have heart failure. I grabbed for that damn belt buckle again, ready to tear it off with my teeth if I had to. I'd just gotten it undone and the button to his trousers open when I heard an ominous buzzing.

"Tell me that's not a cell phone," I said, my fingers on his zipper.

JT withdrew his hand from under my skirt and leaned on the desk, his head hanging down. "No, it's not.

It's my pager." He took a long, steady breath, then reached down to fumble the small device out of the pocket in his jacket. For a long minute he stared at the message on the tiny screen. "Damn." He straightened up.

I wanted to scream. I was *this* close to an orgasm and the man was moving away. He gave me a despairing glance, then pulled his cell phone out of the holder on his belt, turning from me to open it.

For a minute I thought I'd be sick. Waves of disappointment crashed through me so intensely I was dizzy. I hooked my bra and found my camisole where I'd tossed it on top of a nearby basketball. By the time he turned back to me, I was dressed. His face was grim and I could tell he was miles away.

"I have to go," he said.

I nodded. "Did something happen?" I slid off the desk unsteadily. He put an arm around me, hugging me to him.

"I need to deal with this." He sounded distracted and upset. "I want you to go to Yolanda's house tonight. I'm still not sure you should be alone. I'll try to call you later or come over if I can." He ran a hand through my hair, caressing me with his touch. "Make sure you stay with people tonight until I can be with you. Don't be alone." He touched my cheek. "I love you, Molly. I always will."

I put my arms around his neck. We had one lingering, longing kiss. Then he straightened his tie, buttoned his coat, and we left the small room. As we walked down the darkened corridor, I asked, "Can you tell me what happened? Did you catch who killed Sam and who tried to kill me? Is that what the phone call was about?"

He opened the door that led to the dance floor, glancing inside. We slipped back in unnoticed, blending with the rest of the party crowd moving along the darkened perimeter of the gym. "It didn't work out the way I thought," he said, his voice barely audible above Boyd's Boys.

"What do you mean?"

"He wasn't supposed to die." We paused by the door leading to the parking lot. "Stay with people tonight, Molly," JT said, looking intently at me. "Don't go anywhere alone. I'll call you as soon as I can."

"JT, what—" But he was gone.

I was disoriented. Festive people surrounded me, most of them laughing or chatting with others. What had just happened? Who was dead? My little beaded purse bumped against my leg and I thought of Ike. I took out the camera and snapped some pictures, moving on autopilot like a robot. Most of the crowd was gravitating toward the bleacher side of the gym. I spotted Ike and he spotted me at the same time. He waved me over.

"Ike, you won't believe what happened," I said as soon as I got close enough.

"No kidding," he said. "Look."

I followed his gaze. A woman was walking through the parted crowd toward me, like Moses/Charlton Heston approaching Pharaoh/Yul Brynner through the Red Sea.

"Hello, Molly," said Bobbi Jo Rinderhoff, my late ex-husband's lover.

Chapter 17

My first thought was, *Somebody get JT so he can arrest this bitch.*

Then I realized what this meant. Bobbi Jo was here. She wasn't dead. That meant she hadn't killed Sam. She wouldn't have come back here if she'd killed Sam.

"Where the hell have you been, Bobbi Jo?" I demanded.

"Oh my God," someone cried out from the other side of the crowd surrounding us. "That can't be—oh, that's awful."

I glared into the crowd. "Stop being so melodramatic, whoever you are." I turned back to Bobbi Jo. "Well— where have you been?" Ike moved to a group of people who were huddled nearby, stricken expressions on their faces. "What the hell is going on?"

Bobbi Jo moved closer to me. I had to admit, she looked good. She'd lost weight and looked lean and fit. She was casually dressed in jeans and a sweater, which showed off her figure to advantage. Her hair, which had once been overly blonde, was now a soft shade of brown and she wore little noticeable makeup. Overall, she was svelte, sophisticated and put-together. I wondered fleetingly if Sam would have chased after this new Bobbi Jo and decided that no, he probably wouldn't have. She was too classy for him now.

"I'm sorry, Molly," she said, speaking in a low voice,

after glancing at the curious faces that surrounded us. "I heard JT was looking for me, so I decided to come back and face it."

"Face what?" I glanced around for Ike, hoping for a witness to this event, but he was talking to some people nearby.

"I saw what happened the day Sam died."

"What?" Holy shit, I couldn't believe this. "You knew he was dead? You knew he hadn't just run away? Why didn't you tell somebody?"

"I was afraid he'd kill me, too. I was afraid of the killer. I thought—" Her voice trembled and I could see the fear in her brown eyes. "He was so mad. I hid, and when he was gone, I took Sam's car and ran away."

"Wait a minute, wait a minute." I was thinking furiously, trying to make sense of it. "Who did it? Where have you been? Why didn't—"

"Molly, we need to go." Ike was tugging on my sleeve.

"Go? Where?"

"Chuck Anderson's been shot. They're saying it was the same person who shot you."

"What?" I whirled, almost falling down. "Who shot him?"

"An intruder. That's all we know right now." Ike was grabbing for my purse. "I need the camera, we have to get over there and take pictures."

"Damn it, Ike, Bobbi Jo says she knows who killed Sam." I turned back to Bobbi Jo, who was staring at us with eyes as big as plates. "We have to find JT."

"You were shot?" she whispered.

"Yeah." I tugged down the collar of my jacket so she could see my bandage. "Flesh wound," I said with all the casual bravado I could muster under the circumstances. "Now listen, we need to find JT. You have to—"

"I thought he was here." Bobbi Jo stared around the gym and the people who had stopped in their tracks to stare at her.

Mark Devlin was pushing through the crowd toward us. "Molly, what's happening?"

I took his arm. "You need to come with us. We're going to Chuck Anderson's house. Bobbi Jo has to see JT. Chuck's been shot." I started tugging Mark toward the door. "Come on, we have to go."

"But—the party—Shirley—"

"Shirley's a big girl and can take care of herself. We need a lawyer right now. Come on, you're driving." I handed Ike the camera. "We'll meet you at the Anderson house. You be the reporter again, I can't because I'm with Bobbi Jo and I might be a witness."

Ike turned to Dan Bailey and Amelia, who'd joined us, and started issuing instructions. Mark was talking to Shirley and Belinda, who were alternately watching me, Bobbi Jo, and Mark. Belinda appeared pouty and resentful but Shirley surprised me by nodding several times, then giving Mark a little 'get going' push. He kissed her then joined us.

I grabbed Mark's arm again and we hurried toward the door, Bobbi Jo in our wake. "Bobbi Jo says she saw who killed Sam, so she needs a lawyer with her when she tells JT," I explained as we hurried up the staircase to the main level and the front entrance. I almost tripped on my dress in my hurry, but Mark put an arm under mine and steadied me. We got to the coat check girl, and as she retrieved our coats, I had a sudden terrible thought— what if it was Mark? Oh my God. What if Mark was Sam's murderer? Here I was dragging him with me and—

The freshman girl handed me my cape and I automatically bundled myself into it. I glanced over my shoulder at Bobbi Jo as we raced out of the building, but she appeared comfortable about the idea of leaving with Mark. I blew out a sigh of relief as we hurried to Mark's Cadillac SUV. "What is it with men and cars that women have to climb into?" I grumbled as I faced the daunting task of getting into the behemoth in front of me.

He put his hands on my waist and gave me a push. "What is it with tiny women who are bossy and give orders?" Bobbi Jo laughed as she climbed into the back seat. "Where to, Fearless Leader?" Mark asked as he started the big car.

"Chuck Anderson's house. I heard he was shot." I tugged my cape closer around me, then got my pill case out of my purse. I held it out to Bobbi Jo. "M&M?"

She laughed again. "Do you still sort them by color?" She chose a red one.

"Yep. Whenever possible." I held the case out to Mark. "Candy?"

"No, thanks. Will someone explain to me what's going on?"

"Bobbi Jo said she saw who killed Sam."

Mark almost drove the car off the road, or maybe we just hit an icy patch. Either way, the car skidded, then straightened itself. "What?"

"I didn't really see him," Bobbi Jo said from the back seat. "I just caught a glimpse. I think he was blond, though."

Blond. Who did I know who was blond? My eyes moved to Mark who had tawny dark blond hair. I gulped. He met my glance, and for an instant, I know he knew what I was thinking. Then he smiled. "What else did you see?"

"I watched him bury poor Sam." Bobbi Jo was crying. I could hear the tears in her voice. "I didn't know what to do. He and Sam were arguing. I went with Sam to your house, Molly. He wasn't feeling good and I told him he could stay with me until he figured out what to do. We really didn't think you'd get so mad. I mean, it was just some harmless fun."

"Harmless fun?" I tried hard to keep the anger out of my voice but probably failed. "You were screwing him in front of half the town. How was that supposed to make me feel?"

"Oh, that's just how Sam was," she said in dismissal.

I knew she was right, but it still pissed me off to hear her say it. "That's no excuse," I sputtered. "You were having an affair with my husband and I caught you. What did you think I'd do, just—?"

"Molly."

Mark's quiet voice cut through my diatribe.

"Let it go, Molly. It was years ago. You've got better things to do with your emotions now. Forgive and move on. Just let it go."

I looked at him in astonishment. Where did he come off giving me this kind of advice? This was the man who'd propositioned me at least twice and whose wife tried to cheat on him with my old love. I was prepared to give him a piece of my mind, then he smiled again. That's when I realized—he and Shirley had come to some sort of understanding. They had somehow found a middle ground where they could co-exist. They'd moved on.

"Did you hear the argument?" Mark asked, glancing in the rear view mirror at Bobbi Jo.

"It was about money," she said, her voice still choked.

"Money?" Of all the possible things to kill Sam over, money was one I hadn't considered. "Sam didn't have any money. I mean, nothing worth killing over."

"There was that land," Mark said.

"No, it wasn't anything like that." Bobbi Jo sniffled. I grabbed a tissue from the box on the console next to me and handed it back to her. "Thanks. It was something about embezzlement."

"Embezzle..." My voice trailed away. I slid my glance to the outside world, relieved to see we were heading in the right direction. For a minute, I'd had a fear that Mark was taking us out to the country somewhere. "But who would care about embezzlement?"

"I can think of two groups of people," Mark said, steering the car down Eighth Avenue and the house at the end of the block with all the police cars outside. "Lawyers and bankers."

"Chuck?" I stared in stunned astonishment at the big frame two-story house.

Mark parked the SUV near the alley that separated the Anderson house from its neighbor in the back. "Let me go in and see if JT can come out to see you," he said, turning in his seat to gaze at Bobbi Jo. When I started to speak, he said, "It's a crime scene, Molly. He doesn't want people just rushing in."

"But maybe I can help," I said. "Charlene might need someone—"

"I'll volunteer you, but don't be surprised if he doesn't take you up on it." Mark slipped out of the door before I could stop him, leaving the car running so we'd have heat. He started across the lawn to the house, using a worn path through the snow, but two deputies appeared and gestured him to the street and the sidewalk in front of the house.

I peered out the SUV window at the side of the house where Bucky Thornton was walking along the small paved pathway to meet Mark. He and Mark conferred, then Mark waited while Bucky disappeared into the house. In a minute, JT appeared and talked to Mark, glancing at the SUV where Bobbi Jo and I sat huddled. The two men then came out, taking that circuitous route around the front of the house on the shoveled walk. JT looked professional and businesslike with his dark suit and tie. Then I remembered unbuckling his belt and I blushed hotly, a rush of heat going through me that left me dizzy.

I pressed the 'down' button on my window. "What happened to Chuck?" I asked.

"We're not sure yet," JT said, putting his hand over mine on the window frame. He peered in the back seat. "Bobbi Jo, I'm glad you came back. I was hoping you'd hear I was looking for you. Are you ready to tell me what happened that night?"

I twisted to regard Bobbi Jo, whose face appeared blotchy and damp in the light from the squad car's flashers. "I am," she said in a little voice.

"Good." JT gestured to someone. "I want you and Molly to go to the station and wait for me there. Larry will drive you."

"I can drive them," Mark said. He was standing behind JT, peering into the car over JT's shoulder.

"I'd rather they go with a deputy," JT said. His eyes met mine. "It's procedure."

I wasn't sure how to interpret his expression, so I just nodded. "Okay, if you say so. When will you get there?"

"As soon as I can." He gazed back at the house, a puzzled expression in his eyes. "We'll have to process the scene for a while longer, then I'll join you." He turned to Bobbi Jo. "Don't make any more statements until we have a chance to talk."

She looked at Mark, who was frowning at this comment. "Can Mark be there? I'd feel better if I had a lawyer with me."

"Of course. I just want information, Bobbi Jo." JT's voice sounded reassuring and I almost believed him. I knew him too well, though, to be fooled. He was a cop and he wanted to solve this case. Bobbi Jo's worries weren't going to get in his way.

JT opened my door and helped me out of the SUV, then did the same for Bobbi Jo. We walked to the squad car nearby. "Mark, you can meet them at the station," JT said as we got into the car. I didn't hear Mark's reply, but the two men shook hands, so I guess it wasn't acrimonious. I turned to watch JT as our squad car drove away. He was standing in the street staring at us. Then he turned and went back into Charlene's house.

We waited for hours at the police station, sipping coffee and talking while Larry Foster, the deputy, listened in. Bobbi Jo had been living in a suburb of St. Paul, working at a health club, which explained why she was so fit. She was apparently dating someone and they were getting serious. It was he who'd told her a cop had been asking about her at the gas station where he worked. They'd talked it over and she decided she had to come home to Tangle Butte and tell JT what she knew. "I owed Sam that much," she said. "I liked him a lot." Then she made a face. "And I owe you for his car."

I'd forgotten all about it. "I think that's the least of our worries right now."

It was almost midnight when JT came in, shaking snow off his topcoat. He conferred in a low voice with Larry, then came into the room where Mark, Bobbi Jo, and I were sitting. "Bucky's out front. He'll drive you over to Yolanda's house," he said to me. "I'd still feel better if you weren't alone tonight."

"But I want to stay. Sam was my husband, I have a right to know what happened."

"And you will. But you can't sit in on a conversation that I have with a witness."

"Procedure again?" I snapped, jumping to my feet.

He looked briefly pained, then nodded. "Yeah, as a matter of fact, it is."

I stomped to the door, grabbing my little beaded handbag and cape as I went. "If that's all the thanks I get for helping out and—"

He gently propelled me toward the exit, away from Bobbi Jo and Mark. "You have to realize that you can't be in the same room when I'm questioning the woman who witnessed your husband's death," he said in a firm voice.

"The only reason I let you stay here as long as you did was because I wasn't sure it was safe for you to be alone at your mother's. And because I knew Larry would keep track of any conversation you and Bobbi Jo had."

When I started to argue he said, his voice even louder, "If I get enough evidence for a murder case, I'm not going to have it thrown out of court because someone says I was showing favoritism to you, do you understand me?"

I stopped so suddenly I almost jerked him to a stop with me. "I keep forgetting."

"Forgetting what?"

"You're a cop."

We paused by the front door. I glimpsed Bucky outside, the squad car running and sending plumes of exhaust into the frigid air. "Yeah," he said. "I'm a cop." He lowered his voice. "I'm going to try to see you tonight if I can. It'll be a few hours and it all depends on what Bobbi Jo tells me. I want plenty of witnesses to my conversation with her and I don't want you anywhere around." I opened my mouth, but he shook my arm gently. "Trust me, Molly."

He had me and he knew it. I wouldn't jeopardize his job or his credibility. "Okay. But call me if you can't come over, all right? I just want to know—" Know what? I wasn't sure. "I just want to know you're around."

He grinned suddenly. "Oh, I'm around. You can count on that." He opened the door as I draped my cape around me. "You were beautiful tonight, Molly. I want a rain check."

I gave him a coy glance. "On the dance or the equipment room?"

"Both." His voice was low and caressing. "I'll call you."

He watched me climb into the squad car, but when I turned to wave to him, he was gone. Bucky drove me to Yolanda's house, where I was met at the door. "What is going on?" my mother demanded. "I can't believe it, the one time in three decades that I don't go to that dance and all hell breaks loose."

I laughed out loud as I shed my cape and shoes and settled with a sigh on her couch. My shoulder was hurting, probably because I hadn't had any pain pills in a while. I considered popping one, but then Mom pressed a bourbon drink into my hand and I decided to rely on a liquid analgesic. I told Mom what I knew, then we called Ike, who I knew would be at the office.

I was right. "Chuck Anderson was killed by persons unknown," he told us. I was on the phone in the living room and Yolanda was on the extension in the kitchen. "Charlene called it in at about nine o'clock. She said she was upstairs with the kids, heard a gunshot, came downstairs and found Chuck in the kitchen, dead."

"Is it the same person who shot Molly?" Yolanda demanded.

"I couldn't get an official comment out of anybody but I heard Bucky talking to Bob Warner and it sounds like it was the same caliber gun. The police must think he came in from the outside because they had the yard roped off."

I remembered the circuitous route Mark and JT had taken at Charlene's house. "Did any of the neighbors see anything?" I asked.

"Nope. The Billings were at the dance and Mr. Gilroy was asleep in front of his TV. Those are the only two who might have seen or heard anything." I heard the distinctive click of keys being tapped and knew Ike was writing the story as he spoke. "What did Bobbi Jo have to say? Did she say who killed Sam?"

I summarized the little Bobbi Jo had told me as Ike took notes. When I finished, he said, "Can you come in to the office in the morning? We've got a lot of work to do for Monday's edition."

I assured him I could and hung up. I was just settling down on the couch with my second drink when the doorbell rang. Yolanda answered it and ushered JT into the living room. I held up my glass. "Drink?"

He shook his head. "Nope. I saw the lights on and thought I might give you a ride home."

I straightened up in surprise. "Really?"

He smiled. "Really. I've gotten formal statements from Bobbi Jo and from Charlene Anderson. There's nothing else to be done until we get some test results back."

"What happened?" Yolanda asked, sipping her second

bourbon drink from the comfort of her position in the recliner. She looked like a little Buddha all wrapped up in her afghan.

"I've already given Ike a statement for the paper, so it won't hurt to tell you. We're investigating the possibility that someone broke into the house and shot Chuck Anderson. But we won't know for sure what happened until we analyze some evidence from the scene and that may take days. We gave it to the county lab to process."

"But Charlene says someone broke in?" I asked.

JT nodded. "Yeah, but we have to confirm that with evidence."

"And Bobbi Jo?" I prompted.

"I can't give you details, but..." He shook his head. "She didn't see who killed Sam. She came to the house with Sam and went upstairs to pack a weekend bag for him while he wrote you a note, Molly. She said he wasn't feeling good, so she wanted to help."

"I didn't get a handwritten note."

JT nodded. "I think there were two notes. You got the one the killer wrote. Bobbi Jo was upstairs and she heard voices, arguing. She checked outside and saw Sam and another man by the hole, arguing. That man was wearing a cap, so she couldn't see his face. Sam fell in the hole and that's when she saw the blood. Bobbi Jo saw this man call someone on a cell phone, then he put some planking over Sam's body, covering it with a thin layer of dirt. Then she heard him downstairs. She hid in a closet, scared he'd come upstairs. Where'd he leave the note?"

"Hunh? Note?" I was trying to imagine the scene that day, Bobbi Jo cowering in the upstairs den while poor Sam was being pitchforked. It made me a bit nauseous to think of it.

"The note Sam left you."

"Oh, that. It was on the kitchen table. Oh. So you think the killer came in and left a note? One already written?" My mind was in overdrive. "That means premeditation."

JT nodded. "Yeah. Anyway, Bobbi Jo hid and when she felt the coast was clear, she snuck back downstairs, got in the car, and drove away."

"There's more to it than that, isn't there, JT?" Yolanda asked.

"Nothing that I can discuss, Landie." He turned his attention to me. "And I'm sure you'll be glad to know you've been officially cleared of any involvement in Sam's death."

I almost choked on my drink. "I was under suspicion?" I wasn't sure whether to be mad, scared, or pleased.

"I had to consider it." He grinned at me. "Want a ride?"

I sprang to my feet. "Let's get going."

Yolanda finished her drink and set down her glass. "I guess that means you won't need me on guard duty any longer."

JT laughed. I was heartened by the carefree sound of it. "Nope, we won't. Thanks, Landie. For everything."

She stood on her tiptoes and put a kiss on his cheek. "I always liked you, JT, even when you were a shit. I'm glad to see you turned out so good." She waved a hand good-bye over one shoulder as she toddled off to bed.

I bundled into my cape and we went out into the frigid air. JT's truck stood outside. "Not again," I grouched as I started down the slippery sidewalk.

He scooped me up into his arms. "Oh, yeah," he said, his breath hot on my neck. "Again."

Chapter 18

JT and I made it to my bedroom, but it was a near thing.

We left a trail of clothing in our wake—shoes, jackets, shirt, skirt, slacks and camisole lying on the couch, a chair, and the stairs. JT insisted I keep on my thigh-high stockings, bra, and panties until he could peel them off me himself. I was happy to oblige. I insisted he put his gun in the nightstand near the bed, and he obliged.

And then we obliged each other.

We tumbled on the bed, laughing. His body on mine was electric, as though a spark connected us. I pulsed, feeling wild, hot and ready. Lord, it was fantastic. My memories came back in a rush and were almost immediately replaced by new experiences.

Was it as good as it was twenty years ago?

No.

It was better.

****

Later we lay in bed, temporarily exhausted. "I didn't think you'd ever forgive me," John said, nuzzling into my neck.

I felt weightless with happiness, barely tethered to the earth. "I didn't think I would either," I admitted, dragging the covers up to protect against the early morning cold. "I've never been hurt like that before. Even when Sam cheated on me, it wasn't like that." I touched the ropey scar that ran down his chest, the only reminder of the terrible wound he'd had. It seemed so small for something that had almost killed him.

"I loved you, Molly." His breath was hot on my neck, his whispers like ghosts floating in the air. "But I wanted to be something more, something better. I didn't want to be the half-breed kid who wouldn't amount to much. I thought I had to have money and the right people backing me." He laughed softly. "I married Shirley for her money and her body, in that order. Once I got them, I found I didn't want them. I only wanted you. You were the only one who believed in me, who believed I could make something of myself. I felt you deserted me when you went away after Delbert died."

"I had to leave." I remembered the humiliating bitterness that had dogged me when I found out Shirley and JT were getting married. I'd wanted to fly to the ends of the earth, but I had no money, three years of college and no ambitions in life except to marry him and settle down. Delbert's offer of marriage was a lifeline. "When Delbert died, I had to get out of here. I couldn't stand to be here and see you and Shirley together."

"I know. And I'm glad, in a way. With you gone, I realized what a mistake I'd made. It forced me to understand that if I wanted to do something with my life, I had to do it on my own. I had to believe in myself. I couldn't rely on anyone else for help." He took a ragged breath, his arm encircling me so that I felt the long expanse of his body against mine. "It's because of that and what happened with Shirley that I got the ambition to go back to school, go into law enforcement, to do something I really wanted to do."

"And it's because of you I left, got a degree, got a good job and started writing." I kissed his mussed hair, amazed at the serendipity of fate. "I guess we had to go through a lot of shit in order to enjoy this."

"Let's not do it any more, though, okay?" He peeked up at me, his dark eyes mischievous and inviting. "Let's just enjoy ourselves from now on, okay?"

"How's John Thomas feel about that?" I asked. This had been an old joke of ours. He hadn't known that 'John

Thomas' was a euphemism for penis. I'd enjoyed teasing him about it.

"John Thomas is feeling very fine," JT said, turning over.

"Oh, my." I stroked his stomach, then touched the object of our conversation. "Yes, I can see that. He is indeed feeling fine."

"You'd better be careful. I'm an older guy. I may need some recovery time."

"You appear to be nicely recovered."

JT pushed me back to the warm sheets. I tugged him on top of me, angling my pelvis up to meet him. He paused to slip on the condom, then he slid into me, deep and filling.

"You're always so tight," he gasped as he entered me.

"You're such a good fit." It felt as though his penis was filling every inch of my body, every molecule touched by him, every moist, tiny inch being massaged as he pushed deeper.

I relaxed and he grinned wickedly at me. This was when I was truly ready, when my muscles slackened that last little bit. I always tensed up at first. But as soon as I felt him in me, my body took over. He knew it, too. I saw the memory in his eyes. He slid in just that little bit more. It was an incredible sensation, as though some missing, anxious, important part had returned to me, as though I was being completed in a way I hadn't known was possible.

I tightened my muscles around him and held him as he slowly stroked back out. He did it again and again, pushing deeply in then pulling back, so that I could caress him. That hot unfurling began, starting in my stomach and spreading outward like a molten tide. He recognized the signs and quickened his stroking. I tensed, wound so tight I was sure I'd break.

Then, suddenly, it happened. That delicious relaxation, that release began, wrenching all tension out of me. And John was with me just a split second later, crying out as he drove into me one last time. It seemed to last forever and then we clung to each other, listening to our breathing as it quieted.

We must have dozed, because it was lighter in the

room when I opened my eyes. John was cuddled against me, watching me in the half-light of dawn.

"Hey you," I murmured, inching down under the covers, wondering belatedly what I looked like. It had been a long time since I'd had a night of sex.

He kissed the tip of my nose. "I was just thinking we need to get out of bed, but I don't want to." He ran a hand down my hip, then back to cover my breast. "This is so much more fun."

"Do you have to go to the office?"

"Yeah. What about you?"

"I told Ike I'd come in." John frowned. "It'll be okay, won't it?" I thought of poor Charlene. "It's over. You think Chuck did it, don't you?"

"I don't know," he said.

"What about Bobbi Jo? What else did she say?"

He laughed, snuggling under the covers with me. "I already gave Ike a statement about how Miss Rinderhoff has come back to town to help the police in their investigation. Do I need to give you one, too?"

I shot him an outraged glance. "What else?"

"What she said confirms what I thought. There are some things that don't make sense, but I want to wait until I see the evidence. No matter what, I have to go in. To be on the safe side, I want you to stick close to Ike today."

"No problem. We'll have our hands full getting the paper ready."

John's hand caressed my breast. "Speaking of full hands..."

****

I called Ike after JT and I showered. As I expected, he was already at the office. "Come any time you can," he said. "Amelia's coming in this afternoon. Dan can't come in, he's got something to do at the school, but I said you'd handle the pictures."

"Sure." I felt guilty, leaving Ike to man the office alone. We usually set up the Monday paper on Sunday afternoon because it took little effort, but this would be special today and he'd need all the help he could get. "I'll be there soon."

JT went outside to feed Barn Cat while I fixed

180

breakfast for the resident house cat and two humans. When I picked up Augie's keys, JT shook his head. "I'll drive you."

"You can follow me," I said. "This way if it turns out I don't need an escort, I'll have my car with me. Ike may need me to run some errands." JT appeared unconvinced. "You can drive behind me to the office. Come on, JT."

He put his arms around me. "I just got you back, I don't want to lose you again." His voice was rough and deep.

I squeezed him as hard as my bruised arm would allow. "Not to worry."

He did worry, I could tell, but he didn't push it. We left the house before the sun was fully up. I should have been exhausted since I'd only slept about two hours, but instead I felt like a million bucks. As JT followed me to town, I kept glancing into my rear view mirror to reassure myself that he was still there. I couldn't believe it. What a difference a day makes.

Yeah, there were a couple of minutes where I was worried. I know when he first saw me naked, he was looking for the Molly he used to know. I know that for just a minute he, like me, had felt the memories creep up and threaten to take us over.

But then—man oh man. Then all of a sudden it was NOW and what a now it was. I'd forgotten how much fun it could be—laughing, and moaning and plain feeling good. Yesterday I'd been anxious and nervous. And now I owned the world, relaxed and confident.

Well, sort of. True, JT and I had a heck of a lot of fun, but would it last? Let's face it. JT was still a handsome guy with a body to die for. His eye might roam or he might—

Would JT get bored and move on?

No.

I was as certain of that as I was of spring arriving in a few months. He and I may have problems in the future, but he wasn't going to dump me. He wasn't worried about his status in the community any more. The boy I loved was gone.

Now I loved the man he'd become.

I was so wrapped up in steamy memory that I almost

overshot the newspaper office. I slammed on the brakes and slid into my usual spot. JT pulled up next to me as I got out of the car. I hopped up on the running board of his truck.

"There's Ike's Chevy," I said, pointing to the white SUV in the 'Reserved' spot around the corner. "So I've got my bodyguard for the morning."

He leaned on the open window. "And I'm your bodyguard for later," JT whispered. He kissed me. "I'll call as soon as I know anything for sure."

"Okay." I stepped away and watched him drive down the street. I sniffed the cold, bitter air. Man, I felt great. Yeah, I sort of ached but it was a good ache. I whistled as I went into the back door. "Yo, Ike?" I called out as I walked past the empty back offices into the main office.

His computer was on but Ike wasn't there. I went to my desk. As I turned on my computer, I saw the sticky note in the middle of my monitor.

Kiwanis breakfast, back soon.

Damn. I'd forgotten. The breakfast started at eight and ran until noon. Ike was probably over at the Legion Hall getting his fill of pancakes and gossip. I considered joining him, then saw the digital camera in my *in* basket. I popped a couple of red M&Ms (*love, passion, joy*), then settled down to finish my work as quickly as I could. Even though JT would be busy all morning I wanted to be available just in case.

When I thought about why he'd be busy, it made me pause. Poor Chuck. And poor Charlene! Good Lord, what she must be going through. I couldn't imagine it. She'd never worked outside the home—what would she do for money? With Chuck gone, what could Charlene do? Sure, she had a college degree in botany, but that wouldn't buy her much, would it?

I downloaded the pictures from the digital camera, sorting them into folders on my computer. Dan had taken a lot of pictures of the floats as they sat in the high school parking lot awaiting judging yesterday afternoon. Crowds of people were standing around the floats, watching as the judges did their thing. I printed out some of the better pictures, zooming in to check the details. Then I turned to the pictures I'd taken at the party. I panned through them, searching for ones that had the best focus or interest. As I did, I noticed Chuck Anderson in one of the shots. He was in the background in the gym, behind an arbor. It appeared like he was talking to someone.

I zoomed in on the picture some more, blowing it up on my computer screen. I hadn't used the photo software very much, so I wasn't sure how to enhance it, but after a few false starts, I found the right icon. The fuzzy picture on the screen slowly became clearer.

It was Chuck talking to Charlene. She was standing with her arms crossed in front of her, looking angry. I checked the timestamp on the picture. It had been taken at eight-thirty last night during the Fling dance. Just a half-hour later, poor Chuck was dead. I printed the picture, thinking I'd give it to Charlene. Then I reconsidered. If they were arguing, I didn't want to remind the poor woman. What a terrible thing—to argue with someone, then find him dead a few minutes later. It was sort of like finding Sam, but at least I'd had five years to help me mitigate the guilt.

The phone rang and I picked it up, grabbing two yellow M&Ms on the way. "Trib," I mumbled.

"Is Ike there?" an unfamiliar female voice asked.

"Nope. He'll be back in a minute, can I take a message?"

"No, I'll call later."

I hung up and checked the next picture in the sequence. I must have changed positions, because this time I couldn't see Chuck's face, just Charlene's as she said something to him. Chuck's shoulders sagged, and for some reason I thought he looked beaten down. He was staring at the floor while Charlene leaned over him, obviously speaking intently.

I got up for coffee, passing by the desk where our scavenger hunt treasures sat. The rhododendron leaf I'd cut was still perky in its water glass. I made a mental note to myself to throw the glass away when we finished with it. Rhododendrons were highly toxic and the water might taint the glass.

I stopped in my tracks and turned to stare at the dusty green leaf.

Rhodos were one of the most poisonous plants to be

found in the home garden. It was right up there with nightshade, hemlock, lily of the valley or monkshood—all of which I had growing in my garden as decorative ornamental plants. Water from vases containing lily of the valley was so toxic a sip could kill. All parts of nightshade were deadly. I remembered my instructor talking about it in Landscaping 101, when we discussed the legalities of landscaping with poisonous ornamentals.

"A lot of plants are dangerous," he'd said. "You have to make sure your clients understand what is edible and what isn't. You should always have them sign a wavier of responsibility, so they don't come back ten years later and try to blame you for their child's death when the kid decides to chew on a rhododendron flower."

His matter-of-fact way of talking about it had been chilling, more so because I frequently brought rhodo branches into my house because they were so pretty. I'd never done so after that, worrying one of my pets might chew on it.

I poured myself a cup of coffee from the pot sitting on the burner and carried it back to my desk. I'd done some poison research for my third book and I still had the web sites bookmarked. I accessed the Aggie Horticulture web site and there it was:

Laurels, Rhododendrons, Azaleas: All parts: Fatal. Produces nausea and vomiting, prostration, coma.

Had Sam been poisoned by something from the garden? I tried to remember what JT had said about the poison—did he say it wasn't man-made? Hadn't it been organic? I brought up the computer file that held my research, skimming through the various poisons I'd considered for bumping off the bad guy in my book.

There it was. Honey cakes. If bees harvested pollen from poisonous plants, their honey would be poisonous. That's why commercial beekeepers were so careful about where they set their hives. I'd researched it for Book Two, which I had set in a rural town. I hadn't used the honey angle, opting instead for a relatively straightforward pesticide death. But I'd mentally earmarked the information, thinking I might use it in a later story. There was also a note about a killer who had made tea from rhododendron flowers, then used the tea in a cake.

"Molly?"

I jerked away from my computer, spilling my coffee and nearly upending my M&Ms. "In here," I called out.

Charlene Anderson came in through the back door.

"What are you doing here?" I asked, jumping up. "Good God, Charlene, what are you doing out? You should be at home or—" I stopped, not sure where she should be. Her husband was dead, in their home—where could she go? I suppose the house was still a crime scene. Could she even stay there?

She laughed shakily. Her coat today was a nondescript brown man's jacket, not her stylish Michelin Tire Woman jacket she'd worn the other day. To my surprise, she also wore jeans. I couldn't remember if I'd ever seen Charlene in jeans; she always wore slacks or a skirt. It was distracting, like seeing a person who was traveling incognito or something.

"I just couldn't stand to stay there any more," she said, sort of staggering into the room. Her eyes were red and raw-looking and she was even more washed out than usual, her limp hair in tangles around her face. "I wanted to talk to Pastor Martin, but I forgot it was Sunday and he'd be busy at the church."

"Come on, sit down." I was afraid she might fall down. I reached out a hand to steady her but she jerked away, walking woodenly toward my desk. "Where are the kids? Are they okay?"

"They're with Joe."

"Joe?" I reached for my M&Ms, thinking a shot of chocolate wouldn't hurt her.

"My brother. Joe Hunt."

I stared at her blankly. Charlene Hunt. That's right. Jimmy and Joe Hunt were her brothers. And she and Sam had dated before she married Chuck.

CH.

CH in Sam's date book.

The Hunt desk where we stored our scavenger hunt finds, including a rhodo leaf.

Charlene had a botany degree.

Her eyes zeroed in on the coffee mug sitting on my desk, then to the Scavenger desk where the rhodo leaf sat.

"How's the coffee?" she asked.

Chapter 19

I had a hard time breathing. Sweat popped out on my forehead and I fought nausea. "What about the coffee?" I managed to ask.

She glanced around the office. "Is Ike gone?"

Ike. Oh my God. If she poisoned the coffee, was Ike— Wait a minute, wait a minute. Why would Charlene poison the coffee?

Charlene had a botany degree.

"I'm not sure," I said, inching away from my desk. I hazarded a glance at Ike's desk but it just confirmed what I knew. Ike wasn't there. Was he in the bathroom? I hadn't heard anything. What if he was sick? What if he was unconscious, lying on the linoleum floor and writhing in pain? Good Lord, what if he was dead? "Why are you here, Charlene?" I took a baby step to the left, hoping to outflank her.

"I wanted to check that CD you have."

Her words made no sense. "CD?" I glanced at the CD player on my desk and the stack of rock and roll next to it.

"Sam's computer?" she asked patiently. The stunned surprise on my face must have tipped my hand. "You don't have it?" she demanded, striding forward.

I took a step back. That brought me up against the counter that ran along the front of the main office. "Not with me."

"Damn it, you said it was in your purse. Chuck said

you had it in your purse."

I said the first thing that popped into my head. "Charlene, you swore." This was as stunning as seeing Charlene wear jeans. Susie Homemaker never swore.

"I'm under just a tiny bit of stress," she snapped.

"I can appreciate that," I said, edging toward the side of the counter and the drop gate. "That's why I think you should go home and—"

"I can't go home. Don't you understand? I can't go home. I don't have a home."

She sounded so desperate. The poor girl, she looked it, too. Her eyes were darting around the office, moving here and there like a trapped coon. I didn't know what she wanted. "Of course you do, Charlene," I said soothingly. "You've got a home."

"It's your fault, Molly." She took another step toward me, bumping into my desk. My M&Ms teetered on their lazy Susan. I made a grab toward them but stopped at the expression on her face. Her eyes were wide, her jaw was set and I swear, she looked like Jack Nicholson in *The Shining* right before he went crazy. There was that weird, unfocused *other* person in her eyes. I retreated, letting my M&Ms fend for themselves.

"Why is it my fault, Charlene?" I glanced around, searching for an out. She was between the back door and me. The counter prevented me from getting to the front door. I edged toward the side of the counter and the drop gate there. If I could get to the front door, I could get out. Not that I thought she was dangerous. What could she do? Charlene was about four inches taller than me and maybe twenty pounds heavier. She was harmless.

"Because of the audit."

"Huh?" I shook my head. "What audit?"

"The audit you're having done. Sam kept records, you know. About everything."

"How do you know?" As soon as I spoke, I wanted to slap myself up the side of the head. I needed to get out of there. I didn't need to pry information out of her. She was starting to worry me. I glanced at my desk and froze.

The pictures of her and Chuck were sitting there. "Did you enjoy the dance last night?" I said, trying to seem casual as I leaned on the counter.

She looked confused. "Dance?"

"You know, the dance." I laughed, but I think it came out sounding like a strangled choke. "The Fling Fairyland?"

"We couldn't make it," she said. "I wasn't feeling well, so we canceled the babysitter. Why did you request an audit?"

Why was she lying about being at the dance? "I thought you were there."

"I stayed home all night. Chuck went and came home early."

Why was she lying? I resumed inching toward the gate. "So you didn't hear all the excitement?"

"About what?"

"Bobbi Jo." I sidled away from my desk.

"Bobbi Jo?"

Her eyes flickered around the office. I recognized an upcoming lie when I saw it. "No. What about her?"

"She's back."

"Oh. Well, who cares what that slut does?"

Oh, my. There was a little more than moralistic righteousness in her voice. She sounded vengeful and bitter. Good Lord. Were Charlene and Sam—

"What about the audit? Why did you request one?" she demanded.

"I didn't."

"Don't lie." Her voice was loud and harsh. She took a long step forward, away from my desk and the pictures lying there.

"I'm not lying." I shrugged. "I trust Mark."

That stopped her. "Mark?"

"Sure. Who else would I audit?"

She paused by the Hunt desk. We both noticed the fencing sword at the same moment. Our eyes met. She made a move toward the sword. I made a move toward the front door.

"Charlene?"

I whirled. JT was coming in the back door. Ike was behind him, peering around JT's arm as JT pulled his gun. It all happened so fast. Charlene grabbed the sword, pulling it out of its sheath. It wasn't sharp. I knew that.

Charlene didn't. She ran at me, brandishing the

sword.

"Charlene!" JT was shouting now, rushing into the room.

I ducked as the sword came down, crashing into the counter where I'd been standing seconds before. "Holy shit!" I dodged her again as she took a swing at me, using the sword like a baseball bat and aiming for the side of my head. Even if it wasn't sharp, it could do a lot of damage. I cringed, raising one arm.

"Drop it, now!"

I don't think she heard JT. I caught a glimpse of her crazed eyes as she raised the sword again. "Damn it," she grated out as she brought the sword down.

I dropped to my knees and slid under the drop gate at the same moment the explosion ripped through the room. I peeked up from my hidey-hole.

Charlene wavered above me, the sword falling from her hand. Her legs buckled when a small stream of blood starting pulsing down her leg. She stared at me, her face blank. Then she stared at her leg, looked at JT, then passed out right next to me.

I wanted to do the same. Instead, I stood up.

And hit my head on the drop gate. I fell back on the floor.

"Molly?"

Someone was shouting. JT was peering down at me. I blinked at him. "I'm fine," I said. I closed my eyes and passed out.

****

There's a lot of red tape involved when somebody is shot. I had to go to the hospital to be examined, then I had to give statements to the State Patrol, who was called in because some outside agency had to verify that it was a clean shooting. Or at least that's how Yolanda described it—'a clean shooting'. I suspected I heard Bucky Thornton's phrasing there. Then I went to the police station. JT was in a room talking to some men. I was led into another room and had to give my statement. About halfway through, Mark Devlin showed up, so I re-gave my statement with him present.

When I got done, Mark and I went out to the waiting room where Ike and Yolanda were sitting. Ike appeared every one of his seventy-five years and Mom was just about the same. I flopped down in a chair next to them. "Now what?" I asked nobody in particular.

"Now you go home," Mark said. "You get some rest."

"How's Charlene?" I remembered how she'd dropped, without a word, in front of me. I remembered the blood. I tried to peer into the room where JT was sitting, but the door was partially closed.

"It was a good shot," Mark said with a clinical detachment that I thought was a bit too cold. "He broke the bone, but she'll live."

"Is JT going to get in trouble?"

"I doubt it. It was a good shot."

"I wish you'd quit saying that," I snapped. "No shot is a good shot."

Mark looked embarrassed. "Sorry. I'm a bit out of my element here. I normally prepare wills and land deeds, I don't defend people against murder."

"I know." I rubbed my forehead, where a monster headache was forming. "I'm sorry." I stared back into the police station. "He'll be okay, right?"

Mark followed my gaze. "Yeah. He'll be fine. You need to go home, though, Molly. There's nothing you can do here."

He was right and I knew it, but I hated to leave. "Are you going to stay?"

Mark nodded. "I can't defend him because I'm your lawyer, but I have some friends who will take his case—if it's needed," he added, when he saw my outraged look. "Don't worry, Molly. I'll handle it."

Yolanda stood up and put her arm around me. "Come on, honey. Let's go."

She and Ike led me out to Ike's waiting SUV. "I want you to rest tonight," Ike said as he tucked me into the back seat. "Don't worry about anything."

"You're not going to try to get the paper out, are you?" I asked, leaning against the seat. "Isn't the office a crime scene or something?"

"Yeah, it is. But they let me take my files with me. Danny got me a spot up at the high school, in the school newspaper office. I can use their computers. Amelia's already there with the editor of the school paper. We'll get something ready for tomorrow." He sounded energized by the idea. I could imagine him awake all night and cranking out the paper on a mimeograph machine if needed. Ike loved challenges like this.

When we got to Yolanda's townhouse, I finally took the pain pills the doctor had prescribed. I dropped into a sleep that was as deep as a coma, waking once when JT crept into the spare room where I lay. He sat on the edge of the bed, peering down at me in the feeble light that came in through the opened door.

"Are you okay?" he whispered, smoothing back my hair from the stitches on my scalp.

"I've got a headache. Other than that, I'm fine. What happened, JT? I don't understand." I sounded slurred, but I couldn't help myself. The drug I'd taken knocked out the pain, but it also was knocking me out.

He kissed me on the cheek. "We'll talk tomorrow. Sleep now."

I tried to hold onto his arm, but he slipped away.

I slept.

****

"I told Paula that you'd have to miss Mr. Sex tonight," Yolanda said as she came back into the living room from talking on the phone in the kitchen.

It was Monday night. Amelia, Ike and I were sitting in my living room, replete from a meal of donated casserole and cake. Amelia shuffled her Tarot cards on the nearby end table. "So Charlene poisoned Sam for Chuck and Chuck killed Sam for Charlene?" She made a 'tsk' noise. "It's like that 'Gift of the Magi' story from O. Henry."

We were trying to figure out what had happened at the Flower Show, five years before. I'd gotten a bit of the information from JT, who had come to see me that afternoon in order to pick up Sam's date book. Some of it I pieced together from what Bobbi Jo told me when she came to see me that morning. And the rest was just guesswork.

"Sam and Charlene dated before she married Chuck. And they never stopped seeing each other." I made a face. "I swear, was Sam the most over-sexed man on this planet?" Wisely, no one answered me.

"Then Chuck got in trouble with gambling. He stole some money from the bank and tried to cover it up. Sam must have found out somehow. Maybe Charlene let something drop. Maybe Sam threatened to go to the police." I shrugged. "What we do know is that on the morning of the Flower Show, Charlene had an appointment with Sam in his office. It was listed in his datebook. Now this last bit is guesswork, but...remember, we were having a bake sale?"

Yolanda nodded. "Part of every Flower Show, to raise money for the hospital."

"I think Charlene went to his office and tried to convince him not to tell anyone about Chuck. I think she brought some brownies for him made with ground up rhododendron leaves. The sugar and chocolate would mask any taste. Sam was a sucker for desserts and he probably thought she was just being nice, trying to sway him. It doesn't take much to kill a man with a poison like that. One brownie would have done it."

"But the rest of them? Didn't the police find something?"

I blew out a sigh. "I didn't call the police. I just figured Sam took off. I did file an official missing person's report, but it was weeks later, so I could start the paperwork for a divorce. No, I found the brownies." I ploughed on when I saw Ike's disbelieving expression. "I went to his office a week later and the paper plate with half a brownie was still there—with some dead flies on it. I figured some client gave Sam a 'thank-you' treat. People were always doing that. I pitched the plate, packed up his stuff, and brought it all home."

"Holy shit," Yolanda breathed. "Was she counting on that?"

"I don't know. Remember, nobody had reason to suspect Sam was anything but gone. Even if someone had found the brownies—like me—they'd just toss them."

"So Sam goes to the Flower Show, probably originally to see Molly, but he meets up with Bobbi Jo," Ike said, jotting down notes on the pad balanced on his knee. "Charlene followed him and made sure Molly saw Sam and Bobbi Jo together. Molly tells him off and Sam goes home. By now he's feeling sick."

I nodded. "And he gets to the house and finds the construction crew. He tells them to leave because he doesn't feel good." I took a handful of yellow M&Ms and crunched them as I spoke. "Charlene had told Chuck that Sam knew about the embezzling and he'd be at home, alone. Chuck went out there and argued with Sam. They struggled, the pitchfork was there—" I winced, imagining it. "I'm not sure if it was an accident or deliberate, but Sam got stabbed. And died. But he was already dying from the poison, although Chuck didn't know that." I paused in my chewing. "I wonder if Charlene was setting Chuck up?"

We all silently contemplated that for a minute.

"Chuck panicked." Ike picked up the story. "Charlene told him what to do. Chuck covered up the body with some planking and piled some dirt on top. Charlene had given him a note that he left on the kitchen table. As soon as Chuck called her, Charlene called her brother, Joe, and pretended to be Molly. Joe said it was a bad connection but he could understand what she said. She said she wanted a crew out there right away to finish covering that hole. Joe tried to find Jimmy, but he'd gone for the day. So Joe figured somebody got his signals crossed and he went out and filled in the hole. He signed Jimmy's name on the punch sheet and left a copy for Molly."

"And there poor Sam lay all this time until Melvin came along," Amelia said. She cut the cards and glanced at the one in her hand. "But what about Chuck? Who killed him?" She put that card back and pulled out another. She smiled when she saw it.

"Chuck killed himself." I said this with certainty. JT had told me as much. "Charlene tried to make it appear like an intruder, because otherwise she wouldn't get any insurance money."

Yolanda nodded in agreement. "Insurance won't pay out on suicide or murder, for that matter. So if Chuck were found to be the murderer or to have committed suicide, she'd be out the money. How big a policy was it?"

I wasn't sure if I should say. Ike beat me to it. "Half a million." He must have seen our startled expressions. "Public record. It's the first thing the police do—they check the policies."

"One of the oldest motives in the book." Amelia drew out another card and frowned when she saw it. She put it back and kept shuffling the deck. I wondered what she was searching for.

"Chuck couldn't stand the strain anymore." I chose a red M&M. "When Sam supposedly disappeared, Chuck kept waiting for the shoe to drop—he was probably wondering all this time if Sam had left something behind that might incriminate him. I didn't bother to look at everything Sam had. I just figured he'd skipped town with Bobbi Jo. So time passed and nothing happened. Chuck and Charlene relaxed. Chuck used Sam's disappearance as the cover-up he needed to hide the money he stole from the bank, pretending that Sam had taken it. When Sam's body was found, Chuck knew there'd be an audit. JT started checking Sam's papers. Chuck was waiting for it all to unravel."

"But what about the fire? And the shooting?" Ike asked, tapping his notepad. "Chuck?"

I nodded. "I think so. I think Charlene knew Chuck was going to do something and she came back, either to see if he'd succeeded or to save me, I'm not sure which. And when I talked to him, he was on his cell phone." I gestured toward the window with my head. "Right out there in the yard."

We all sat in quiet thought. "Poor bastard," Yolanda finally said. "Imagine how it felt, all those years, to wait and wait to be found out. I'm surprised he didn't kill himself sooner."

"Oh, my." Amelia was staring down at the card in her hand, her pale hazel eyes wide.

"Don't tell me. Death, right?" I took a handful of true blue M&Ms.

"No. It's the two of cups." She held it up for me to see the Owl and the Pussycat in their pea green boat. "Time to make plans to end that solitary life."

All eyes turned to me. I shrugged. "Any good Teasers this week?" I asked Ike as he got to his feet.

"A new anonymous one. I'm not sure what to make of it. It's not from Lost Love."

"Hmm." I speed-popped three M&Ms. "Interesting."

"Will we see you in the office tomorrow?" Amelia

asked, as she zipped her cards into their velveteen bag and tucked them into her purse.

"You bet. Bright and early." I struggled off the couch and escorted my guests to the mudroom door.

"Is JT coming over tonight?" Yolanda asked as she bundled up in her faux leopard.

"No, he's still got business in town. I think the State Patrol are keeping him busy." I knew we'd have to be circumspect until the investigation wrapped up. I had to content myself with a few phone calls and a brief meeting in JT's office to 'discuss the case.' My body still tingled from that discussion.

Yolanda hugged me so tightly, I almost lost my breath. "I'm so happy for you," she whispered in my ear. "And plan a Christmas wedding. Don't keep us all in suspense."

"He hasn't asked me, Ma," I protested. "You gotta have an invitation before you can go to the party."

She kissed me. "Then you ask him. I'm getting too old to wait around for you to be happy. Do it to please an old woman."

"Okay, I will. Just for you."

I almost told her my secret, then I decided to let her find out for herself. We only had a few hours to wait.

The next morning, I got to the office at nine. I knew that the early editions of the TBTrib would land on desks at about ten, specifically on a desk at the police station around the corner. My advance copy was sitting on my desk already. I opened it to the Teasers and saw my ad. It was in the center of the page, edged in hearts.

You asked how I feel. I love you. Your Found Love.

"Interesting ad."

I almost tipped over backwards in my chair. JT was standing at the side of my desk. "Where did you come from?"

He took the seat next to mine and examined my M&M tray. "I was in the back office, chatting with Ike. We were just waiting for you to come in, lazy bones."

"Hmm." I eyed him. He was wearing his uniform again, so I guess that meant he hadn't lost his job. He selected a blue M&M and crunched into it. "Well?" I prompted.

"What?"

"Did you like the ad?"

JT took another blue M&M. I watched him, then did a double-take. My entire M&M tray was filled with blue M&Ms. "What the hell?" I muttered.

"Did you like my present?" he asked as I grabbed the M&M tray and started fingering through them.

"Who put all these blue—" I picked up one M&M. *Marry me, Molly* was printed in three tiny lines. I picked up another one. *I Love You.* Yet another one read *Please marry me.* I looked up at him. "Did you do this?"

He rolled his eyes. "Don't tell me somebody else is proposing to you." He twirled the tray and pointed to the middle slot.

I pulled out the small gold band with enameled M&M characters on it, arms linked and smiling up at me. One was blue and one was red. "There's a wedding band that matches it," he said softly. "I told you I had some shopping to do when I went out of town that day."

I stared down at the ring, then held it out to him. He slipped it on my finger.

A flash went off. Ike grinned at us from behind the digital camera. Amelia brandished her Tarot cards. "What did I tell you? The cards never lie."

I smiled at JT. "I may need to give that damn pig a present."

He leaned forward, his eyes intent on mine. "Why?"

"Without him, we never would have gotten back together."

JT laughed. "Yeah," he said. "It's all the pig's fault."

A word about the author...

I was born in a small town in Iowa, and have traveled extensively in the U.S. and overseas, finally ending up back in the Midwest where I'm married to a glass artist who spends a lot of time in the studio, making amazingly beautiful things. We have assorted animals who live with us and who make regular appearances in my books under various pseudonyms (they know who they are). In 2003, I read my first romance novel and immediately decided this was the genre for me. But there was a problem: the books I read all featured young heroines, interested in starting a family and having babies. So I started writing romantic suspense (with an occasional side trip into paranormal fantasy) about older women, with some age on 'em, who are interested in men and sex and having a good relationship (which may or may not include a marriage). I hope you enjoy reading about them as much as I enjoy writing about them.

Contact JL at jaye@jayellwilson.com

Visit JL at www.jayellwilson.com